THE QUEEN OF DIAMONDS

The Affair of the Diamond Necklace shook the throne of France and, some say, precipitated the French Revolution and so helped to bring Louis XVI and Marie Antoinette to the guillotine. But why did these fantastic and ultimately sensational events fall so neatly into place? Why should a Prince of the Royal House of France become so credulous and without question play the almost incredible part prepared for him? Why was an ambitious and predatory woman allowed to steal that famous piece of jewellery that represented a fortune? Who were the secret instigators of the plot?

In this novel Jean Plaidy offers one solution to an historical mystery, the motives behind which have long puzzled students and amateur detectives of history.

For a complete list
of books by Jean Plaidy
please see pages 255–256

JEAN PLAIDY

The Queen of Diamonds

ROBERT HALE · LONDON

© Jean Plaidy 1958 and 1995
First published in 1958 under the pseudonym of Ellalice Tate
This edition 1995

ISBN 0 7090 5769 5

Robert Hale Limited
Clerkenwell House
Clerkenwell Green
London EC1R 0HT

Printed and bound in Great Britain by
Mackays of Chatham plc., Chatham, Kent.

Contents

AUTHOR'S NOTE

I wish to acknowledge most gratefully the help I have had from the following works :—

History of France	M. Guizot, Translated by Robert Black, M.A.
The French Revolution	Thomas Carlyle.
The French Revolution	Nesta H. Webster.
The Waiting City, Paris 1782-88. An Abridgement of Louis-Sébastien Mercier's "Le Tableau de Paris"	Translated and edited with Preface and notes by Helen Simpson.
Historical Mysteries	Andrew Lang.
Secret Societies and Subversive Movements	Nesta H. Webster.
Famous Secret Societies	John Heron Lepper.
Marie Antoinette	Stefan Zweig.
Louis XVI and Marie Antoinette Before the Revolution	Nesta H. Webster.
Marie Antoinette and the Diamond Necklace from Another Point of View	F. De Albini.
Nooks and Corners of Old Paris	Georges Cain.
Critical and Miscellaneous Essays	Thomas Carlyle.
France	William Henry Hudson.
The Old Régime in France	Frantz Funck-Brentano.

E.T.

I

THE ILLUMINATI

(*The Cards Are Dealt*)

AROUND A TABLE IN AN UNDERGROUND ROOM OF A BUILDING on the outskirts of the city of Frankfurt, a group of men was sitting. They had met in secret, for their business was of the utmost privacy. Each one of them was watching the stranger in their midst.

This stranger was of striking appearance, although he was neither tall nor short; his skin was dark and it was clear that he was not a native of Germany; his nostrils were wide, and this gave an impression of suppressed energy; but it was his eyes which were his most outstanding feature; they were dark, slightly prominent, and those learned in such matters realized after one glance at him that he was almost certain to possess hypnotic powers. He would be a worthy member of the Illuminati.

Adam Weishaupt, that ambitious man from the Bavarian University of Ingolstadt who was now sitting at the head of the table, had assured his fellow-masons that the new-comer was to be trusted. He was a Freemason and a Rosicrucian, and he merited initiation into the secret society of the Illuminati; he was a man who had travelled all over the world, and he had the entrée into those households where he could do good work. They need have no fear; he was one of them, ready to work for the cause.

An iron box, which had been placed on the table, was opened by Adam Weishaupt who took papers from it, and, glancing at the stranger, began to read the oath.

His voice rolled round the underground chamber, at

7

the door of which stood one of their number on guard. There were no windows, and the only illumination was provided by the light of several candles.

"I swear to reveal all secrets, which may be confided to me, or which I discover, to the Head of the Order."

"I swear," said the stranger.

"I swear to pursue all knowledge which it may be necessary to acquire for the sake of the Order, and I swear to employ, if necessary, poison or the sword, and to render imbecile those whom it would be imprudent to remove."

"I swear."

"I swear to submit all decisions to the Head of the Order, to contract no engagement, make no bargains; and to give the power of death to whoever can convict me of betraying the secrets which have been confided."

There was the slightest hesitation. All in the room seemed to catch their breath as they waited; all eyes were on that distinguished-looking figure with the magnetic dark eyes. For only those who swore to serve the Illuminati could be allowed to learn the Society's secrets and live.

There was a faint twitch of the stranger's lips, betraying his love of mischief. He looked at the anxious faces about the table contemplatively for a few seconds before he said: "I swear."

Their relief was obvious.

Adam had risen. He had taken the man's hands and cried: "You, my friend, Freemason and Rosicrucian, are now a member of the honourable Illuminati, whom you will serve with your life and the lives of others. You will now sign your name on this document."

The scroll was unrolled. A quill was dipped into a container, and in red blood the stranger wrote his name at the top of the scroll. Solemnly and one by one all those in the room added their names to the scroll; and when the last had signed, Adam Weishaupt turned to the newcomer, embraced him, and told him that they welcomed him warmly for the story of his talents had travelled before him, and they wished him to work as one of them without delay.

He knew the aims of the Order, which was to promote the well-being and freedom of mankind; he knew that members of the Illuminati never flattered the great, had no desire to serve princes and that their motto was Virtue, Wisdom and Liberty. Liberty! The world was in need of that at this time. There were many nations who suffered under the yokes of tyrants, and it was the purpose of the members of the Society to give freedom to the people. The Society of the Illuminati was possessed of large funds in many countries. It had accumulated these funds with a purpose; the freedom of the people and the abolition of tyrants.

As Adam was speaking his eyes flashed, not so much with virtue as with ambition. He was seeing himself as successor to one of those rulers whom he would displace; he saw first one country then another fall to the domination of the Illuminati. And there was not one man among them who did not, to some extent, share in that ambition. Adam visualized a Europe ruled by the Society which, amalgamating with similar societies such as the Free-masons and the Rosicrucians, should have himself as its head. Those henchmen of his knew that, if this should come about, they would have a big share in that power.

Therefore they were determined that one by one the monarchies and governments of Europe should fall, and it was natural that the weakest should be dealt with first.

Adam had drawn closer to his friends and glanced about the room anxiously, for these were indeed deadly secrets of which he was about to speak.

"The weakest," he said, "may seem at this time to be one of the strongest. My friends, you know the country of which I speak. Its court is the most extravagant, the most elegant in the world. Its King is a weakling; it is said the Queen rules, but the Queen is the most frivolous woman on Earth and it is not she who rules but those who influence her. There we see a glittering monarchy, such splendour as has never been seen in any other court; but the foundations are creaking, my friends; the foundations are rotting and ready to collapse."

The stranger said: "You speak of the Court of Versailles?"

"Aye!" was the answer. "And peace-loving Louis, the gentle fool who is unaware of his creaking throne. . . . I speak of him and Marie Antoinette, the frivolous woman who is galloping to destruction and dragging Louis and the monarchy with her. Grand Masters, I tell you this: our great task is to sweep away the monarchies of the world and set up republics in their stead; we will abolish tyranny and establish freedom. And our first objective shall be that which seems so great and, like an over-ripe plum, all bloom, all beauty outwardly, all rotten within, is ready to fall into our hands at a vigorous shaking of the tree. The people of France are ready. We have our friends in France. We have had our rehearsal in the recent *Guerre des Farines*. We saw in this how ready for revolt are the people of France. Every day now in the City of Paris, in Versailles, in Lyons, Poissy, Saint-Germain—in fact, my friends, all over France we hear the rumbling of revolution. Each day somewhere, somehow, rumours are circulated, songs are sung in the streets, epigrams are written on walls. I tell you our first objective is Versailles."

"Versailles!" echoed his followers.

"We have a good friend in the Duc de Chartres— cousin of stupid Louis—a man of mighty influence in

France. He leads the Grand Orient of France, blood-brother to the Illuminati. There is Mirabeau ... he is ready to be one of us. There is Choderlos de Laclos ... he is another. An important man, because he is a writer; and of all those who can be of importance to us, writers and women are the foremost. The writer can bring understanding to men more easily than the soldier, for it is certain that the pen is as great a weapon as the sword. Therefore we reward those writers who serve us, and decry as petty scribblers those who are against us; and if they do not mend their ways we must find means of removing them. Then there are women. They have great influence on certain men. Flatter women, for they are more influenced by flattery than anything else. Flatter them, use them. They can be our most useful allies."

One of the Grand Masters said then: "So all efforts are to be directed against Versailles?"

"The *main* effort," amended Adam. "We do not meanwhile forget other objectives. There is England, but that is a strange land. Its people will be the most difficult to convince. They are lazy; they overeat; they are smugly contented with their state. Not the stuff of which good revolutionaries are made! They will be last to fall. First France. Then Italy. But let us now turn our thoughts to Versailles."

Adam was now talking directly to the newcomer.

"With your reputation you should do good work, and it is our wish that you think deeply on these matters of which we have spoken. We are rich, and riches are useful. You will not be stinted. We suggest that you travel to Strasbourg and there make the acquaintance of the resident Cardinal. He is a connection of the French Royal house. You know of whom I speak?"

The dark eyes seemed more prominent; they gleamed with amusement. "You mean the Cardinal de Rohan?"

"I do. A man who is strongly attracted by occultism. Thus you should not find great difficulty in winning his interest."

"And if I should do this, what should my duties be?"

Adam Weishaupt spread his hands. "That, I cannot tell you." He leaned forward and looked into the dark eyes. "But you will discover. You will find his weaknesses. We know of one: women. You will learn how to exploit them. All that you need will be at your disposal. You have the power of Freemasonry behind you; you have the riches of the Illuminati."

"I will set out at once for Strasbourg," was the answer.

Adam smiled. He glanced at the scroll and particularly at that name at the head of it. It was Alessandro, Comte de Cagliostro.

*   *   *

II

THE COMTE AND THE CARDINAL
(*A Pair*)

THE COMTE ALESSANDRO DE CAGLIOSTRO WAS SMILING as he left the underground room. He was aware that people turned to look at him as he passed through the streets of Frankfurt. He was an arresting figure among the German population. He had always admired colour and ostentation from the days when, as a boy, he had lain dreaming of future greatness on the sea-shore at Palermo and looking out over the sickle-shaped bay to the world beyond. The buttons on his waistcoat could have been emerald, and the buckles on his shoes studded with diamonds.

When he walked through the streets he was often followed; he would listen rapturously to the whispering: "It is the great Cagliostro. Do you see his jewels? He made them himself. He is the only man in the world who has found the Philosopher's Stone."

His smile was benign; he would lay his hand on the heads of children and bless them, and their mothers would swear that from that day forth good luck was theirs.

He cured the sick, for in his laboratory he produced potions which were unknown to the rest of the world. There were some who believed that he had always walked this Earth and would do so as long as the planet lasted, for, in addition to the Philosopher's Stone he had discovered the Elixir of Life. Cagliostro smiled at the stories he heard about himself. He was not always sure that he disbelieved them.

He reached his lodgings and looked with some distaste at the tall narrow house which had been lent him during his stay in the town. It was a plain house, and in it he was forced to live simply. He had his laboratory, and that seemed to be all his German friends thought he needed. He longed for splendour, so he would be glad to leave Frankfurt; he hoped that Strasbourg would be more interesting and he believed, from what he had heard this day, that he might soon be going to Paris.

As he entered the house and mounted the stairs to the rooms above those in which he carried out his experiments, a beautiful young woman had heard his approach and hurried to greet him. They embraced affectionately; then he held her at arms' length and looked at her. Lorenza still gave him more delight than all his glittering jewellery. He had not intended to marry and a wife, before he met Lorenza Feliciani, had seemed to have no part in his plans; but she had changed that idea, and he had never regretted marrying Lorenza.

"Well?" she said.

"I am accepted. Behold! You see me—an esteemed member of the Illuminati."

"Why should this mean anything to you?"

"For one thing, my love, it means that we leave Frankfurt. We set out for Strasbourg without delay. Our future lies with the French, and I would rather spend my life among Frenchmen than Germans."

"Alessandro, tell me this. What are we to do in Strasbourg?"

"Cultivate . . . or be cultivated by the great Cardinal de Rohan."

"And this pleases you?"

"He is reputed to be fabulously wealthy, and he is a connection of the French Royal house. His hobbies are dabbling in the occult and amusing himself with women."

He laid his hands on her shoulders. "I will quickly intimate that you are not to be included in the women who may interest His Eminence."

"Thank you, Alessandro. I was hoping we should go back to Rome."

"Ah, Rome! I know of what you dream. You want to wander once more among the ruins of the Colosseum, to go marketing in the Via Canestrari and to pray in Santa Maria del Popolo. In other words, my dear, you want us to slip into obscurity, to deny our destinies, and myself take up some humble trade in your native city, that we may there pass the rest of our days in peace."

She nodded.

"But you know, Lorenza, do you not, that such a life is not for me . . . not for the Comte de Cagliostro?"

"Perhaps for Giuseppe Balsamo."

"Poor Giuseppe! He died long ago when Alessandro, Comte de Cagliostro was born. Do not revive that poor creature, Lorenza."

"No."

He laughed suddenly. " Have faith in your destiny, my love. It is linked with mine. You and I together will rule the world one day. In the meantime prepare for we leave for Strasbourg tomorrow."

*   *   *

She was accustomed to sudden moves. It had been so ever since their marriage. Alessandro was not always popular in the towns wherein they stayed. It was inevitable that such a man should have many enemies.

"Such as I am would always have enemies," he had said in that ringing voice of his which, like everything else about him, seemed to hold something of the supernatural in it. "Consider them not. In the end they shall be defeated."

They had had to leave London hurriedly, although he had declared that he would stay for years in that city. It was full of gaiety and noise; and they had enjoyed their sojourn there. The Comte de Cagliostro had made a certain amount of money selling cures, love philtres, and ointments and lotions to make the old appear young and the ugly beautiful.

How did he do it? she wondered. It was some strange power within him with which he hypnotized his patients so that when they looked into their mirrors they saw their faces, not as they really were but as he willed them to see them.

Was he a charlatan as some said he was; or was he truly a magician, as others fervently believed him to be?

Lorenza, who loved him, could never be sure.

*   *   *

He was not even sure of himself.

Another move, he was thinking; and this time to what?

He was in a pensive mood and at such times he would project himself into the past. Lorenza had talked of Giuseppe Balsamo and she had conjured up the image of a small barefoot boy lying on the shore, dreaming while he should have been helping in his father's shop.

He could recall the past so vividly that he half believed that at such times he lived it again. "Time?" he would say. "What is time? The master of most men, the slave of Cagliostro." He stretched himself on a couch, and he was on the shore. He was aware of Monte Pelligrino and Monte Catalfano which seemed to enfold the town, and he felt again that frustration because he lived on an island yet longed to travel in the great world beyond. He had made mental pictures and he had commanded himself to believe that he was actually looking into the future. They had not understood him, those simple Sicilians; they had merely looked upon him as Pietro Balsamo's queer boy.

He could hear his father's voice—poor Pietro Balsamo, a humble tradesman of Palermo, a Sicilian Jew converted to Christianity because life was perhaps easier for Christians. "What comes over you, Giuseppe? Is it that you do not want to earn your living? Do you want to be a poor beggar who must starve but for charity?"

He had looked at his father and answered haughtily: "Have no fear of that. I will not be a beggar. I will be a great man. But not in Palermo . . . not in Sicily."

"Where then?"

And that small boy had pointed to the sea and beyond.

Pietro Balsamo had spat over his shoulder in contempt. But he was worried, asking himself what one could make of a boy like Giuseppe. He had no need to worry, Giuseppe's looks implied. Such as Giuseppe made their own lives.

He remembered the morning; the sun on the water and the boats bringing in the haul of sardines. He had thought of his father in the shop, trembling with eagerness to make people buy, angry because Giuseppe was not beside him to do his bidding, to smile at the ladies—who never failed to be charmed by those enormous dark eyes.

When he was moved by hunger he went home. He could see his father's eyes watching him as he entered the shop. "So you come home now, Giuseppe! You come home for food, eh? And where have you been this morning when there are many coming into the shop to buy?"

"I was by the sea, Father, thinking. . . ."

"And you imagine thinking will feed you?"

"Yes, Father. It will; and with better food mayhap than barley bread and salt sardines."

"There are times when I cannot believe that you are my son, Giuseppe. Am *I* slothful? Do *I* lie looking at the sea and dreaming?"

Giuseppe shook his head.

B

"Then you . . . if you do these things, must be punished, Giuseppe. That is why there will be no food for you this day. Instead you shall have a taste of my stick. For food is the reward of industry, and the stick that of sloth."

Then Pietro Balsamo took off his coat and prepared to punish his son, but even as he lifted his stick, those great dark eyes held his. Giuseppe said not a word, but those prominent eyes seemed to speak for him. "Pietro Balsamo," they warned, "who are you? A small trader of Palermo, a Jew who has denied his religion, denied his birthright for the sake of a living. Think twice before you attempt to heap indignity upon one whose shoes you are unworthy to dust."

Pietro's arm dropped to his side. He was uneasy. What was this strange creature he had begotten? What power lay within that small body? He felt now a compulsion to obey the command, to refrain from using the stick, which he read in Giuseppe's dark eyes.

Giuseppe threw off his father's grip with a dignity which was bewildering in one so young.

Then he went to the table and began to eat sardines and barley bread.

It was at that time that he became aware of his power. As he subdued his father, so would he subdue the world.

*   *   *

The Comte and Comtesse de Cagliostro travelled in some state from Frankfurt on the journey south to Strasbourg. They should not, the Comte had assured the Illuminati, arrive in Strasbourg in humble style. If he came with all the pomp of rank he would more quickly become the friend of the great Cardinal.

This had seemed sound sense, and money was put at his disposal; yet the practical Germans had wondered why, since the Comte had discovered the Philosopher's Stone, he could not make enough gold to satisfy his wants.

The operation, had replied the Comte, was by nature of its intricacy a long and delicate one. If the Masters would allow him a few years in which to provide the gold, he would willingly dedicate himself to this task. If, however, his mission was as urgent as they had implied, and if he might give his opinion, he must say that his services were more valuable in winning the confidence of the great Cardinal than in providing the society with treasure such as it already possessed in abundance.

The money had been given and the journey begun. The carriage provided was magnificent; drawn by four horses it was of an elegant style and lined with brocade. On the doors was engraved the crest of Cagliostro, and inside the carriage was a special compartment in which his great jewel-box could be securely stowed.

The Comte had arranged that a rider should precede them into the towns through which they passed—and it would be his duty to warn the townsfolk that the famous Comte de Cagliostro was coming their way. This would ensure that crowds gathered to surround the carriage as it made its way to the posting stations; and that while the horses were being changed the great man could step from the carriage and show himself to the crowds. All a-dazzle with the brilliant jewels which it was said he had made himself, he would hold them with his magnetic eyes, lay his hands on the sick, talk to them in that deep resonant voice of his which hypnotized them; so that after he had passed they set about making their lives conform to that pattern which he had prophesied for them, which empowered the lame to walk naturally, even if only in the great man's presence.

It was imperative that Strasbourg should be prepared

for his coming, and that the news that Cagliostro was about to enter the town should be brought to the ears of the great Cardinal.

He sat back in the carriage smiling. He was content. It was at such times as this that he tasted success. Gazing from the window he lifted a hand in salute to the people who stood by the roadside; and he trusted—although he revelled in such homage—that none at this stage would kneel in the road and prevent the carriage's passing on before its illustrious occupant had alighted to bless them. He was eager to reach Worms before nightfall.

He looked at his Comtesse. She was beautiful, but no more so than she had been in her humble Roman home. Her delicate features did not need the enormous gems which he insisted she must wear to set off her beauty. The ruby, the size of a pigeon's egg, at her throat would cause no more admiration than her delicate profile. He felt tender at the sight of her. He even felt that he would like to grant her wish, to throw away the title with which he had endowed himself and become plain Giuseppe Balsamo again for her sake.

But no, my love, he thought, this is my destiny, and perforce yours.

How could he, the great Cagliostro, bear to live the life of an ordinary citizen, to become a man such as his father had been, bowing obsequiously to those who he hoped would buy the goods he had to sell? He had been born with unusual talents; should he preserve them with care and never use them, as had the man in the parable of the talents? Should he end with what he started? Indeed no. He, Cagliostro, intended to write his name on at least one page of history; there were many who believed he had discovered the Elixir of Life, and this to some extent he had for he would live in the memories of those who came after him, even if his physical body went the way of all flesh and bone. That was the true Elixir; that was the spiritual manifestation of what the simple people thought they could buy in a bottle. "Yes," he would declare to them, "I, Cagliostro, have discovered the Elixir of Life."

It was true. And if, when people looked at these enormous gems which adorned the persons of himself and his Comtesse, they said: "Cagliostro has learned the art of making jewels, he can transmute base metals into gold!" that also was true; for in the eyes of those who beheld them the jewels were real jewels, the glittering metal real gold. He had the power to make these people see as he wished them to see. Thus he was in possession of the Philosopher's Stone.

There were shouts from the road.

"He is coming! He is coming! It is the great Cagliostro himself. See! There he sits. Look at his jewels. He made them. He will live for ever."

His white hand was lifted; the glitter of diamonds was dazzling in the sunlight.

"He carries a fortune on him!"

"Would you not think he would be afraid of robbers?"

"Who would dare rob Cagliostro? They say, too, that as soon as the jewels leave his possession he has the power to transform them to worthless lumps of stone."

This was the materialization of a dream. He wanted now to relive his early life in brief episodes which should seem like the stepping-stones across a river; the river was that which separated penniless Giuseppe Balsamo from the Comte de Cagliostro.

The jolting carriage and the cries of acclaim lulled him into that sense of trance which carried him back over the years.

*　　　　*　　　　*

Now he was Giuseppe, coming up from the seashore. It was a hot day and he could feel the warmth of the sun on his dark head. He believed that he sensed a change coming into his life. Foreboding? No, not that. He had known that whatever happened to him he would turn it to advantage. It was a sense of change, nothing more.

It was the son of their neighbour who came running to him as he stood there looking out at the sea.

"Giuseppe, Giuseppe, come quickly. Your father is ill."

They walked through the town together, the son of his neighbour white-faced, teeth chattering with the excited horror peculiar to the bearers of bad news.

"My father is more than ill," Giuseppe had said. "He is dead."

How had he known it? Was it because his father had had these attacks before? He had said: "One day, Giuseppe, they will carry me off, and then what will become of you?"

His father was not dead when he reached the shop; but he died later that day.

He could feel the atmosphere of gloomy excitement, all that death meant. He could see his father's body, dressed in its best clothes, lying in the room behind the shop; he could smell the tallow of the candles, hear the whispering voices of those who sat and watched, read the question in their eyes. What will become of Giuseppe now?

His uncle was there—Balsamo the chemist, larger, more successful than Pietro. He looked at the boy and shook his head. He had heard from his brother that Giuseppe was a problem, that he spent his days in dreaming rather than work. "You are a fool, brother," he had said again and again. "That boy rules you. Is he the father? Are you the son?" He was a business man, astute and shrewd. If he took a boy into his shop, he wanted one who would earn his bread and sardines and his bed on the floor under the counter.

What was to be done with penniless Giuseppe?

"We will put him in the care of the Ben Fratelli," said Uncle Balsamo. "He is a boy who is given to contemplation. Where better could he contemplate than with the monks? He is a boy who is said to be possessed of talents which we simple people cannot understand. The monks are learned; let them discover what is best for the boy."

"Uncle," said Giuseppe, "allow me to live with you. I wish to learn of medicines."

He turned those brilliant eyes upon his uncle, but Uncle Balsamo was not looking at him; he was thinking that in his business there was no room for idlers.

Giuseppe understood then that his powers were not effective with all, and he was determined to discover why this was so.

Now he opened his eyes for a while. He did not want to accompany that boy on the journey from the shop to the monastery. A fear had come to him; and because at that time he had been unable to use his powers on his uncle as he had on his father, he had suddenly felt small, weak and very much alone.

But the pictures once called up, would not fade. They presented themselves and he must look at them; moreover he must live again that period of loneliness and terror which he had experienced during those first days in the monastery when he had thought that he was imprisoned there for ever and that one day he would walk silently through those cold stone-floored rooms, the swish of his habit the only sound as silent-footed he made his way to his cell; he had imagined that his black hair would be shaved from his head and his brilliant eyes would grow sunken as were those of Brother Girolamo.

But soon he was rising above despair. The monks were kind. They had no wish to incarcerate him for ever in their monastery; they merely wanted to obey the wishes of the good chemist, Balsamo, who gathered his herbs in the monastery grounds and who was ready to give advice and help to their monastery apothecary when he needed it.

"Could I not study under Brother Giovanni?" asked the young Giuseppe.

The monks saw no reason to refuse him; they were astonished by the way in which this boy—whom they had expected to be wayward—applied himself to all that Brother Giovanni had to teach.

He became the delight of Brother Giovanni, whose plump cheeks would quiver with pleasure when he talked of him, whose eyes would glisten as they rested on the small figure, seated on a stool, pounding away with a pestle and mortar.

"What I should do, without my young assistant, I know not," he declared.

There had been months of contentment, during which the boy even grew to love the sound of the continual ringing of bells because he knew that he had but a short time to hear them. The silent-footed monks, who seemed to glide through the cold rooms, were like ghosts to him; they were shadows who peopled this quiet half-world in which he must stay awhile during his apprenticeship. He could sit at the table and listen to their talk of the kitchens and gardens, and all the domestic problems of a self-supporting community, and when Brother Giovanni talked of his herbs and his medicines, there were times when Giuseppe would have a word or two to say. Then there would be the days of silence when not a word was spoken, and he would sit, eyes downcast, as he drank his soup or ate his hunk of bread baked by Brother Francesco in the great monastery kitchen. But all this he had

done because he had known that it was a period of tran-
sience, which would be nothing more to him than travelling a quiet stretch of the road. Yet in passing along
that road, because of its quietness he had had time to
pause and pluck the flowers which grew at the wayside.
Flowers of wisdom; flowers of knowledge. He had learned
the use of simple herbs and plants; he knew how to extract
what was useful, and he knew for what purposes it could
be used.

And when he realized that there was nothing else the
Ben Fratelli could teach him, he walked quietly out to
the herb garden—to gather herbs, so Brother Giovanni
fondly thought—but when he reached the garden,
Giuseppe threw down his sack and walked out of the
garden, out of the monastery, back to his uncle's shop
and the streets of Palermo.

*   *   *

The carriage drew up. The postilion was at the window.

"My lord, it is a poor man who begs that you lay your
healing hands upon him."

He sighed; he turned to his wife. "It seems we shall
not reach Worms this night. But what can I do? Can I
refuse this poor man?"

He smiled at her. He saw the doubts in her eyes.

She did not know, his charming Lorenza; she was
not yet sure what manner of man she had married. His
hand, which he laid over hers, rested on the great emerald
she wore on her finger. Fleetingly he looked down at it.
There was not a man or woman waiting by the roadside
who would not believe the emerald on the finger of the
Comtesse de Cagliostro was anything but genuine.

That was as it should be.

As he stepped down from the carriage, there was a
hushed silence throughout the crowd. Hastily he surveyed

them. Some lowered their eyes; some even fell to their knees; but there were some who stared at him brazenly. There would always be the incredulous, he thought. When there were no disbelievers, all the powers he felt seething within him would come to maturity. All he had to do was convert the sceptics.

The man was leaning on his crutch. His face was white, his eyes glazed, and he was calling: "My lord Comte ... Your Grace ... Your Excellency ... have pity. ..."

A hysterical subject, thought the Comte; undoubtedly a believer.

"What ails you, my son?" he asked.

There was a gasp through the crowds as he lifted his hand, for the sparkle of the gems thereon seemed dazzling to many, although there were some to declare they had seen false gems shine as brightly. Cagliostro sensed their hostility even as he sensed the faith of others. Doubt and faith came to him as tangible objects. It was one of his gifts to sense to a degree the feeling in the crowd.

"My Lord, Your Excellency," gibbered the man, "I was struck down by a passing carriage, and since then I have been unable to walk."

"Your leg was broken?" asked the Comte.

"Nay, Excellency. But I tried to rise from the road and I could not move."

Cagliostro nodded.

"And you believe that I can cure you?"

"I believe, Excellency."

"And you put yourself in the road ... in the way of my carriage. What if we had heeded you not?"

"My Lord, Your Excellency, I have waited long for you to pass this way; and when I heard that you were to come, I placed myself in the road, having no fear that your horses would ride me down. I knew that you would come to cure me."

"Then give me your crutch," said the Comte.

He was watching, alert for the manner in which the man obeyed. That was all-important. He exulted. There was not a second's hesitation. The crutch was put in his hand. He broke it easily and threw it into the road.

"Go your way in peace," he said. "Your faith has cured you."

A dazzling smile illuminated the face of the man. The Comte knew he had succeeded. He had removed the cause of paralysis; the man's belief that he was crippled.

He made his way briskly back to his carriage. He was continually afraid that one day a broken limb would be offered him to cure.

He heard the whisperings. "He is as a god."

"He is as God Himself. Did you not hear his words? The words are almost the same. It is the Son of God walking on Earth again."

He was in the carriage. He shouted: "Whip up the horses and away. We must reach Worms this night."

Through the windows he saw the people kneeling by the roadside; he saw the man whose crutch he had taken, the tears of gratitude streaming down his face.

He looked at Lorenza. Could she now be longing for the quiet life of Rome? Could she, after such scenes, look on and not embrace the destiny allied with his own?

For such moments he had lived through many trials and humiliations.

He closed his eyes again and the past was with him once more.

*   *   *

Humiliations. Yes, there had been humiliations. The first had come through the Jew, Marano.

He was now leaving the monastery, arriving at his uncle's shop. It was mid-morning and his uncle was waiting for customers, when Giuseppe presented himself. Uncle Balsamo could not believe his eyes.

"Giuseppe! What means this? The monks have sent you away?"

"I have run away from the monks."

"Then back you shall go, this very day."

"No, my uncle."

It was useless for Giuseppe to turn his black eyes upon him. He was unimpressed. He was the first of those unbelievers, the forerunner of many who declared his diamonds paste and the glittering metal which looked like gold but a base substance after all.

"I say yes," said Uncle Balsamo. "You'll turn right round and go back this very minute."

"I have learned all that they can teach me, Uncle. I long to learn more. Here in your shop I could be of use to you. I want to learn all it is possible to learn about curing the sick. I could be of use to you here."

Uncle Balsamo was shrewd; he was a man who had an eye for business; he was not like his brother Pietro who, when he died, had had nothing to leave. He had heard good accounts of Giuseppe. If Brother Giovanni found the boy useful, perhaps his uncle would also.

Very well then, he should stay. But if he brought his slothful habits into the shop of Uncle Balsamo, it would be back to the monastery with him.

These were important scenes—those which brought changes into his life.

And the next? It was years after, when he had learned much of herbs and lotions and philtres, when he knew all that he could learn in his uncle's shop and more also, that he grew restive and once again there stirred within him those longings for adventure.

He dreamed of sailing away from Sicily. For this he needed money; he had worked for many years for his uncle, and during that time he had acquired a reputation of being something more than an ordinary apothecary.

He had always been aware of his effect on some people. Merely by staring at some men and women he could dominate them, and then, should he command them to act in a certain way, however foolish this might be to their interests, they would obey him.

He had learned the art of speaking without moving his lips; and he could make it appear that his voice came from a direction where he was not.

He had journeyed across to Messina where, he had heard, lived a man of mystery, a certain Altotas whom he was eager to meet. Altotas the Greek had been as eager to meet him and had welcomed him as a friend, had taken him into his house, and many conversations had there been over bottles of wine. Altotas had stories of the world beyond Sicily. There was no doubt, he had said, that men such as himself and Giuseppe Balsamo were gifted. They were possessed of extra-sensory perceptions; they were in touch with something outside this world; such men had been called occultists, and there were societies to which they could belong, to their advantage.

They compared their gifts, their hypnotic powers, that quality within them which sometimes foretold them what was about to happen.

They had both been made aware that they possessed these gifts and were eager to discover more about them.

Sometimes Giuseppe visited Messina; sometimes Altotas visited Palermo. Giuseppe had been wise, Altotas assured him, in studying the apothecary's trade, for that would be of use to the alchemist he was to become, and through the cures he had effected he had been given an insight into human nature.

So passed the days in the island of Sicily until Giuseppe, dreaming of leaving the island and seeking his fortune in the world outside, took to pocketing money which belonged to his uncle; and in this fraud he was eventually discovered. Uncle Balsamo had no wish to turn the young man out, for he had become too useful; business had prospered since Giuseppe had worked with him and the whole island talked of his extraordinary powers.

But such a man had his enemies. He could not steal indiscriminately and, when he cheated a Jew named Marano and the fraud was discovered, Giuseppe knew that he was in danger.

Marano had harangued his friends, stirring them to hatred against this upstart Balsamo who, because he had a pair of flashing black eyes which seemed to bring him favour from the women, because he could perform tricks and was an apothecary's boy, seemed to think that he ruled the island.

It was time he was taught a lesson. How would it be if a group of them armed themselves and set out to do this one dark night?

Giuseppe knew then that he was in danger. That extra sense warned him; and if it had not, there was his friend Altotas who was alarmed on his account. All Giuseppe's charm, all his power would be of no avail against a band of lusty men who thought they had something to avenge.

Altotas came to Palermo; and as soon as he arrived in the town he went to Giuseppe and said to him: "Every night you stay in this place you run great risk. They will kill you if they can. You must not let that happen."

"What can I do?" asked Giuseppe. "If I avoid them tonight there will still be tomorrow."

"I have arranged for a boat to take us to the mainland. It leaves at dusk. We will go together. Bring all the money and valuables you can put your hands on. Why do you look so startled? Is it not what you always wanted to do? Did we not know that one day you and I would sail away from Sicily together?"

Yes, they had always known it. The island had no more to offer.

So, on a dark night Giuseppe Balsamo and Altotas crossed to the mainland and began their lives together.

A glorious life it had been. Altotas was his good friend, and from him he learned many of the secrets of the alchemist as well as how to speak many languages with fluency. They went to Greece and Altotas introduced him to those whom he called the wise men of the world. Their friends were Occultists, Freemasons, Rosicrucians and members of other secret societies. They, like all wise men of the age, were seeking those two goals—the discovery of the Philosopher's Stone which could transmute base metals to gold, and that Elixir which could give eternal life.

They travelled the world, he and Altotas—Greece, Egypt, Arabia, Persia, Rhodes and Malta; they lingered in the Orient for it was there that occultism was more advanced than in the West. They were received by secret societies whose secrets were revealed to them. Giuseppe declared that the mystery of the Great Pyramid had been revealed to him in Egypt, and it was during his years of travel that he became known to Grand Masters and Freemasons throughout the world.

In Malta he suffered a grievous loss in the death of Altotas. This was more than the loss of a friend; it was the loss of an ideal. They had planned to live for ever, he and Altotas, but death defeated them.

In a mood of deep depression he travelled to Rome and, whilst staying there, met Lorenza Feliciani, whose gentle charm enslaved him so that—folly though it seemed even at the time—he must give himself the comfort of marriage with her.

So they were married and, wishing to make her a Comtesse, he renamed himself. He was no longer Giuseppe Balsamo who hailed from the little shop in Palermo, but Alessandro, Comte de Cagliostro. He must dispense with Giuseppe whose roots were so clearly to be discovered in the island close to the toe of Italy. He must be a man of mystery, a man in whom none could trace a beginning, none see an end.

Comte Alessandro now set out on his travels. Altotas had left him the wisdom of a lifetime's research. A Freemason and a Rosicrucian, he was accepted with acclaim in the Lodges throughout Europe.

Only in England was he looked upon with suspicion. Freemasonry in England was in truth the simple and innocent society it purported to be in other countries. It was inaugurated in order to free people from religious prejudice, to cultivate the social virtues and bring universal happiness in a state of liberty and moral equality.

In England the Comte's great success was with the ordinary people, who knew little of, and cared nothing for, the Grand Lodges. They were ready to believe in a sorcerer who could turn base metal into gold; they wanted a man who would sell them his Elixir of Life and those philtres which would bring their lovers back to them or give them eternal beauty.

But it was better not to think of England. There had been the unsavoury affair of a Chelsea lady's diamond necklace which the Comte had urged her to buy so that he might make the stones three times their original size. This, declared the stupid authorities of London when the lady mentioned her doubts to them, was an impossible feat and anyone who attempted it was, they were convinced, also attempting fraud. A very unpleasant incident, with the mysterious Comte de Cagliostro actually confined for a time in a noisome London jail!

But he had his good friends, the Masons; and they would not allow him to be found guilty of fraud. All the same, he was forced to leave the country in a hurry.

No! Memories of England were not pleasant.

But in Europe fresh honours awaited him. He was well received by the Rabbi Falk and the Grand Masters of the Stricte Observance; Thomas Ximenes, in St. Petersburg, showed by his welcome and his willingness to share secrets that he had the utmost respect for the Comte de Cagliostro.

And so to the initiation into the Illuminati at Frankfurt and now ... to Strasbourg.

*   *   *

Into the town came the carriage.

"Make way! Make way!" cried that servant who must ride ahead. "Make way for the great Comte de Cagliostro!"

The people hurried into the streets to see the carriage pass, to chatter together, to ask each other whether it was true that the notorious Cagliostro was going to stay awhile in Strasbourg itself. Would they see him in their streets? Would he heal the sick? Would he show them the way to keep eternally young?

They waited in the shadow of the Gothic Cathedral to watch the carriage pass. Germans forgot to feel resentful, and Frenchmen triumphant, because this town of Strasbourg had passed from the hands of Germany to those of France during the conquest of the Grand Monarque. They could only talk of Cagliostro.

And there was the carriage—as magnificent as that of the Cardinal himself—and seated in it were the Comte and his Comtesse. The Comte was strikingly handsome, the Comtesse beautiful; and not even the Cardinal himself wore jewels such as these two wore.

Excitement spread through the town. People followed

c

the carriage, running to keep up with it as the equipage rumbled through the narrow streets.

And there, before one of the grandest mansions of the town, the carriage stopped and out of it stepped the Comte, gracefully turning to hand out his lady.

The crowd caught its breath to see such dazzling jewels, and the Comte turned to them all, and smiling, raised his hand and blessed them.

Many declared, after he had passed into the house, that they felt some healing spirit enter them. Those people believed that a Master had come among them. But there were, of course, the sceptics.

"Jewels!" cried the believers. "Did you ever see such jewels?"

"No," retorted the unbelievers. "Nor did anyone. Fakes, that's what they are. Paste and painted stones."

But the believers continued to believe and there were many quarrels in the streets that day, but even the unbelievers were expectant; they might believe that Cagliostro was incapable of making rubies, emeralds and diamonds; but they were certain that he could create excitement wherever he went.

Prince Louis Réné Edouard de Rohan-Guéménée, known throughout Strasbourg as the Cardinal de Rohan and Archbishop of Strasbourg, driving in his carriage to the cathedral, could not but be aware of the expectant crowds in the streets.

As he alighted he said to one of his attendants: "What is today that so many are abroad?"

"Monseigneur, the Comte de Cagliostro has arrived in Strasbourg this day."

"Ah," mused the Cardinal, "I have heard of the man." He smiled. "And since he is in Strasbourg I doubt not that ere long we shall meet."

*   *   *

In the shadow of the cathedral a group of men had started a brawl. There were many such in Strasbourg.

It may have begun when two exuberant Frenchmen jostled a German as they passed.

"Out of my way, pig of a German!"

"Have a care to whom you speak, French hyena!"

It could happen so easily; memories were long and stories of conquering armies had been handed down from fathers to sons.

The crowds gathered, each side with its supporters. The noise was great and the carriage was upon them before they heard its coming.

It halted before the group of men and, when its occupant alighted, there was immediate silence. One man, bleeding from the nose, lay on the cobbles as though transfixed. His opponent stood over him, fists raised, yet motionless like a statue.

Cagliostro walked with slow dignity towards the fighters.

All eyes were on him. The people of Strasbourg were as yet unaccustomed to see so much splendour. His taffeta coat, which swung open as he walked, was lined with cloth of gold; his waistcoat of scarlet was richly embroidered with gold thread; his silk stockings glistened with jewels as he walked, and the diamond buckles on his shoes were dazzling.

"My children," cried a resonant voice which seemed to come, not from the mouth of this man but from the doors of the cathedral itself, so that all turned to look in that direction and, seeing no one there who could have spoken, turned once more to gape at great Cagliostro. "Wherefore must you fight together? Listen to Cagliostro who will give you the benefit of his wisdom."

It was as though they were in the presence of a god. Cagliostro was of medium height but by very reason of his glittering presence he seemed to tower above all others. There were many in the crowd to swear afterwards that those words had come from heaven.

Then Cagliostro spoke, and this time those about him saw his lips move. "Let the injured man come to me here."

He was aware now of the arrival of a carriage on the edge of the crowd—a carriage of great magnificence— and he caught a glimpse of the scarlet-clad figure within it. Cagliostro was aware that the man, to make whose acquaintance he had come to Strasbourg, was a spectator of this scene.

No one turned to look at the Cardinal in the more impressive presence of Cagliostro.

The man who had been sprawling on the ground rose slowly and, as if drawn by some invisible rope, he came towards Cagliostro.

The man's shirt was torn away from his forearm, and he was bleeding profusely from a wound he had received there.

Cagliostro looked at the man; he took a silk kerchief from his pocket and waved it three times; then he took out a small stick like a wand. He said: "Stretch out your arm, my son."

The man obeyed him. He then tied the handkerchief about the brachial artery and tightened it by means of the stick until the blood ceased to flow. He then deftly tied the bandage and examined the man's grazed face.

"You know my house?" asked Cagliostro.

"Lord, all know your house."

"Come to me three hours from now." He laid his fingers on the man's head. "Let the man who fought with this one come forward," he said; and when the other came to stand before him, he continued: "You too, my son, have suffered from your outburst of anger. Come also to my house three hours from now. In three days you will be fit to fight again, but do no such thing. I should not be inclined to help you twice. Go now."

· The men moved away. Cagliostro turned to the people. "Do not look as though you have seen a miracle. You have seen nothing but that which any skilled doctor would have done. Miracles, my friends, are for those men and women of faith. They are rare and beautiful and not to be squandered on petty brawlers."

The Cardinal had now stepped from his carriage, and the people remembered the homage they owed to him. Many went to him and kneeling asked his blessing.

Over the bowed heads the Cardinal de Rohan met the gaze of Cagliostro. The great Cardinal; the great magician! There were some in the crowd who waited eagerly to see who would pay homage to whom.

Cagliostro had bowed his head slightly, as he would to an equal. The Cardinal hesitated. The fame of this man had travelled before him and he was eager to make his acquaintance.

Cagliostro then turned away. He must show the people of Strasbourg that he paid homage to none—neither cardinals nor even kings.

The Cardinal's love of the occult went beyond his dignity. He was after all a Prince of the Royal house and known throughout France and Germany as such. He had less need to cling to dignity than had the mysterious Cagliostro. So it was the Cardinal who went forward.

"My lord Comte," he said, "welcome to Strasbourg."

"My lord Cardinal, I am honoured to meet you."

"I had heard of your arrival in the town, and planned to ask you to visit me at Saverne."

"Then as my house is but a few steps away, would you not honour me by visiting me first?"

"I am delighted to take advantage of your hospitality."

"Then I pray you come with me. My house is but a few steps from the cathedral."

The people fell back to allow them to pass—the elegant Cardinal, Royal Prince, and the mysterious Cagliostro. They compared the Cardinal's diamonds with those of his companion. Cagliostro's were three times as large, three times as glittering.

"These brawls," said the Cardinal. "So unfortunate. Inevitable, I fear."

"But they become rarer with the years," murmured Cagliostro. "I remember the day Louis rode into the city . . . its conqueror. Oh, what a handsome man he was—le Roi Soleil in very truth!"

The Cardinal said with a laugh: "You must indeed be a very old man. Yet you would seem at least ten years younger than I am."

"Age, what is age? What is time? I would be the master of time, not its slave."

"So would we all. But time defeats us in the end."

"All?" asked Cagliostro lightly.

"Your words interest me," said the Cardinal. "You have said you were here when my ancestor, Louis Quatorze, took this city from the Germans. You cannot mean that. Do you know when it occurred?"

"I remember the occasion well."

"You astonish me, Comte. How could you, a man of not more than thirty, have seen something which happened a hundred years ago? What is your age?"

"I am the age which those who regard me think me to be," said Cagliostro.

"But to live for more than a hundred years . . . as you must have done if you remember such things . . . it is a miracle."

"What are miracles, Your Eminence? What indeed! Why, I declare you have a look of your noble ancestor.

What a king! I think of him as Apollo in the ballet. Now that would be before he had built the Palace of Versailles. How the people loved him! It would seem there have not since been kings like that in France."

"Is it true then," asked the Cardinal, "that you have discovered the Elixir of Life? Is it true that you have walked this Earth for hundreds of years . . . always a young man in your prime?"

"Your Eminence, you ask questions which it is not humanly possible to answer. Time and space—they are the very stuff of which the mysteries of life are made. I have spent lifetimes studying, and yet even I do not understand the entire mystery of the universe. That is why I work ceaselessly in my little room. There are problems, Eminence, which are not to be explained in words. There are secrets to be communicated from mind to mind and not through the worldly medium of words —for words are man-made, and the secrets of the universe are beyond the comprehension of ordinary men. But come, here we are. A humble dwelling, I fear, and one which must seem poor in the eyes of a noble prince."

The Cardinal looked about the great hall; it was hung with Gobelin tapestry and furnished with elegance.

Cagliostro clapped his hands and a dwarf in rich scarlet brocade, dressed in the Persian style, with an enormous emerald set in his turban, came running into the hall.

"Wine," said Cagliostro. "Oh . . . and Djem, send one of the Comtesse's women to her apartment to tell her that we are honoured by the presence of a most eminent visitor."

Djem stretched his arms, the fingers of both hands touching, and bowed so low that his turban touched the floor.

"My lord has spoken," he said, and he hurried silently away.

"You have an unusual household, I perceive," said the Cardinal.

"Djem? His grandfather served me in Persia."

The Cardinal was nonplussed. His common sense told him to be wary of a charlatan, but he was intrigued at the thought of being in the presence of a sorcerer. There were certain things in life which the Cardinal desired and was ready to pay a great price for: power—not as a man of the Church but as a statesman—youth and good looks. With these, in addition to the wealth with which he was adequately provided, he believed he could be the most important man in France.

Of what great use could such as Cagliostro be to a man of ambition, providing of course that Cagliostro was not a charlatan!

A lady was coming down the great staircase. She was young and beautiful; about her neck was a chain set with rubies and emeralds; on her slender white hands diamonds glittered.

The Cardinal's eyes shone as he contemplated the Comtesse de Cagliostro, but the Comte had gone to her and placed an arm about her shoulder.

"My wife," he said; and his dark prominent eyes held those of the Cardinal. The eyes held a warning which the Cardinal found that he understood. He was shaken. In that moment Cagliostro had begun to establish his power over the Cardinal, for de Rohan discovered that his thoughts had been read and that it was possible to say certain things to this man without the use of words.

The Cardinal took the Comtesse's hand and bowed low over it, his lips lightly brushing her skin.

She was charming. But she was not for him.

Well, thought the Cardinal, there are many women in the world.

Cagliostro nodded as though he had spoken aloud.

"Now," said the Comte, "we will refresh ourselves, and later I will show the Cardinal my laboratories. I know that he will be interested to see what work I do therein."

The Comtesse drank with them; and they talked of Strasbourg and Rome, the Comtesse's native city. They must visit him at Saverne, declared the Cardinal. They should not stay another week in Strasbourg without being his guests.

And when the Comtesse left them, the Cardinal accompanied Cagliostro into his laboratory and there they talked of the alchemists' secrets, the wonders of the universe which had been discovered and those which had yet to be understood.

When the Cardinal left the house of Cagliostro, it was arranged that the following day the Comte and his wife should be the guests of Cardinal de Rohan.

*   *   *

When the Cardinal had left, Cagliostro went to Lorenza and, taking her hands in his, laughed aloud with triumph.

"And so ... to Saverne! We are to be guests of the great Cardinal. I will look into the future, my love. I will tell you this: Before many weeks have passed you and I will leave this house."

"Leave ... but Alessandro, where should we find another in Strasbourg to compare with this?"

"We shall find apartments more suited to us at Saverne."

"At the Cardinal's palace!"

"At the Cardinal's palace. He will so yearn to know my secrets, he will be so eager to have me work for him, that he will not be able to bear my being out of his sight."

Cagliostro's eyes had taken on the glazed look which made Lorenza uneasy.

"No," she cried. "Stop. Say no more."

He laughed. "It shall come to pass." Then he embraced

her. "We have taken the first step," he said. "I am pleased with our progress."

"Giuseppe . . ." she said fearfully, for she used the old name when off her guard; but he held up an admonishing finger. "Alessandro," she corrected herself, "what are you going to do here in Strasbourg?"

"We shall cultivate the acquaintance of this eminent man," said Cagliostro. "And then . . . it will be revealed to us what we have to do."

*   *   *

In the Palace of Saverne the Cardinal de Rohan was waiting for his guests. He was entertaining no others this day but Cagliostro and his wife, and he wished to convey to them that he intended this as a compliment; for he was so eager for conversation with the Comte that he could not spare the time to devote himself to other guests.

His table was magnificent with its ornate dishes and glittering gold candlesticks. Ten of his twenty-five footmen would wait upon them; his many cooks were at work in his kitchens preparing a meal with which he hoped to astonish the Comte and Comtesse. The best of his wines were being brought up from his cellars.

He himself was impatient. He longed for that moment when the meal would be over and they might withdraw to the small study of luxury and comfort where they could talk in complete privacy. The Comtesse was a charming woman, but the Cardinal wished that it had not been necessary to include her in the invitation. Women attracted him so strongly that he could never be unconscious of them, no matter how exciting the project in which he was absorbed. He wondered what would happen to him if he seduced the wife of Cagliostro—and he shivered at the thought. He was not a coward, but he would not wish to arouse the wrath of such a sorcerer.

On his fingers gleamed the most magnificent of his jewels. He longed to possess diamonds the size of those worn by Cagliostro. It was clear that the Comte had discovered the Philosopher's Stone. Would he be prepared to pass on his secrets?

The carriage had arrived and the Cardinal was all impatience, but several minutes seemed to elapse before one of his many pages threw open the door and announced: "His Excellency, the Comte de Cagliostro."

They were standing face to face, the Cardinal seeming soberly clad in the robes of the Church. He noticed on Cagliostro's finger the largest diamond he had ever seen set in a ring.

"Greetings, Excellency," said the Cardinal.

"Greetings, Eminence."

"And the Comtesse?"

Cagliostro's eyes held those of his host, and once more the Cardinal had the uncanny feeling that his thoughts had been read and that Cagliostro, knowing he had hoped he would come alone, had done this.

"A little indisposed. She craves your Eminence's pardon and sends her deepest regrets."

"It is indeed a sorrow," said the Cardinal, but he could not meet Cagliostro's eyes.

Cagliostro smiled. "But you and I, Your Eminence, will have much to talk of."

"That is so."

They sat at the long table. "I would have no guests this night," the Cardinal began.

"Because," finished Cagliostro, "you knew that there would be much we had to say, one to the other, and you wished that there should be none other present to hear it."

"It is true," admitted the Cardinal.

"I am happy that it should be so," said Cagliostro.

"When we have eaten," said the Cardinal, "we could retire to the intimacy of my private chamber."

"That would give me great pleasure, for what we shall say must be for the ears of none other but ourselves."

De Rohan lifted a hand and signed to the minstrels in the gallery, and their music made a pleasant background to the conversation, which concerned life in Strasbourg and travels abroad.

The silent menservants moved expertly about the hall. Cagliostro ate well and drank deep. It was long since he had enjoyed such well-cooked food. The Cardinal was delighted with his appreciation, but he was eagerly awaiting that moment when they should retire.

Cagliostro, whilst tackling the fish covered with a highly flavoured sauce, the meat which was equally garnished, whilst drinking the wine which the Cardinal told him was from his own vineyards, was taking stock of his companion. He did not forget for one moment that his reason for coming to Strasbourg was to know this man, to know him completely and to understand his innermost thoughts. To anticipate those thoughts? To put desires into the Cardinal's mind? To make the Cardinal clay in the hands of Cagliostro?

He was eager to do this because in return he would learn all the secrets of the Illuminati. He must show them that in choosing Cagliostro for this delicate task they had chosen the only man who could perform it.

The object? To undermine the throne of France, which, according to these men whose knowledge came from secret places, was more ready to fall than any other in Europe. Every minute which he spent in the company of Cardinal de Rohan brought him nearer to understanding why he had been chosen as an instrument in this devious game.

Louis de Rohan believed in the occult. He believed

because he fervently wished to believe. And such men were dissatisfied with the world as it was—or perhaps their place in it. They would mould the world to their own desires; for only by so doing could they bring to themselves those honours which they were so sure were theirs by right. This, they had discovered, could not be done by earthly means; therefore they sought wider powers.

All ambitious men who felt themselves to be failing would be ready to seek powers beyond the control of ordinary men; and surely all such men must in some measure be weak men, for, if they had all the gifts with which in their imagination they endowed themselves they would not have failed.

The Cardinal's eyes were shining with excitement as he said: "And would it please you now to retire to my small chamber where we may talk in privacy?"

"It would give me the utmost pleasure. I confess it is what I have been waiting for. Your cooks, Eminence, are excellent; I trust you will not think me churlish if I say that I long to explore what is in your mind rather than what is on your table."

"I see that we are of the same mind in this matter," said de Rohan, smiling. "Come, my friend."

It was a small panelled room, silent and luxurious. The signs of the zodiac had been painted on the ceiling and in the centre of these was that of the Scales, the Cardinal's own sign. A skull, several books, and charts of the heavens, which lay on a gilded table set with precious stones, proclaimed the Cardinal's interest in the occult.

"Charming," murmured Cagliostro.

"I retire here for complete solitude," answered the Cardinal. "I pray you, be seated."

"You ... first," said Cagliostro, and by those words he implied that he was in command. In the great hall before the eyes of the servants he had been the guest, talking with animation of his travels; here in the presence, he implied, of the occult, he was the master.

The Cardinal looked mildly surprised but sat down on a couch embroidered with the arms of Rohan-Guéménée.

"I sometimes like to walk about while I talk," said Cagliostro. "A little foible, you understand?"

"Pray do as you wish," the Cardinal begged him.

Cagliostro turned his magnetic eyes upon his host. "Eminence," he said, "you are a little weary. You are a man on whom great demands are made. You, a Prince of the Royal house, should not be here in Strasbourg."

De Rohan tried to open his eyes wide, but he found that it was not easy to do so. Completely fascinated as he was, much as he had looked forward to this encounter, he found that he was decidedly sleepy.

"I . . . I do not understand you, Comte," he said.

"I mean, Eminence, that your place should be in Versailles . . . in Paris . . . in the capital. Not here in this town which is not worthy of you."

"I became Archbishop of Strasbourg on the death of my uncle, Constantine. . . ."

"And you are a cardinal," said Cagliostro softly, keeping his eyes on de Rohan as he spoke. "A cardinal, a man of the Church. I fancy, Eminence, that you would better have served your country at the head of state affairs."

Over the Cardinal's face had crept an expression of pride and anger. I am right, thought Cagliostro. His mind is as an open book to me.

"And," went on Cagliostro, "why should not a cardinal rule France? There have been cardinals. Richelieu! What a man! What a genius! And Mazarin—not even a Frenchman, though he always declared he became one in . . . let me think again . . . ah, 1642. The Queen was fond of Mazarin . . . over-fond? Perhaps . . . but that is their secret. Richelieu! Mazarin! Why not de Rohan?"

The Cardinal was slightly flushed. His knuckles showed white among the jewels on his fingers.

"I see no reason," went on Cagliostro who had now turned his eyes from the Cardinal's face and was staring blankly before him, "why France should not have the benefit of yet another cardinal's wisdom. I see Cardinal de Rohan at Versailles."

"You see the future?" said the Cardinal. He had risen and, taking Cagliostro's arm, seemed almost to be pleading with him. "Tell me . . . you see the future?"

Cagliostro laid his hands on de Rohan's shoulders and gently pushed him back on to the couch. "The future?" he said. "The future is within our grasp." He was staring at his own hands which were curved as though holding a globe which the Cardinal almost felt he saw. "We make it as we wish it to be," he added.

"I am not loved at the court," said the Cardinal almost sullenly.

"It is true."

"At every turn I am frustrated. I have my enemies. And the greatest of these is. . . ."

"The Queen," said Cagliostro.

"It's true. The frivolous Austrian woman has decided to spurn me. The King is a fool . . . wax in her hands."

Cagliostro thought: So he desires the Austrian woman. And almost as though he had bidden the Cardinal speak of her, he began to do so.

"I saw her first when she came into France. Before Louis saw her, I touched her hands. It was. . . ."

"In the year 1770," supplied Cagliostro. "When she came to hear Mass at your cathedral."

"My uncle could not officiate and I took his place. She was but a child . . . a frivolous child, and the manner in which she looked at me, the manner in which she put her hand in mine. . . ."

Aroused that desire, thought Cagliostro, which is always so ready to be aroused. But he said: "Warned you then of the coquette she would become."

There was silence. He was willing the Cardinal to recall that scene: the young girl—on her way to her husband—the new Dauphine who might do much for an ambitious man.

It seemed to the Cardinal that another scene was superimposed on that of the room. Instead of the glittering figure of Cagliostro, he saw that of a young girl—fair-haired, the daintiest creature he had ever set eyes on, and she was lifting her blue eyes to the face of the young and handsome priest to whom, his uncle being indisposed, had fallen the great honour of receiving her. He saw his own hands lift the monstrance for the benediction; he heard his own voice praising her and the union with the Dauphin which was going to bring peace to France and Austria. The scene shifted to this very Palace of Saverne where he had entertained her after the ceremony in the cathedral. She had sat beside him at the table and she had talked, sometimes in German, sometimes in her quaint, but attractive French. He had thought about her long after she had gone; and he had laughed derisively to think of his clumsy kinsman—the Duc de Berry, who had since become Louis XVI of France—as the husband of such a charming creature. How much more suitable to that role would have been Prince Louis de Rohan-Guéménée!

A faint laugh close to him brought him back to reality. Cagliostro had sat down in a chair with a high, ornamental back. He was holding his hands together, tips of fingers touching, palms apart, and over them he continued to study the Cardinal.

"That happened more than ten years ago," he was saying. "And during those ten years much has happened ... to you ... to her ... and to France."

"To France, I fear, not much that is good."

"That is why she needs great men to rule her."

"There was a time," mused the Cardinal, "when I believed that I should be one of those men."

"It was two years after the arrival of our little Dauphine," murmured Cagliostro. "You were sent on an embassy to Vienna."

"It would seem that you know a great deal about my life."

Cagliostro's eyes expressed surprise, which, the Cardinal understood, implied his astonishment that a man of intellect should waste time commenting on the obvious. Of course he knew all; he was a magician.

"Vienna," mused Cagliostro, "and the Empress."

De Rohan laughed. "A battle-axe of a woman."

"Not one who was likely to give pleasure to a man of such fastidious tastes as Your Eminence. She disapproved."

"Heartily," agreed the Cardinal.

"She wrote of you that you were without prudence, talent and morals."

"The woman was obsessed by virtue. Unless a man spent half his life on his knees he was counted profligate."

"A pity, Eminence, that you aroused the indignation of that *good* woman."

"Had I but foreseen the future. . . ."

"Ah!" interjected Cagliostro.

"As you do," went on the Cardinal, "I should have acted differently. I verily believe that my dissatisfaction with my present state dates from my visit to Vienna."

"Every little action leaves its mark on our lives, Eminence. Every little ripple disturbs the serenity of the lake."

"One is young . . . one does not guess what the ambitions of the future will be."

"Unless one is possessed of great wisdom. But it is

D

never too late. The past can be redressed by the future."

"I have tried." The Cardinal clenched his hands. "I have done all in my power to reinstate myself. I think that if it rested with the King I should be there, at Versailles. But she does not forget. She has sworn to be my enemy. Who would have thought that a girl . . . a young, frivolous girl . . . could have such power?"

"You speak of her with great feeling," whispered Cagliostro.

De Rohan did not immediately answer. To him it was as though she were in the room. She seemed to materialize, in her gown of shimmering silver, the enormous skirt covered with lauriers roses, the bodice falling away from slender shoulders. Diamonds glittered at her throat and neck. Her fair hair was piled above her high forehead, a chain of diamonds wound about it, and white plumes, gracefully drooping over it, shaded that face which was so small, so dainty yet full of animation. She seemed to him —partly because he felt her to be unattainable—the most desirable woman in the world.

"It is she who stands between me and my ambitions," he said, and his voice shook with fury. "She has declared she will never forgive me, that I shall never be received at court if it is in her power to prevent me. She uses her influence against me continually. She did all in her power to stop my being made Grand Almoner."

"Without success," added Cagliostro, so faintly that the Cardinal scarcely heard him.

"She would have prevented my receiving my cardinal's hat; but there again she failed."

"One understands her anger against Your Eminence. I pray you, do not frown. It is only if I speak the truth that I can be of use to you. While you were in Vienna, did you not boast a little of the impression you had made on the Dauphine during that first meeting with her?"

"I swear I made an impression."

"But to boast of it—and she Dauphine of France! It is something which she finds it hard to forgive. But you are a handsome man. I would say that many women find you irresistible. You might have been forgiven, but you attacked the sacred Empress, did you not?"

"A light remark in a letter."

"Poking fun at Maria Theresa, at the Dauphine's mother! Marie Antoinette reveres her mother; did you not know that? Delighted as she is to escape from those stern eyes, receiving letters of admonition, as she does every few days, she yet respects her sainted mother as no one else. That was your mistake, Cardinal. You poked fun at her ... in writing ... which gave our little Dauphine's greatest enemy, the du Barry, the opportunity of reading aloud what you had written ... aloud, I repeat ... at one of her supper parties." Cagliostro spread his hands and stared at the magnificent diamond on his forefinger. "That was where you made one of the greatest mistakes of your life, Eminence."

There was silence in the room. The Cardinal was aware of the ticking of his favourite clock; he felt sure that the intervals between the ticks were longer than usual. He believed that in some way Cagliostro was holding back the passage of time, and that every second which was now passing was full of importance for himself.

"Yes," he said slowly, "it was the greatest mistake in my life."

"There are certain factors which have not occurred to you," continued Cagliostro. "The little Dauphine who has now become our Queen did all in her power, you say, to prevent your becoming Grand Almoner and receiving your cardinal's hat. *All* in her power? Then since she did not succeed, how great is her power? Ponder this. She tried ... she failed. She is a beautiful woman.

She could influence the King. Yet she fails. Do you not realize, Eminence, that she is like a gay butterfly? She wants this ... she does not want that ... oh, but not deeply. Not enough to use all her influence to obtain it ... or prevent it. Such a woman stamps her foot and says 'I will not'. But ... a little gentle persuasion, a little diplomacy, and in a short time 'I will not' becomes 'I will'."

Again he had curved his hands and the Cardinal believed he saw a crystal globe held in them.

"You look into the future," he said hoarsely.

"My friend," said Cagliostro, and the appellation seemed fraught with meaning to the alert ears of the Cardinal, "the future is in our hands."

Cagliostro had risen abruptly. Now the room seemed lighter to de Rohan; he noticed the familiar objects. He felt as though he had been put into a trance, and that trance was now at an end. He put his hand to his forehead; he touched the beads of sweat there.

"I have tired you," said Cagliostro.

"It is long since I have felt so stimulated by conversation," answered the Cardinal.

"But I will leave you now."

"I pray you, do not go. There are so many subjects which I wish to discuss with you. It is not often that one is aware of so much wisdom within one's grasp."

"Then we shall meet again."

"But when?"

Cagliostro laughed. "I reside in Strasbourg. We shall visit frequently, if the desire to do so is mutual."

"I beg of you ... visit me here tomorrow."

"So soon?"

"I will invite no other guests. It shall be as it has been this day. I want to ask you so many questions. Is it true that you have discovered the Philosopher's Stone and the Elixir of Life?"

Cagliostro smiled. "My lord, you are a prince and a cardinal. You have your duties in this place, and I have mine. Do you know that, since I have been here, I am visited daily by those who are sick in mind and body?"

"I know that you bring new hope to many of the suffering people of Strasbourg."

"It gives me the utmost pleasure to spend my time with a man of your intellect, with a man destined for greatness. But I have my duties, Eminence."

"But tomorrow . . . ?"

"I will send a messenger to tell you when I can come to you."

The Cardinal could not hide his apprehension. He was afraid that the wise man, who had in some strange way implied that he could help him achieve his heart's desire, was about to slip through his fingers.

*   *   *

Cagliostro went to Lorenza's apartments when he returned to his house in Strasbourg.

She was waiting for him. He laughed and embraced her. "You look blooming, my love."

"It is well that your Cardinal cannot see me now, Alessandro."

"He would think that I had cured you, and I believe he imagines I laid upon you that little indisposition so that he and I might be alone together."

"You are pleased with what took place?"

"My work here is going to be amusing, my love, amusing and very pleasant."

"He was amiable?"

"More than amiable. He is enamoured of all I stand for. He hopes that through me he will achieve that which so far he has sought in vain."

"And will he, Alessandro?"

He took her chin in his hand and smiled at her. "Are you too asking me to look into the future? This much I can tell you. We shall live here like a prince and princess, Lorenza. No . . . not here . . . but in the Episcopal Palace itself. A magnificent mansion, my dearest, and one worthy of us."

"He has asked us to join him there?"

"Not yet. That will come."

"Alessandro. . . ."

"Let us say, my love, that I have put the thought into his head. Now we will wait for it to take root and blossom."

*   *   *

All next day and the one that followed, the Cardinal waited for a message from Cagliostro.

In his house near the cathedral the believers waited to see the Comte. He received them one by one. His discerning eyes and that extra sense quickly summed up the man or woman with whom he had to deal. For those whom he could reach through that hypnotism which he had studied so assiduously in various countries under the guidance of Altotas, he worked his miraculous cures. For those who could not be so reached he had his pills and philtres, which were as effective as anything available from the doctors. It was only necessary, for a credulous crowd, to see one miraculous cure and forthwith accept him as a Master of the Occult, a benevolent magician— all that he wished to seem in their eyes.

"You, my friend," he would say to those whom his experience told him he could not cure by suggestion, "are without faith. Even my Great Master, who walked this Earth many years ago, could not have helped you as He did the daughter of Jairus. So I give you this lotion. You would pay dearly for it to a court physician. Go your way in peace and, my friend, if you would benefit from the miracles of the universe, have faith . . . have faith."

Many went away weeping, and throughout Strasbourg the fame of the great Cagliostro was spreading.

But still no news came to the Cardinal of that promised visit.

The Cardinal sent one of his servants into the town to discover what was happening, and the man came back to tell him of the crowd who assembled night and day outside the house of Cagliostro.

"He cures the sick, Eminence, and there is scarcely time for him to eat or sleep; so many people call upon him to speak with him, to glean some wisdom and to be cured of their sickness."

The servant then began to tell of the miraculous cures which the whole town was discussing and added little flourishes of his own—for he knew they would please his master—to the exaggerations of the townsfolk.

"Go to the house of the Comte de Cagliostro," said the Cardinal. "Tell him that I am sick of a pain in the throat which prevents my breathing with ease. Go to him immediately and beg him to come to visit me, not as guest but as a physician."

Within three hours Cagliostro was presenting himself at the Palace of Saverne.

The Cardinal was lying on a couch in the private room in which they had talked on that night when Cagliostro had been his guest.

"Do not rise," said Cagliostro, taking the chair which the servant had drawn up for him. "I pray you, leave us," he said to the serving man. "And close the door."

The servant bowed and departed, and when they were alone, Cagliostro smiled at the Cardinal.

"You are cured," he said. "Your pains are no longer with you." He burst into loud laughter. "Did you think to deceive me, Eminence? Did you think to put me to the test?"

The Cardinal joined in the laughter and rose from the couch. "I had to find some way to bring you here."

"I am honoured, and most humbly do I crave your pardon. There has been no opportunity, you understand. I felt that those others had greater need of me."

"No one," said the Cardinal firmly, "has greater need of you than I."

"Well, I have come."

"There is so much I have to say to you. Our conversation of that night stays with me. I hear it again and again, and it seems fraught with meaning. You can help me, Comte. I know you can help me ... even as you help those poor creatures who come to your house."

"The help must come from within each person," said Cagliostro. "All I can do, is show the way."

"Then show me the way, I beg of you."

"Your way," said Cagliostro, "is long and devious. You are not possessed with an idea of sickness which manifests itself in the body, as are those ignorant people with whom I have been dealing. You must find your way up to the pinnacle of ambition ... alone. I could only point the way."

The Cardinal had risen; he had grasped Cagliostro's arm. "Then show me the way. I beg you, show me the way."

"Back to Versailles. Back to greatness," mused Cagliostro. "Richelieu, Mazarin, de Rohan!"

"You can help me. I know it."

Cagliostro had released himself from the Cardinal's grip. "To live at court one must be rich. You are rich, Cardinal."

"Men would call me so."

"You have a large income."

"Two and a half million francs a year."

"You must be one of the richest men in France."

"I have never been prudent. I have many debts."

Cagliostro was turning one of the rings on his fingers and staring at the great diamond set therein. The Cardinal followed his gaze and said: "That stone must be worth twenty-thousand livres."

"I would I could show you the workroom which was once mine," said Cagliostro. "Here ... in my house I have a small room. In Frankfurt, where I resided awhile before I came to Strasbourg, I was given laboratories to delight the heart of any alchemist."

"I should like to show you mine."

"Ah, your laboratories. You, like every gentleman in Europe, are busy with your experiments."

"The man who discovers those two great benefits will be ready to explore the secrets of the universe."

Cagliostro turned to the Cardinal and laid his hands on his shoulders. "I feel," he said, "a mingling of our souls. They are worthy of each other. Eminence, you are a man with whom I could share many secrets."

"I know it!" cried the elated Cardinal.

"Take me now to those rooms in which you have conducted your experiments."

"They are at the top of the palace. Follow me. I will take you there immediately."

Cagliostro smiled. There, were all the tools of the alchemist, everything finely wrought, as luxurious as wealth could provide.

"I see," he said, "that you are indeed fortunate. You have everything an alchemist could need. And yet ... you are as far from the discovery as the humblest man who dreams over his crucible in a rat-ridden cellar. I'll confess to you that I myself have never worked in rooms of such magnificence. I'll confess something else. I could find it in my heart to envy you, Cardinal."

"These poor rooms, Comte, are of course at your disposal."

"That is a generous offer. But the alchemist must live with his crucible for days and nights."

"Then leave your house. Come here . . . you, your wife . . . your servants. Be my guests. Nothing would delight me more. . . ."

"Cardinal, I thank you with all my heart. But I think of the poor of Strasbourg."

"They have enjoyed your presence for several days. What do you owe the people of Strasbourg more than those of any other town? I swear that if you will come to Saverne as my guest I will do everything in my power to make you comfortable. My laboratories are at your disposal. Comte, I implore you, come to Saverne."

Cagliostro was silent; he smothered his elation and forced a show of reluctance into his eyes, his gestures, the very tone of his voice.

"I do not seek luxury, my friend."

Silence fell between them. With the Cardinal it was the silence of despair.

Then he heard Cagliostro whispering something under his breath. It was "Richelieu, Mazarin, de Rohan!"

A great excitement seized the Cardinal then. He was sure that he could not achieve his ambition without the occult power which he would draw from this man.

When Cagliostro left he had given him no answer.

He had decided to let him wait at least a week before he moved into the Episcopal Palace.

*   *   *

Never during the whole of his career had Cagliostro found an easier subject than the Cardinal de Rohan. It seemed incredible that a man of education and experience, a Prince of the Royal House of France, could be so simple. Cagliostro was the first to realize that it was ambition coupled with an inordinate vanity which had softened the Cardinal's mind.

Cagliostro and his wife now had their apartments in the Palace of Saverne and the Cardinal spread all the luxury of his establishment at their feet. Rarely in the whole of his life had he been so excited.

Cagliostro quickly established his ascendancy over his dupe. There were times, he implied, when he needed long hours of meditation in which as yet the Cardinal was unfitted to accompany him. De Rohan meekly accepted this and humbly waited for those precious hours when Cagliostro could devote himself to his host.

Then they talked long of the Cardinal's past and Cagliostro found a certain pleasure in pointing out at what stages of his life he had swerved from the path to greatness. Always in these conversations they would return to the Queen. She was the focal point of the Cardinal's failure; when he mentioned her name his voice became infused with an intense passion which the man would have Cagliostro believe was hatred. The hatred, mused Cagliostro, was a cloak covering desire. Once the Queen had smiled on the amorous prelate, the hatred would fall away as though it were a cloak that had been unclasped and discarded. The Cardinal's great dream was of power with which he would rule France as other cardinals had; but he would achieve this power through the beautiful young Queen who appealed so strongly to his senses. He did not mention this to Cagliostro, nor did Cagliostro think it wise as yet to mention it to him, for he was not certain that the Cardinal had faced the truth; but the desires of the Cardinal would not be satisfied until he was the lover of Marie Antoinette, the Queen of France.

In the attics Cagliostro, among whose many talents was a sleight of hand which he had perfected when he had learned his ventriloquial art and had practised ever since, 'made' diamonds before the astonished eyes of the Cardinal. It was a long process, Cagliostro explained, and an exhausting one. He had no intention of performing this trick often; but he had realized that once he had taken up his residence in the Cardinal's palace he would be required to do it now and then.

He produced a dazzling stone which, had it been a diamond, would have been worth twenty-thousand livres. He handed it to the enraptured Cardinal.

"It is yours, my friend," he said.

The Cardinal implored his friend to allow him to use the crucible and the material in the way that Cagliostro had, but he found when he did so that his efforts were fruitless.

Cagliostro laughed. "There is more to it than what is seen by the eyes, my friend," he pointed out.

And the Cardinal believed this. He sent for his jeweller, a man who Cagliostro quickly realized was as credulous as his master and would be an easy subject for suggestion.

"You see this stone?" said the Cardinal, holding it out to the man. "What would you say it is worth?"

The jeweller looked at the stone, and as he did so he was aware of the magnetic influence of Cagliostro. He had seen the miracles in Strasbourg.

He said: "I have never before seen a stone to compare with this one, my lord."

Cagliostro laughed. "His Eminence thinks it to be worth many thousand livres. I suggest twenty-three thousand."

The jeweller lifted his eyes and met the dark ones of Cagliostro. He seemed to lose himself in them. Then he answered: "It is so, of course, my lord Comte."

The diamond was set into a ring, and the Cardinal wore it always.

"Never," he declared, "shall I allow it to pass from my possession."

Cagliostro made a little 'gold' for his friend; but here again the process was long and the Cardinal was more interested in his ambitions than in the accumulation of wealth with which, in spite of debts, he was already well supplied. He greatly preferred those hours when they walked in the gardens or were alone in his private room discussing the glorious future which would be his.

Lorenza was scarcely seen by the Cardinal. She did not wish to be. She could not cast off her fear of the strange things which had happened in her life since she had married Cagliostro. Sometimes the Cardinal saw her walking in the gardens but he could do so without emotion. His thoughts were obsessed by one figure—the daintiest and most arrogant in France.

Friends came to visit de Rohan at Saverne. They were astonished and alarmed not only to find Cagliostro established so firmly in the Episcopal Palace, but that the Cardinal was completely in thrall to the man whom, although they were aware of his extraordinary qualities, they suspected of being one of the most cunning scoundrels of the age.

They warned de Rohan to be wary, but he laughed at their suspicions.

"I tell you Cagliostro is a god," he said. "There are times when I believe he is God Himself. He makes diamonds and gold before my eyes. Who else in the world can do that? They are miracles. He also cures the sick. There are many in Strasbourg who will testify to the miracles of this man."

"He is clever," was the sceptical answer. "We doubt that not. But there are many who swear he is a trickster."

"As there was of One other who walked the Earth seventeen hundred years ago. I tell you Cagliostro has deep knowledge of matters beyond the understanding of ordinary men. He is as familiar with the past as he is with the present and, I suspect, the future. He will make me the richest man in Europe."

"Take care, Monseigneur," he was warned. "It has been said that he demands full payment for what he gives."

"He asks me nothing . . . nothing."

"Yet he lives in your palace, he and his household, at your expense."

The Cardinal snapped his fingers and displayed the jewel on his finger. "This he gave me. It is worth more than twenty-thousand livres. My jeweller confirms this. Yet the Comte handed it to me as though it were a flower he had carelessly picked in the gardens; and you say he will demand more than he will give!"

"Take care," was the repeated warning.

But the Cardinal merely laughed at these warnings.

He invited a sculptor to the palace and begged Cagliostro to sit for him.

Indulgently, Cagliostro agreed, and the result was a bust of the magician beneath which de Rohan caused the words 'The divine Cagliostro' to be engraved.

It was placed in the hall of the palace, so that when guests entered it was the first thing which caught their eyes.

*   *   *

Cagliostro had been residing at Saverne several months and each day the mind of the Cardinal became more and more under his control. The Cardinal now accepted him without doubt as divine, and Cagliostro marvelled at the conceit of the man while he rejoiced in it, as he must rejoice in everything that made his task easier.

De Rohan saw himself as the greatest figure in France, now under a cloud through the perversity of one woman;

he believed that the Divine Powers had therefore sent Cagliostro to him that he might by occult means be placed on that high eminence to which by nature he belonged. It did not seem incredible that Divine Providence should select him as the instrument to save France from disaster, but merely natural that this should be so. He was a prince and a cardinal, a man twice the size, so he believed, of those other minor statesmen who buzzed about the court like so many benevolent bees or infuriated wasps.

He was enough of a politician to realize that France was in an uneasy state. He was aware that never in its existence had the country been in such danger as it was in these 1780s. There were certain men of power in France who, it seemed, were working together to destroy the monarchy. The chief of these was the Duc de Chartres, son of the Duc d'Orléans, who had founded a secret society—the Orient of France—the motives of which were not widely known but were undoubtedly subversive and directed against the throne. There was also the Lodge of the Amis Réunis, and it was whispered in some quarters that, under the cloak of Freemasonry, many plots were afoot to destroy all monarchy throughout Europe and bring about a state of equality.

The Cardinal wished to save France; he was conscious of great powers within him. He believed that he was destined to rule France, with the Queen as his most ardent supporter—Louis did not count—as Mazarin had once ruled with Anne of Austria. And with the passing of each day he believed more firmly that it was no mere chance which had brought Cagliostro to Strasbourg.

One day he came to Cagliostro with the news that he expected a visitor.

"It is the Marquise de Boulainvilliers, the wife of an old friend. She is passing through Strasbourg and says she cannot do so without calling on me. I believe that, knowing you are with me, she is making the journey especially to see you. If you would rather not endure her woman's chatter I will make your excuses."

Cagliostro smiled gently. "I would not seem churlish to your friends," he said.

*   *   *

The Cardinal received his visitor with his usual grace.

"My dear Marquise, it is indeed a pleasure to see you here at Saverne, and I am delighted that you have found the time to visit me."

"I could not pass so near and not do so, my lord," she answered.

He had invited a few guests to the intimate banquet; and it was when they were all assembled that Cagliostro made his entry.

He was magnificently attired in velvet and cloth of gold, but as usual it was his dazzling array of jewels which attracted everyone's attention.

"His Excellency, the Comte de Cagliostro!" announced the footman; and as the Comte slowly advanced, the Cardinal went to meet him, his hands outstretched, and murmuring: "It is indeed gracious of you to honour us with your presence, Master."

Cagliostro smiled and laid his hand affectionately on the Cardinal's shoulder. Then he turned and surveyed the assembled guests.

"Present me," he said, "to the Marquise de Boulain-villiers. I would show the world that your friends are mine."

So the Cardinal presented Cagliostro, first to the Marquise, and when the others had one by one greeted him with that respect which the Cardinal demanded for him, he took his place beside the Marquise.

All attention was directed to Cagliostro, and this he

accepted as his right. He set himself to entertain them with tales of his travels, introducing into the conversation accounts of miraculous happenings with that nonchalance which never failed to impress an audience. He had discovered over the years that, by referring to such events as though they were natural, he was almost certain to win the confidence of his hearers.

But he was really thinking of the Marquise, and after the company had feasted he suggested they stroll in the grounds of the palace; and he made sure that he walked beside the lady. He led her away from the others with a firmness which the Cardinal always respected and would, on such an occasion, make sure that his guests respected also.

Cagliostro believed that the visit of the Marquise had been arranged, and he was determined to find out why. It occurred to him that the Illuminati might have sent their own spy to discover what was happening at Saverne. He realized that although they would hear reports they would want something more than rumours. He was fully aware that, so far, they had not confided to him their innermost secrets, and he imagined that the subjugation of the Cardinal de Rohan was a test of his ability to which they were putting him.

He knew that the Marquise's husband was a member of several secret societies, and that he was a Freemason of the Amis Réunis. He knew also that it was the desire of the Illuminati to bring all secret societies under one head, that they might work towards a common end.

"Your husband's grandfather was a great man," said Cagliostro. "I admired him. There was a bond between us, for he was a Jew, and I have a great fondness for Jews. I consider them one of the cleverest races on this Earth."

"That is indeed kind of you, Comte. The Jews are not loved by all."

E

"They are reviled . . . by fools. Have you not noticed that those who ill-treat them are invariably overtaken by disaster? But your family has come to greatness. I trust your husband's grandfather's services have not been forgotten by the crown."

"Oh, we are not favourites at court as my husband's grandfather was."

"Le Roi Soleil could be grateful. He did not forget Samuel Bernard's help."

"You speak as though you knew them both, my husband's grandfather and Louis Quatorze."

Cagliostro smiled. "How concerned so many are with time! But do not let it disturb you. I know this, that Louis was grateful to Samuel Bernard and in return for financial help made him a Chevalier of France. It was through the gratitude of Louis Quatorze that Samuel Bernard's grandson was able to buy the estate of Boulainvilliers and make his charming wife a Marquise."

"You know so much about us, Comte."

"I know also that a certain impulse sent you here."

She looked startled, but ignored that remark.

"I would ask your advice, Comte. It concerns a protégée of mine."

Cagliostro waited. He could not ask of whom she was speaking, for he must appear omniscient.

"It is a certain young woman for whom I feel very sorry. She is handsome, young, and of aristocratic birth. I fear life has been very cruel to her. She is married, but she and her husband have little means of support. He is a young officer." Madame de Boulainvilliers lifted her shoulders. "You know how it is with these young people. I should like to do something for her, and I wonder whether the Cardinal would help her."

"It is your opinion that the Cardinal could help her?"

"He is a man of influence."

"Then . . . since he is your friend, why do you not talk to him of your protégée?"

"The Cardinal would be more influenced by you, Comte. It is clear that you have but to lift a finger and he obeys."

"So you would have me persuade him to help this young woman and her husband?"

"If you would graciously consent to do so, you would have not only my gratitude but that of . . . others."

Cagliostro was silent for a few seconds. He thought he understood. There was some reason why this young woman should be brought to the Cardinal's notice. This might be an order from those who had financed him that he might insinuate himself into the Cardinal's household. He could not ask outright if this were so, for he must appear to know.

He said: "I see no reason why this young woman should not be brought to the notice of His Eminence."

"How can I thank you, Comte?"

"It is little you ask," he told her gallantly. "I would so willingly do more."

*   *   *

The Cardinal and Cagliostro were driving on the road between Saverne and Strasbourg when they saw a carriage coming towards them.

The Cardinal said: "I declare it is that of Madame de Boulainvilliers. She must be driving out to visit us."

The carriages drew up on the roadside. The Cardinal and Cagliostro alighted, and as they did so the Marquise stepped out of her own carriage.

"Well met!" cried the Cardinal bowing gracefully over her hand. "I should have been desolate if you had driven to Saverne, only to find us not at home."

"It is true that I was calling on you," said the Marquise.

"And the fault is entirely mine. I should have sent a messenger first to ask your permission. I have a friend with me whom I was bringing to meet you."

Cagliostro had come forward and, bowing to the Marquise, laid his hand on the Cardinal's arm.

"Madame la Marquise is eager to present her friend. She knows you will receive her kindly."

"So it is a lady?" said the Cardinal.

"Yes," said the Marquise. "It is a lady. Jeanne," she called, "you may come out, my dear. The Comte and the Cardinal will receive you."

She stepped out of the carriage and the Cardinal's eyes lit up as they fell upon her, for she was tall, slender, and very pretty. Her hair was dark, her skin very clear, and her eyes blue. Her lashes and eyebrows were dark, and the contrast to her eyes was startling and made of her a beauty.

"Monsieur le Comte, Monsieur le Cardinal, may I present Mademoiselle de Valois?"

The Cardinal took the girl's hands as she dropped a low curtsy. He kissed them both lingeringly. She was the prettiest girl he had seen for a long time, and for those few seconds he even forgot Cagliostro standing beside him.

Cagliostro did not take her hands; he laid his on her shoulders. She curtsyed and raised those beautiful blue eyes to his face. The dark prominent eyes held hers as Cagliostro tried to discover what sort of woman this was. It was as though the girl understood this and was determined to shut him out of her thoughts.

She is a schemer, thought Cagliostro. An adventuress. I must beware of this one.

"Mademoiselle de Valois," the Cardinal was saying, "you have a distinguished name and one which makes a member of the House of Bourbon ponder."

"I have a right to that name, Eminence," said the girl almost pertly.

"Indeed she has," put in the Marquise. "Jeanne is descended from Henri Deux."

Cagliostro laughed lightly. "As unlike a King of France as ever sat upon the throne. He was a simple man. Your ancestress was a charming girl." He smiled at Jeanne. "She had a look of you. His *affaire* with her was one of those little lapses which beset even men such as faithful Henri. Madame Diane was not very pleased, but she was a clever woman, wise enough to know that when he was not near her there must be ladies to charm him . . . as your ancestress did."

The girl said slowly: "How can you know so much?"

"It is clear," said the Cardinal, "that you cannot realize you are in the presence of the Comte de Cagliostro."

Jeanne lowered her eyes and dropped another curtsy.

"I did not realize it, my lord." She looked boldly at Cagliostro. "Then you understand, Master, that I speak truth . . . that I am indeed descended from the Royal House of Valois."

"Those who seek to deceive me are foolish," said Cagliostro. "You, my child, are not a fool."

The Marquise and the Cardinal looked on with delight.

"The road," said the Cardinal, "is scarcely the place for meetings such as this. I trust, Marquise, that you will bring Mademoiselle de Valois to visit me at Saverne."

"With the utmost pleasure," said the Marquise.

Then they returned to their carriages; and the Marquise's was turned to follow the Cardinal's into Strasbourg.

The Cardinal was pensive. It was obvious that his mind was more occupied with thoughts of the charming young woman than with his future greatness.

*   *   *

Cagliostro and Madame de Boulainvilliers strolled in the gardens of the Palace of Saverne. They had left Jeanne alone with the Cardinal.

"She will the better plead her cause alone," said Cagliostro. And once more he was right.

The Cardinal had taken her into that intimate room of his.

"Here, my child," he said, "we can be undisturbed, and I can listen in peace to what you have to tell me."

Jeanne hesitated.

"You are afraid?"

The blue eyes were innocent. "Not of you, my lord Cardinal."

Her innocence was enchanting. He took her hand and made her sit beside him on his couch.

"Now . . . tell me what it is you want."

She was silent, and he put an arm lightly about her shoulders to encourage her.

"It is hard to . . . to ask favours. . . ."

"You have such charming lips. Surely they were meant to ask favours."

"Your Eminence is so kind. I find it very difficult to tell you that I am almost penniless and very much afraid that I shall soon be reduced to begging in the streets. It would seem as though I were asking for your help."

"But is that not what you came to ask?"

"It was Madame de Boulainvilliers who suggested I should speak to you. I myself would never have dared."

"Then, I pray you, be grateful to Madame de Boulainvilliers . . . for I am."

"Why so?" she asked artlessly.

He drew her to him and placed a chaste kiss on her forehead. He was immediately excited. He had been neglecting women during his obsession with Cagliostro.

"You are charming," he said, "and it is my pleasure to help charming girls such as you are."

"I do not ask for money," she said proudly.

"For what do you ask?"

"For . . . for help. I have been brought up to know that I belong to a royal house. The Valois were as great kings as the Bourbons, and it seems an insult to the house of Valois that one of its members should be reduced to penury. My husband and I. . . ."

"Your husband? So you are married!"

She turned away and looked sorrowful. "It is true, my lord Cardinal. I was very young. It was a great mistake; but it happened and I must therefore admit it."

Madame de Boulainvilliers said nothing of a husband, mused the Cardinal. But he was not displeased. He was determined that the girl should be his mistress, and he preferred married women to fill such roles. They were more knowledgeable, more philosophical than young girls, and there was usually less delay. "Tell me," he said, "who is this husband of yours?"

"He is the Comte de la Motte, an officer in the army."

"And where is he now?"

"He is in Strasbourg."

"He did not see fit to come with you to ask my aid?"

"No, my lord. He is too proud. It was Madame de Boulainvilliers' idea that you might help me. My husband is insensible to . . . to the honour of being connected, through marriage, with the Valois family. He does not realize its importance. The Valois no longer rule, he says; therefore they are of no importance to France. That is not true, is it, my lord?"

"Of a certainty it is not. For Valois and Bourbon are closely knit, my child. They trace their descent back to the same stem, the same roots."

"So I thought."

"What would you have me do for you, my dear?"

"Find me a place at court, where I can live as my name demands I should."

"Did you not know that I am out of favour at court?"

"It will not always be so."

"No," said the Cardinal fiercely, "it shall not always be so."

"And when you are in your rightful place, my lord. . . ."

He smiled down at her. "I will do all in my power to give you that to which you are entitled. In the meantime you must not be proud, my dear. I shall give you a sum of money which I trust will be of use to you."

"My lord, your goodness is such that I do not know how I can repay you."

His hand had come to rest on her throat. She was an enchantress.

"Let there be no talk of gratitude between . . . good friends," he said.

He kissed her again; this time on the mouth, and it was not the chaste kiss of a cardinal.

She struggled a little in his arms.

"My lord, I had not thought. . . ."

"Time is fleeting," he answered, "and opportunities should not be missed."

"I am overwhelmed, my lord," she protested. "You are the great Cardinal and, in spite of my name, I am but a humble woman . . . I did not think. . . ."

But while she protested she yet promised, and the Cardinal knew that he was going to find great pleasure in their relationship.

She had betrayed—was it by that sly glance of her eyes or from the response to his kisses?—that she was not as innocent as she had at first seemed, that she had come here for a purpose, and that purpose was to ask him to help a pretty woman who was ready to be his mistress.

Afterwards she said: "I am overwhelmed with . . . both shame and honour. It is a strange mingling."

"It has been delightful . . . for us both," said the Cardinal.

"When I return to Paris, as I must, Your Eminence will forget all about me."

"Nay," said the Cardinal. "I shall not forget. Moreover, I think it is time I visited Paris."

When they joined Cagliostro and the Marquise, the latter was quickly aware that the encounter between the Cardinal de Rohan and Jeanne de la Motte-Valois had been satisfactory to them both.

*   *   *

When the Marquise de Boulainvilliers returned to Paris, Jeanne de la Motte-Valois accompanying her, the Cardinal was fretful. He had only begun to know his new mistress and he had found her full of surprises. It was irritating that she should so soon be taken from him.

But it was easy for a man in his position to find it imperative to leave Strasbourg for Paris.

Cagliostro, understanding de Rohan's mind, knew that he was a little less interested in matters of the occult than he had been before the coming of Jeanne, and realized that the amorous side of the Cardinal's nature was probably as strong as the ambitious side; it was very likely due to this weakness that he was in his present frustrated state. But it was not for Cagliostro to teach the Cardinal wisdom. If he were a wiser man he would not be such a docile subject.

Therefore Cagliostro decided to forestall the Cardinal's announcement. It would be disappointing to have to give up the luxury of Saverne, but he could see that it was necessary.

"It has occurred to me," he told the Cardinal, "that you would do well to show yourself in Paris."

"In Paris!" The Cardinal was unable to hide his delight.

"Indeed in Paris. It is not good that you should be shut away here. There should at least be occasional visits. As Grand Almoner you should be seen now and then at court."

"You anticipate my thoughts, Master."

"It may be so."

"When shall we leave?"

"It is for you to say," said Cagliostro.

"Then we will prepare to leave at once. You are right, as usual. It is small wonder that Versailles neglects me when I neglect Versailles."

*　　　　*　　　　*

So to Paris they went; and although the people of the capital were less easily deceived than those of Strasbourg, Cagliostro had a large following there. He gave himself up to the healing of the sick, seeking those neurotic types who could best serve him and spread his fame. He would wander along the Pont Neuf, past Notre Dame and the Hôtel Dieu to that squalid quarter beyond the Rue de la Juiverie and the Rue aux Fèves, to the Rue des Marmousets and the Rue de la Calandre; there he would beckon ragged men and women to his side, lay his hands on them and bid them go their way in peace and health. He would step over the dyes—reds, greens, blues—which ran between the cobbles from the great tubs set up by the dyers in this quarter; and he would be smiling, flashing his jewels, letting all Paris know that the noisome airs of this quarter of the city had no effect upon him.

He would be seen among the elegant in Dauphine Square or strolling across the Cour du Mai or in the Jardin des Plantes. There was often a crowd following him; even in Paris, the most intellectual of cities, there was a place for Cagliostro.

But he had not been long in the city when word was

brought to him that he had done his work well. He had so firmly established himself in the mind and affections of the Cardinal de Rohan that he need no longer stay close to him. He might go travelling again. He would of course keep in constant touch with the Cardinal, for there must be continual correspondence between them.

He understood. The Cardinal was to devote himself to his love affair with Jeanne de la Motte-Valois. Cagliostro, it seemed, came between the lovers.

When the Cardinal was told of his decision to go away, he was desolate.

"But I have planned that you should always be a member of my household."

"And so I shall be. I have in some measure explained to you that time is not necessarily the slave of man. The same is also true of space. I may be far away, but I am still beside you."

"You mean that you will show me some means of communicating with you although you are miles away?" asked the Cardinal eagerly.

"You would go too fast. Your mind is alert and wise but, my friend, you are not yet capable of such communication. For the time being we will rely on letters."

"You will swear to keep in touch with me?"

Cagliostro smiled into the Cardinal's eyes. "I demand," he said, "that you keep in touch with me. You must write to me of every little detail in our plan."

"But what need is there for that when you will know already? For do you not read my thoughts?"

"I have not all the secrets of the universe at my disposal yet. It would be better if you wrote to me. Write frequently, and thus it will appear to you that we are not parted."

"I will do that," said the Cardinal. "Indeed I must. I should hesitate to take one step without your advice."

"Here at Versailles we are on dangerous ground," said Cagliostro. "So . . . I have your promise?"

"You have it, Master."

"Adieu, my friend. We shall meet again ere long. And by then you will be on your way . . . to greatness."

So Cagliostro left Paris and travelled to Lyons, where he stayed several months in order to establish a Lodge of Egyptian Masonry. He took the title of Grand Cophte there and was acclaimed wherever he went.

Meanwhile the Cardinal was often in Paris, sometimes in Saverne; he found that his encounter with Cagliostro had inflated his ambitions; and he was continually on the alert to find the means of fulfilling them.

*   *   *

III

JEANNE, DE LA MOTTE, RÉTAUX DE VILLETTE
(*Three of a Kind*)

JEANNE DE LA MOTTE-VALOIS HAD A GRIEVANCE AGAINST the world.

Was it fair, she would ask herself a hundred times a day, that she—a royal Valois—should have nothing but a miserable eight hundred francs a year and have to scheme for every little luxury she desired?

She should have her own carriage—she would one day —and it should bear the golden lilies of France on it, for she had as much right to them as anyone else.

She was determined to acquire that state which had belonged to her ancestors in the days following the death of Henri Deux.

But it was a superhuman task. There seemed to be no way in which she could climb into her rightful place. Yet she had come a long way since those days when she had stood by the roadside begging with her brother and little sister from the rich whose carriages splashed them as they passed. Often she had stood there weeping, not with hunger, not with cold, as those who had stopped to talk to her so stupidly imagined, but with humiliation and anger against the world, against the people in their carriages, against the ladies and gentlemen who had what she considered to be hers by right.

But there were times when Jeanne could stop and consider, and then she congratulated herself on the distance she had come.

Jeanne de Saint-Rémy de Valois had been born at Bar-sur-Aube in Champagne, the child of a serving girl and a father who, born with the knowledge that he was of royal blood, had been unable to adjust himself to a life of poverty. Jeanne had little affection for her parents. Why should they have been so stupid? Her father was of the noble family of Valois and there was not a grander name in the country except that of Bourbon—and the Valois were as royal as the Bourbons any day! But what did he do? Did he try to regain what was his by right? Did he consider the future of his children? No! He was content to drink himself—whenever he had a sou or two to pay for it—into a state of maudlin misery. Then he would talk of the grandeurs of the past, of the estates of Fontette, Verpillière and Essoyes which had once been in the possession of his family.

The three children—Jeanne, her sister who was a year or so younger, and her little brother—would listen, but none listened so avidly as Jeanne, and even in those days she determined to get back all that was due to them.

It was decided that begging might be a more profitable trade in the town than in the country, and the family moved to Paris, but Jeanne's father did not long enjoy the amenities of town life. He died a few months after their arrival in that place of horror and squalor, the Hôtel Dieu.

Jeanne's mother had then formed a friendship with a soldier turned professional beggar. He saw possibilities in the name of Valois which he liked so much that he adopted it for himself and swaggered about the town calling himself Baron de Valois. He taught the children to use the name when they went out on begging expeditions. Jeanne was willing. Never for a moment did she forget that she had descended from royalty; from the age of four she walked as though she were wrapped in ermine. She lost no opportunity of watching royal processions; and each time, although her eyes would glisten with admiration, she would be seized with a bitterness which was so great that it made her speechless, and she could only recover by assuring herself that one day she would win all that was lost to her family.

And, considering those early days when she and her sister and brother had begged for a living, she had not done badly.

But at this stage she was frustrated, not knowing which way to turn.

The great Cardinal de Rohan was her lover, but he had made it clear that their relationship would be only a light one. She had seen him once when the Queen was passing through Paris on her way to the opera. The Austrian woman had looked charming. Who would not, Jeanne fiercely demanded of herself, in such extravagant gowns? It was said in the streets that Madame Bertin, the Queen's dressmaker, had made a fortune and that she was on such terms with the Queen that she was almost like a queen herself. Who indeed would not look magnificent, gowned by Madame Bertin, and with hair dressed in such an exaggerated but so attractive manner by Monsieur Léonard?

The Cardinal had been unable to keep his eyes from her face.

"So that is it!" Jeanne had said to herself; and while the Cardinal watched the Queen, Jeanne watched the Cardinal.

He was aware of no one else. His eyes were limpid with desire. This was a good joke, thought Jeanne. The Cardinal longed to be the lover of the Queen!

And what hope had he! Lover of that haughty creature? All Paris knew that she was furious with him for laughing at her old mother and, it was said, whispering scandal about herself.

Cardinal de Rohan must think again if he was thinking of becoming the lover of Marie Antoinette.

Oh, to be a queen, to ride in a royal carriage! To say "Send for Madame Bertin, for Monsieur Léonard." To snap one's fingers at a haughty cardinal who dreamed of becoming one's lover.

Jeanne must have her dresses made by the half-starved little seamstress in the Rue de la Juiverie, must do her hair herself, and be very gracious to Monsieur le Cardinal when he deigned to notice her.

It was cruelly unfair. She could weep with anger at the thought of it all.

And what now? she asked herself. Whither should she turn?

The Cardinal was tiring of her. Had he done anything to have her recognized at court? Not a thing! For what could he do? He himself was out of favour at court and the very fact that a request came through him would mean that if it should reach the Queen's ears, it would certainly be refused.

Soon he would tire of her completely. And what then? Should she find some other kind gentleman? But where would she find a cardinal?

Life was passing and she was as far from realizing her dream as she had ever been.

Oh no, that was quite wrong. She must not forget those three little beggars who had stood by the road, the younger girl and boy crying because they were cold and their chilblains hurt and they were hungry. Jeanne because the mud from the carriages had splashed her and she hated the people riding in those carriages, because that was where she knew she ought to be.

There was frustration everywhere she turned. But these fits of anger helped her not at all. So she would think of those wretched days of beggary and, looking back, review her progress.

They had stood by the roadside, she and her sister and brother. She remembered how the tears ran down their faces, making clean pathways through the grime.

Silly children! They would have remained beggars all their lives.

Begging was humiliating, but it was no more so than working in the fields or looking after sheep and cows.

"Help!" she would cry to the passer-by. "Help a poor orphan, who has sprung from the loins of the Valois."

Some merely laughed and passed on. Others hesitated, looked at the dirty children and shrugged their shoulders, but they invariably dropped a sou or two into the outstretched grubby palms. There were some who would ask: "What was that you said?" And she would repeat her cry. "That's a fine tale," they would say. And others would add: "It must have been François Premier. It has been said that those in France who do not owe their existence to him owe it to Henri Quatre. We have all then sprung from the loins of the Bourbons if not the Valois." "It is true," she had cried vehemently, "that my father is directly descended from Henri Deux."

But they only laughed at her; yet they also were good for a sou or two.

Then there came the great day. She could remember it in detail, for it was the beginning of the change in her fortunes and she had determined on that day that before she died she would ride in her carriage bearing the arms of Valois.

It was a grand carriage and the roads were particularly bad that day. The mud was thick, and the faces of the three little beggars were splashed with it; but the carriage, by a stroke of great good fortune, was stuck in a rut and brought to a standstill.

Jeanne stepped into the mud and put her face close to the window.

F

"Have pity," she cried. "Have pity on poor orphans who have sprung from the loins of the Valois."

A woman leaned out of the window. She was magnificently dressed, her hair rose high above her forehead, and perched on it was a hat with drooping feathers. Jewels gleamed on her bodice, which was of rose-coloured satin; the little beggars blinked at her finery.

"What was that?" said the lady.

Jeanne repeated her cry.

"Why do you say that?"

"Because it is true, Madame."

"Then who was your father?"

"Jacques de Saint-Rémy de Valois, Madame. He was a poor man, but he was in truth descended from Henri Deux."

"Jacques de Saint-Rémy," repeated the lady. "What has become of him?"

"He is dead, Madame."

"And your mother?"

"She has to get herself a living as best she can. As . . . we must."

The lady's coachman had come to the door.

"We are out of the rut now, Madame. We are awaiting your command to start."

Jeanne's face puckered in dismay. She could have killed the coachman. But the lady said: "Wait for a while." She turned to Jeanne. "Where do you live?"

"In a shed near the Bièvre, Madame."

"And you . . . from the loins of the Valois!" said the lady ironically; but although she smiled, Jeanne realized that she was not entirely ridiculing her. Jeanne expected a large gift from this woman; and she was excited because she knew that she was the first to believe that she spoke the truth about her origins.

But Jeanne received more than money from the lady.

"If I tell you where your mother can find me, will you ask her to come to see me tomorrow?"

"Yes," said Jeanne eagerly.

She gave an address which Jeanne repeated.

"Tell her to present herself there and say that she was sent for by the Marquise de Boulainvilliers."

A few coins were pressed into Jeanne's hand—more than she had ever received before. But that was of small importance. Imperiously she commanded her sister and brother to follow her, and she ran as fast as she could to the shed near the Bièvre.

Intuitively she knew that she had taken the first step towards her goal.

*   *   *

And so it proved. Their mother did not stand in their way. She was only too glad to be rid of them. Here was a great opportunity. A lady ... a real Marquise ... had become interested in them. There was to be no more begging in the streets. The Marquise could not bear to hear that plaintive cry from one who had sprung from the loins of the Valois. The children were to be washed and fed and, at the expense of the Marquise, the two girls were to be sent to a school for gentlewomen in distressed circumstances. The boy should be educated to serve in the army or navy.

"What luck!" cried their mother.

But Jeanne knew that it was not luck. She, with her unusual plea, with her imperious looks, had attracted the attention of the lady. It was not luck. It was Jeanne.

And what she had done once, she would do again.

It was a happier life in the seminary than it had been in the streets and environs of the great city; there was always enough to eat, but Jeanne hated discipline; and she was discovering that the ambitious know little peace because their very nature demands that, one goal having been reached, they must immediately strive for the next.

Still, she was wise enough to know that it would be folly to run away from such comfort . . . as yet. She would wait until she was a woman and able to fend for herself. So she endured the discipline of school buoyed up by the royalty, which she assured all with whom she came into contact on every possible occasion, that she possessed.

By the time Jeanne was fourteen, Madame de Boulain-villiers, making use of her influence in court circles, had managed to bring the needs of the children to the notice of the King. As a result the boy was to be made a lieutenant in the navy and the girls were each given a small pension of eight hundred francs a year. They could not live on this. Hence Madame de Boulainvilliers decided that they must be taught a useful trade. This was a great blow to Jeanne's pride, for she had made herself believe that Madame de Boulainvilliers intended, when they were sufficiently educated, to introduce them at court.

There was a return of that bitterness, but Jeanne was too clever not to know that to spurn her benefactress at this stage would be folly. She applied herself to learning with an energy which was a sublimation of bitterness, and she learned to make clothes (which she realized was going to be of great use to her) as well as to wash and iron like a laundress.

But the time was passing and Jeanne grew uneasy. She was not able to fit herself into the life which her sister seemed to accept with such serenity. And Madame de Boulainvilliers, wondering now what she could do with the two girls who had become young women, put them into a nunnery and, assuring herself that she had done her duty by the old nobility, prepared to forget them.

Jeanne's rage was intense when she understood what was happening. She, who had sworn to ride in her carriage emblazoned with the royal arms, to spend the rest of her days in obscurity! It was not to be borne. She swore she would never take her vows, and one morning when the nuns were at their various duties and Jeanne was thought to be at work in the sewing-room, she and her sister, who had become accustomed to obeying her imperious commands, slipped out of the nunnery and made their way to Madame de Boulainvilliers' house in Paris.

Madame de Boulainvilliers was in the country, and Jeanne haughtily announced herself as Mademoiselle de Valois. That name was like a key to the kingdom of respect and homage.

During the years when she had been shut away from the world she had forgotten the effect it could produce. Moreover the habit of the novice was an asset, for so many noble ladies went into convents and, for those few days before the return of Madame de Boulainvilliers, Jeanne was able to test to the full all that she had taken such pains to learn in the last years. With exultation she realized that the servants had no idea that she was not a lady of the standing of their mistress.

Madame de Boulainvilliers was disconcerted when she returned.

"But Jeanne," she cried, "what made you run away like this?"

Jeanne believed she understood how to treat her benefactress. Madame de Boulainvilliers was a lady with a conscience. It would not let her pass by noble beggars on the road; it would not, surely, allow her to consign them to a convent when they had no aptitude for the life.

Jeanne, spokeswoman for herself and her sister, threw herself at the feet of their benefactress. "I implore you to forgive me," she said. "This must seem to you the basest ingratitude. Forgive us, Madame, we could not take the vows, for we know in our hearts that we are unworthy to live such a life. We have longings which it is impossible to suppress."

Madame de Boulainvilliers, having recovered from the shock of seeing her protégées, begged Jeanne to get up, and they would discuss what must be done.

Madame de Boulainvilliers studied Jeanne. She saw an unusually good-looking girl whose startlingly blue eyes and dark brows made of her almost a beauty. It was small wonder, thought the kindly Marquise, that the poor girls did not want to live all their life in nuns' habits. She was glad that she had had them trained to be useful.

"Let us be your servants," implored Jeanne. "I swear I will serve you faithfully all the days of my life. I would indeed be the most ungrateful wretch in France if I did not."

"You ... my servants ...!" said the Marquise. "No, my dear. We must not forget who you are."

Jeanne's heart leaped in triumph. Then she said: "You are not angry with me then ... for running away and bringing my sister with me. The fault was mine. She would have stayed."

"My child," was the answer, "we must all make our lives in our own way."

Jeanne's desires were always so intense that they sometimes ran on madly ahead of possibility. She saw herself the constant companion of the Marquise, riding with her in her carriage—hair dressed à la Monsieur Léonard, in a gown very like the latest made for the Queen by Madame Rose Bertin. She saw herself bowing this way and that to the gallants in the Champs Élysées. Counts . . . dukes ... were asking for her hand. Penniless she might be, but she was Mademoiselle de Valois, and that was a name which meant something in France. Penniless! The Marquise was no longer a young woman. *Mon Dieu!* thought Jeanne. How she has aged! And she looks ill ... not long for this world. She is rich. Her husband was the grandson of the Jewish banker who had been on terms of friendship with Louis Quatorze. (Jeanne had made a point of learning all she could about her benefactress.) And to whom should she leave her fortune but the girls who had been as daughters to her!

So Mademoiselle de Valois—ex-beggar girl—would not only be of royal lineage, but an heiress.

Those were dreams which could be shattered by a word.

"My dear child, you must not reproach yourself. Certainly you must do what you wish. You are both, I know, very good dressmakers and laundresses, and I feel certain that a friend of mine will be delighted to receive you into her house."

"Receive us into her house. . . . ?"

Madame de Boulainvilliers was smiling benignly at the girl.

"You will have a good home in the country," she said.

*   *   *

Jeanne recalled it now—all the anger, all the bitterness of those days. Because she soared so high in her dreams she could descend to the nadir of despair. But she never despaired for long. She had a complete belief in her own ability to rise above all misfortunes.

Bar-sur-Aube was a pleasant spot; it was not of course Paris, and Jeanne had always believed that Paris would be the background to her successful life. Monsieur and Madame de Surmont, those very good friends of the Marquise de Boulainvilliers, were eager to do all they could to help her protégées. They were kind and sympathetic; but Jeanne despised their house, which lacked the splendour of the establishment of the Marquise.

Her sister might settle down into that pleasant rustic existence. Jeanne never would.

She was twenty-three years of age; which was no longer

young. And what hope had she of making a grand marriage?

The monotony of life at Bar-sur-Aube had been relieved by the coming of Monsieur de la Motte. He was an officer in the army, somewhat feckless, far from handsome, but he brought with him into the rural world a breath of the gay life for which Jeanne craved.

He noticed Jeanne immediately and made himself agreeable; he took to visiting his uncle, Monsieur de Surmont, at regular intervals.

Jeanne did not know how she could have been so foolish, but there was a side to her character which had so far been subdued by her urgent desire to gain what she considered her dues. The young man lured her into the woods and made for her there a bed of bracken. It was summer, and the woods were delightful; and for an hour or so Jeanne forgot everything else but the discovery of her own sensuality. There was now another need in her life to be placated, and so overwhelming was it that it could at times dwarf all others.

So Jeanne was seduced by the dashing young officer.

Now she was looking forward to his visits; there were wanderings through the woods and meadows; he would find his way to the room she shared with her sister, and her sister, who had always obeyed Jeanne, would sigh and make her way to one of the attics or go to that room which the young officer had vacated. It was all very simple, and easily arranged, and during that summer Jeanne was as happy as she had ever been in her life.

But such bliss must be paid for. Jeanne remembered now her anger on discovering that she was pregnant. With this discovery there was a return of frustration. Had she forgotten that she was one day to ride in her carriage emblazoned with the royal arms! Was a mere officer going to lift her as high! Certainly not.

She now began to see the faults in her lover. He was selfish, careless, and not as attractive as he had been in the early days of his courtship. She, Jeanne de Saint-Rémy de Valois, had been trapped as certainly as thousands of other women had been trapped. She had shown the world, by submitting to a lover, that she was merely a weak woman after all.

Meanwhile it was becoming apparent to Madame de Surmont that Jeanne would, in the not very distant future, become a mother; so she called in the aid of that benefactress, Madame de Boulainvilliers.

The Marquise was shocked at first and then declared that it might all be for the best. Jeanne was evidently a lusty young woman, and marriage was necessary for her. De la Motte, officer and gentleman, nephew of Monsieur de Surmont, was not a bad catch when one took into consideration that the first time the Marquise had seen Jeanne she had been a beggar on the roadside.

"You must marry Monsieur de la Motte as soon as possible," said Madame de Boulainvilliers.

Jeanne's anger quickly changed to hope. Marriage would mean escape. She could accompany her husband to Paris. She would insist on keeping her own name. De la Motte was not a worthy substitute for de Valois. In future they would be known as de la Motte-Valois.

She told de la Motte this, and he was quick to realize the advantage of changing to such a useful name. Jeanne was pleased; she was beginning to understand that she would very quickly mould her husband to her way of thinking.

The marriage took place, and a few weeks later Jeanne gave birth to twins. They only lived for a week; and it was then that Jeanne discovered that her husband was so much in debt that it was impossible for her to join him in Paris.

Madame de Boulainvilliers came to the rescue, and Jeanne was allowed to return to the convent and stay there until her husband could make a home for her.

She was at the convent when Madame de Boulainvilliers sent a message to her, that she was on her way to Strasbourg, and Jeanne was to join her there.

When they met—and oddly enough Jeanne's husband had also been called to Strasbourg—the Marquise told them both that she believed the great Cardinal de Rohan might be able to help them. As they knew, he was not only a cardinal but Grand Almoner of France; he was very rich and, although out of favour at the court at this time, there was a feeling about that soon he would be able to overcome the resentment against him in that quarter. Once he had done that, he could be one of the most powerful men in France.

The Marquise had seemed a little diffident and uneasy, as though she were acting against her better judgment. It was rather mysterious but exciting, and Jeanne's spirits had soared while her ambitions were as strong as they ever had been.

The Marquise had said: "Jeanne, it would be better for you to approach the Cardinal. He is more ready to help women than men."

How unlike the virtuous Marquise! She could not have realized what she was saying.

Jeanne had played her part. The Cardinal had been impressed by her beauty. Very quickly he had become her lover. She believed too that he had come to Paris to be near her.

There again the Marquise had acted strangely, for although Jeanne had been obliged to return to her convent after leaving Strasbourg as her husband's position had not changed at all and he was still unable to support her, when the Cardinal was in Paris the Marquise had called Jeanne to her house; and there in the city, she had frequent meetings with the Cardinal.

And here in Paris she had discovered the truth about the Cardinal. The foolish man was in love with the Queen. Much good would that do him! As for herself—she, Jeanne, a Valois, was nothing more to him than the lightest of loves with whom to amuse himself while he dreamed of a queen.

It was humiliating. Moreover it was alarming. When the Cardinal ceased to desire her, she would have no hope whatsoever of advancement through him.

Towards the end of the year the Marquise fell ill of the smallpox, and Jeanne's hopes soared once more.

She decided that she would devote herself to the Marquise, ignoring the dangers of infection, showing the old lady that in Jeanne she had a daughter. Then surely, with that sense of justice which she possessed, she would remember her in her will.

If only, Jeanne often thought, as she sat by the Marquise's sick-bed, I had money! Then I could ,establish myself in a pleasant house; I could give parties and invite to my establishment all the notable people of the day. I would find some means of making more money, and in a short time I should be rich and successful, riding out to Versailles in my own carriage.

De la Motte called at the house. He was slyly eager, but he was a man of no great ability, she had come to understand, and he should take his orders from her. He had one virtue. He realized her superior wisdom and energy and was prepared to do this.

"Why, Jeanne," he said, "the old lady will surely leave you some of her fortune."

"Who can say?"

"But you've nursed her; and hasn't she always been fond of you, eh?"

"She has relations. You know what relations are."

But her husband was smiling at her slyly. He might imagine that the Marquise would leave them a little, but Jeanne's dreams were grandiose. She visualized the whole of that fortune.

When the Marquise did die, Jeanne went about in a state of tension for several days, until she learned that the bulk of the Marquise's great fortune had gone to her family. She had not forgotten the de la Mottes, though, and had left instructions that the whole of de la Motte's debts were to be paid; she also implored her son-in-law, the Baron de Crussol, to plead with his friend, the Comte d'Artois (who was a brother of the King), to give him a place in his guards. This had been achieved and she believed that thus the couple would be able to start afresh and, with Jeanne's good sense, she was sure they would live happily.

There was frustration at every turn, it seemed to Jeanne. And now that her benefactress was dead, there would be no one to turn to in an emergency.

Very well, Jeanne would take charge of her own affairs. She had not given up one part of her ambitions.

Now at least she and her husband would be able to live in Paris unmolested by his creditors.

*   *   *

Living was expensive, and what was the use of ridding oneself of old debts if new ones accumulated?

The home of the la Mottes was a few little rooms in the cheapest of lodging houses in the Rue de la Verrerie. La Motte might be ready to submit to his wife's judgment in most matters but it seemed it was impossible for him to keep out of debt.

They quarrelled over money, and he demanded of her: "Why do you not go and see your old friend the Cardinal? I hear he is in Paris."

She reflected that it might not be a bad idea. In any case she was desperate for money and must do something. What chance had she of living the life she wanted, in these wretched rooms in the Rue de la Verrerie?

So she dressed herself in her most becoming clothes and set out for the Cardinal's house.

He was not displeased to see her. He had forgotten how pretty she was. He recognized her now for not only a pretty woman but a clever one. He no longer considered her an innocent victim of his lust, and could indulge in amorous relations with a clear conscience.

She wanted money; he knew that. He had plenty and he was prepared to give her some.

"It is good of you to come to see me, my dear," he said, as he took off the hat which she had made herself and was a good imitation of the reigning fashion.

She shook out her long dark hair. She knew that she was attractive.

"I heard Your Eminence was in Paris, and I confess I found it difficult to stay away. I so desired a glimpse of Your Eminence. It seems so long since I enjoyed that pleasure."

What else did she so desire? It would be churlish to ask at this juncture. Of course the poor girl needed money. She wanted fine clothes and ornaments, just as did any other woman. The Cardinal would be the first to understand that.

They made love. The Cardinal's manners were always exquisite, and so he did not ask her to leave immediately afterwards; he had tactfully presented her with a purse, the weight of which made her happy.

But she wanted more than money from him. Money evaporated and she wanted something permanent. A position of some sort; something which, with her brains and energy, she could exploit.

"I have heard it said," she told him, "that the Queen is less frivolous than she has been, that she has taken several of those whom she once considered her enemies into her little circle."

The Cardinal could not hide the interest which he always felt at the very mention of the Queen's name.

"Of course," added Jeanne, "one hears these things. There is gossip in the markets. How do these women know? Is it because the servants talk? But who can know better than servants?"

"That is good news," said the Cardinal lightly, quickly recovering himself, "for those who were once the Queen's enemies."

"She is good-hearted, they say, though forgetful. I have been wondering whether I will try to see her. If I could be granted an audience and tell her who I am, I feel sure she would not turn me away."

"It is not easy to obtain an audience with the Queen."

"No, but the name of Valois should carry some weight."

"It certainly should do so."

"I have thought of taking a small apartment at Versailles, so that I could present myself at court and perhaps in time gain an audience." The Cardinal looked interested. "If I could only reach the ear of Her Majesty I am confident that I could bring much good to myself . . . and others. . . ."

"It is just possible," agreed the Cardinal.

"Madame de Polignac, her great favourite, was quite humble when she first came to court."

"It is true," said the Cardinal. "Fortunes are quickly made at Versailles."

"I can but try," said Jeanne. "I feel certain that I must one day be recognized. I believe that then certain of the Valois estates may be given to me."

The Cardinal hesitated for a while; then he said: "You

should do all in your power to obtain that audience. You will need money for the apartment in Versailles. Here is a purse."

"You have already been most generous."

The Cardinal put the purse into her hands.

"I shall be interested to hear if you obtain that interview with the Queen. Remember all she says . . . remember how she looks at you. I shall be very interested to hear."

"As soon as I have gained my object, I shall come with all speed to Your Eminence."

*   *   *

When Jeanne had left him the Cardinal received an unexpected visitor. The man who was ushered into his presence wore a dark cloak, and his hat was drawn well down over his eyes. He was sombrely clad. The Cardinal did not recognize him immediately, and he was astonished when the hat was taken off and the cloak thrown back.

"Cagliostro! Master!" he cried.

"My dear Cardinal! I was eager to avoid the crowds in the streets, so I arrived incognito. But, passing close to your house, I could not miss the opportunity of calling to see you."

"A right hearty welcome awaits you."

Cagliostro took the Cardinal's arm and they walked to an embrasure. From a window they looked out on the streets of Paris.

"And still," Cagliostro said, "you are not invited to Versailles."

"I am as far from it as ever."

"Nay! There I must contradict you. Your star is in the ascendant. Very soon you will be received at Versailles."

"Thank you, Comte. It is what I have longed to hear."

"Thank destiny, Eminence, not me. I am but the instrument of fate."

"Your advice has always been so valuable to me."

"But, as I said, my dear Cardinal, you yourself must find your own road to success. We all must. I have not ceased to think of you while we have been apart. I know more of what is going on than you realize. And I am happy . . . very happy . . . about your future."

"You know something? Tell me."

"The woman, Jeanne de la Motte-Valois, has recently left you."

"That is so."

Cagliostro began to pace the room; he was holding his hands curved before him as though he held something which was visible only to himself. It was the well-known gesture, and it implied that the magician was about to look into the future.

"I was pleased to see she had called on you," he said. "She has a part to play in your life. Oh no . . . not only as mistress. What are mistresses? They amuse for a light half-hour. No, she has a greater part to play than that."

The Cardinal was excited. "She talked of going to Versailles, to try to procure an audience with the Queen."

Cagliostro nodded.

"She is, when all is said, a Valois," went on the Cardinal.

"A path will be opened direct from you to the Queen," said Cagliostro. His lips twitched in a smile. "Who knows, it may well be that that woman will be the one to cut away the weeds and brambles which now make it impassable."

"You are indeed a god. You are omniscient. I believe you are also omnipresent. I beg of you, do not hurry away but give me the pleasure of your company."

"It was a flying visit. It was merely to reassure you. For although I keep constantly in touch with you, you are not yet able to understand that; and there are times when I believe you think I neglect you."

"It is because I miss our conversations."

"Yet you remember them. You are faithful to them. And when men revile me—as they did One other greater than I—you defend me. When they say, 'But the stone in your ring, which you call a diamond, is no diamond!' and you look at it and because your faith is weak it seems to you that it does not sparkle as other diamonds, still you know it to be a true diamond because I have told you so." The dark eyes were looking straight into those of the Cardinal. "Always remember that, my lord Cardinal. It is through your faith that you will come to greatness. You are right; I am always with you. Though this body may be far away, our minds are as one. That is why I am rejoicing now, for the future of my friend is glorious indeed."

"Come, I will send for refreshments. I will have apartments made ready."

"Nay, nay! It is a flying visit."

"Whither do you go?"

"I go to the meetings of wise men."

"There is a certain amount of whispering in the city. I would you could tell me if there is any truth in these rumours. I heard that there was a gathering of secret societies in Germany and that the Comte de Virieu, a young Freemason, withdrew in horror and has resigned his membership."

"He has not forgotten his vows."

"No. He will not say what is discussed at these gatherings, but it is something which has horrified him. Sworn to secrecy, he can do nothing. But it is said that he is terrified when any of the societies are mentioned. I promised myself that I would ask you if this were true."

Cagliostro once more laid his hands on the Cardinal's

G

shoulders and turned on him the full force of those magnetic eyes.

"In time," he said slowly, "I shall reveal much to you, for you are my friend and our minds are as one. But at this time there is one matter which is of greater concern to us both than any other in the world." He began to repeat slowly under his breath: "Richelieu ... Mazarin ... de Rohan. ..."

He led the Cardinal to that couch on which he had recently lain with Jeanne, and made him lie down. He placed his hands gently on the Cardinal's forehead, and the Cardinal felt himself—although no word was spoken—bidden to close his eyes.

When he opened them again, Cagliostro had gone.

*   *   *

Jeanne had returned to the room in the Rue de la Verrerie and was counting the money when the concierge called up the stairs that a gentleman was asking for her.

Hastily she hid the money in a drawer and went to the door. The man was already coming up the stairs. He was wearing a long dark cloak and a hat which concealed his face.

He walked into the room and took off his hat to bow to her.

"Monsieur le Comte!" she cried, and dropped a hasty curtsy.

"You have recently left the Cardinal," stated Cagliostro. "You know this?"

"I know a great deal, Madame de la Motte-Valois."

"You have visited him and he has told you."

Cagliostro regarded her with some impatience. She was not an easy subject for suggestion. If he wanted anything from this woman he would have to speak plainly.

"It is of no importance how I know this," he said a little

impatiently. "Suffice it that I do. The Cardinal has given you money."

Jeanne was silent.

"Do not think," went on Cagliostro, "that I am not your friend. I have an interest in your advancement. You are going to present yourself at Versailles in the hope of attaining audience with the Queen. I doubt not that you have noticed His Eminence's preoccupation with the Queen."

Jeanne nodded without speaking.

Cagliostro smiled at her. "Let us sit down," he said. "We can talk more easily. You must not be afraid of me. I am your friend."

"I am not afraid of you," said Jeanne boldly.

"That is well. Fear is the deadly enemy of all who possess it, and you are a woman who needs to have her wits about her; therefore you cannot afford to be afraid. These rooms . . . they are a poor setting for a woman of your good looks and intelligence."

"You flatter me, Comte."

"It is no flattery. I speak truth. It would be an excellent thing if, through you, the Cardinal could win the favour of the Queen."

Jeanne laughed suddenly. "Through me! A humble woman with scarce a sou to her name? I . . . to bring together the Queen and the richest cardinal in France!"

"Stranger things have happened. The Cardinal would be grateful. His gratitude to you would be excessive. He would not be able to do enough for one who brought back his favour at court." Cagliostro had drawn his chair closer to that of Jeanne. "The Cardinal is an ambitious man. His heart is not in the Church. He dreams of other great cardinals . . . men who in other times ruled France. That is the sort of cardinal he would be. You know nothing of the power of Richelieu, of Mazarin. It is power such as theirs for which our Cardinal longs. Imagine what he would give to the woman who brought it to him. I doubt not, if she were clever enough, she could become one of the richest and most influential women in France."

In spite of herself she was dazzled, not so much by the man, but by what he seemed to be offering her.

He had come even closer. He said: "Consider Madame de Polignac. She, a humble woman, became the Queen's dearest friend. Her relations, all those connected with her, are now rich and important. They have their vast incomes, their positions at court. You are as handsome as Madame de Polignac, my dear. I doubt not that you are also cleverer."

"Could this be?" said Jeanne, and her voice had sunk to a whisper.

"Everything is possible to the one who determines to make it so."

"I fear I shall be unable to gain an audience. I must have that."

Cagliostro was smiling. "There are always ways. . . ."

"But. . . ."

He had risen. "I am paying but a fleeting visit," he said. "I wished to tell you that I have the utmost confidence in your wit and ingenuity. Let the Queen refuse to see you; yet you will gain all that you set out to gain. You will find a way."

"Shall I?" said Jeanne.

"I swear it," said Cagliostro.

Then he rose swiftly and taking her hand kissed it. He was smiling at her slyly. She thought he was like the devil, spreading a temptation before her which she did not fully understand.

And when he had gone, she took out the purse to count the money, but she was too excited to do so.

*   *   *

When her husband came in she showed him the money which the Cardinal had given her; she also told him of the visit of Cagliostro and his strange words.

De la Motte listened eagerly.

"The first thing we must do," she told him, "is to take a small apartment at Versailles. Then I shall present myself at the palace on those occasions when people assemble to make their petitions to the royal family."

"Need we have an apartment?"

"It is hardly likely that I shall obtain an audience immediately, and I cannot keep making the journey back and forth between Versailles and Paris."

"But the money?"

"I have this from the Cardinal and I do not doubt that there will be more to come."

"You think the priest will be ready to pay?"

"He will pay, particularly if he gets good value. I mean if we can give him information about the Queen there is nothing he won't do for us."

"Then let us find this apartment in Versailles at once."

"There is one thing we must do," she told him. "We are going to move into the highest society. Fortunately we are Valois; but it is not enough to be simply Monsieur and Madame. In future we shall be known as the Comte and Comtesse de la Motte-Valois."

De la Motte whistled. "Comte de la Motte-Valois," he repeated.

"It is not a joke," she said sternly. "Why, if we had a Valois instead of a Bourbon on the throne, most certainly you would become a Comte."

De la Motte bowed in a mincing manner which was intended to be an imitation of a court gallant, took her hand and kissed it.

"Madame la Comtesse," he said, "I have come to believe

you are a very determined woman. And," he added, "a clever one."

*   *   *

But all Jeanne's cleverness could not win for her the audience she craved. She had presented herself at Versailles. She had waited with the crowd in the Galerie des Glaces; she had implored the palace officials to give her name to the Queen and beg for an interview, however brief. "Tell her it is the Comtesse de la Motte-Valois who begs an audience," she reiterated. She offered bribes, all to no avail. Every time she presented herself she was told that her name was not on the list of those whom the Queen would see that day.

Jeanne would not be defeated, so she began to plan.

She had noticed that one day in the press of people a woman fainted and, as she fell to the floor, the Queen was passing. Her Majesty had not appeared to notice the confusion caused by this accident; but there were many to succour the woman; and later Jeanne heard that the Queen *had* noticed after all, had asked most kindly about the woman, had sent her money and had granted her an interview.

Back in the lodgings at Versailles, Jeanne told her husband that she would have a fainting fit.

He thought this an excellent idea.

"We must wait until we are sure the Queen is passing," he said.

"No," Jeanne retorted. "That would be too obvious. The last was in the Queen's presence. It shall be in that of her sister-in-law, in Madame Elisabeth's ante-room. Madame Elisabeth is reputed to be a saintly woman who does much work for the poor. She will be more interested than the Queen; she is more likely to grant me an interview.

Then I shall tell her who I am and ask her to present me to the Queen."

"It's an excellent plan," cried de la Motte.

"We must be careful. You must be with me, for when I am fainting I cannot say who I am. You must cry out: 'Holy Mother of God, it is the Comtesse de la Motte-Valois. She has fainted from starvation. Is it not a tragedy that this could happen to one who belongs to a royal house of France!'"

De la Motte could scarcely speak for laughing.

"You will have to be serious," she warned him.

"As serious as Madame Elisabeth."

"We will take the first opportunity," she told him.

And they did.

*   *   *

The splendour of the great palace would have aroused all Jeanne's bitterness had she not felt so certain that very soon she would be ascending the Escalier de Marbre, not as a humble suppliant but as a friend of the Queen.

Now with her husband she joined those crowds who were assembled in the ante-room of the apartments of the King's sister, Madame Elisabeth.

The atmosphere was undoubtedly close, and the press of people was great. It would not be incongruous to faint at such a time.

Jeanne's sharp blue eyes watched the people about her, and she sidled close to those who she thought could be relied upon to make the most of a scene.

At length Madame Elisabeth came out of her apartments and was about to pass into the ante-room. Jeanne groaned and began her act of swooning.

Her husband caught her and cried out: "Help, good people! A lady has fainted. *Mon Dieu*, it is the Comtesse de la Motte-Valois!"

Madame Elisabeth had stopped. She lacked the beauty of the Queen, but she was well known for her pious works and it was only natural that if a woman had fainted in the crowds outside her apartments she should pause and express her sympathy.

"A lady has fainted, Madame," said a garrulous woman in the front of the crowd.

"A royal lady, by the sound of her name, Madame Princesse," declared another.

"I am sorry," said Madame Elisabeth, her kindly face lighting with genuine sympathy. "There is such a crowd to-day, and how hot it is!"

The crowd fell back so that she could make her way to the de la Mottes. Jeanne was partly lying on the floor, partly supported in her husband's arms, while he fanned her with a kerchief.

"It is the Comtesse de la Motte-Valois," said de la Motte hopefully.

"De la Motte-Valois," said Madame Elisabeth musingly. "Poor lady!"

"I fear," said de la Motte, "that it is not the heat, Madame, which is responsible for this. The Comtesse, in spite of her noble name—and she is truly descended from the Valois, Madame—has fainted from starvation."

His manner was a little too eager, and Madame Elisabeth, gentle as she was, had come into contact with beggars often during her life. She recognized them when she saw them. Moreover, the fainting woman was plump and well fed. All the same Madame Elisabeth was ready to give any beggar the benefit of the doubt.

"Let a stretcher be brought," she said, "and take the lady to her home." She turned to one of her ladies. "I pray you, send two hundred livres to her from my purse."

There was a little gasp in the crowd at this munificence; and de la Motte then began to explain how Jeanne was descended from Henri Deux and had nothing but a pension of eight hundred francs a year on which to live. Madame Elisabeth expressed her sympathy and promised to see what could be done.

Jeanne was exultant, particularly when she heard from court that her pension was to be increased from eight hundred to one thousand five hundred francs a year.

When she presented herself in Madame Elisabeth's apartments however to, as she said, express her thanks, she was told that Madame Elisabeth would be informed of her gratitude but could not see her then. Again and again she presented herself; but Madame Elisabeth would not grant the interview and Jeanne came to realize that although she had come very profitably out of her little scheme she was still as far from her goal as ever.

*   *   *

They must try again, suggested de la Motte.

They did. This time outside the apartments of the King's brother's wife, the Comtesse d'Artois. She was less interested in the people than was Madame Elisabeth; and she passed by without appearing to be aware of the fainting lady.

It was very disappointing, and Jeanne decided that the fainting trick could only be tried once more. As it was, she believed that some people who had been in the crowd outside Madame Elisabeth's apartments had also been outside those of Madame d'Artois; and if this were so, they may have recognized her. It would be fatal to gain a reputation as the fainting lady.

However, there should be one more attempt, and this should be in the presence of the Queen herself.

This was the greatest failure of the three, for when the Queen appeared, exquisitely dainty in the latest dress to display Madame Bertin's talent, a laughing merry creature, who seemed to glide rather than walk, everyone in the room was so busy looking at her that they did not even notice Jeanne's faint and, although her husband declared in loud tones that Madame de la Motte-Valois was fainting from starvation, no one even turned a head to look.

It was most discouraging.

"Come along to our lodgings," said Jeanne quietly.

And they hurried out of the palace.

"It's my belief," said de la Motte, "that you'll never have that interview with the Queen."

"Be quiet," she snapped, experiencing again all that bitter fury which she had known in the past.

But I will do something! she told herself. I will make myself known.

*   *   *

The next day she saw Rose Bertin's carriage leaving the palace on its way back to Paris.

There sat Rose, extravagantly dressed, her hair piled high in the latest fashion set by the Queen. People stood about in the streets of Versailles to watch the carriage pass.

As it started from the palace a lady of the court, clearly an attendant of some lady of rank, came hurrying out, crying "Madame Bertin! Madame Bertin!"

Rose Bertin graciously called a halt, and waited for the lady to reach her carriage. When she did so Rose looked imperiously down at her as though she were the Queen herself, being approached by a menial.

"My lady is waiting for you, Madame Bertin," said the panting woman. "You said you would come to her apartments when you left the Queen."

Rose laughed lightly. "Did I? Then I made a promise which I fear I must break. I have promised so many gowns to Her Majesty that I can neither make nor keep my promises to others."

"Oh but, Madame Bertin, you promised. . . ."

"Then I was too kind-hearted." Rose Bertin waved her hand and the carriage went forward, leaving the woman looking after it very disconsolately.

A *dressmaker*! thought Jeanne, and I am the Comtesse de la Motte-Valois!

A woman had sidled up to her. "Did you hear that, eh? It seems that dressmakers have become queens."

"She is arrogant, that dressmaker!"

"And who has made her so? The Queen has her friends, so we hear. *They* can do no wrong. It is thus with the Princesse de Lamballe and Madame de Polignac. They at least are ladies. But that one . . . a dressmaker! Do you know, Madame, they say that in Paris she holds court like a queen. Oh yes, the workrooms of Madame Bertin are as Versailles. Court manners, if you please, and our Queen Rose in the centre. One understands. The woman has power. She can promise favours to this one and that. And she does. She sells more than dresses. She grows rich on selling the Queen's favours. It is: 'I'll persuade Her Majesty to do this that and the other.' Well, she is a clever one, we must admit that, eh?"

"Yes," said Jeanne slowly, "she is a clever woman."

But there were others as clever.

*   *   *

She had made up her mind. It was reckless, but then how could she possibly achieve her aims without reckless-ness? One had to gamble, as she explained to de la Motte.

He was alarmed when she took him to the mansion in the Rue Neuve-Saint-Gilles.

"This," she announced, "is to be our new home."

"We're on the verge of bankruptcy," he cried. "How can we afford to live in such a house? It's a mansion!"

"Precisely because we are on the verge of bankruptcy we shall live in this house."

The owner of the house showed them over it. The rooms were large.

"They will be ideal for the parties we want to give," said Jeanne.

"It is too dear for us," put in de la Motte, who was becoming seriously worried.

"You forget," she told him quickly, "that the Queen has promised to study my claim. Why, the estate is as good as mine already. The Queen herself told me so."

The owner of the house was impressed to think that the prospective tenant was on such terms with the Queen. He believed her. There was her name for one thing, her manner for another.

"Then," said Jeanne, "doubtless we shall want to move from such a small house as this one."

"You will find it a charming house," said the owner, now all eagerness that this interesting woman should become his tenant. "I doubt not that even when you come into your fortune you will wish to keep this one."

"It may well be so," said Jeanne. "And we will take it."

They quickly moved in from the Rue de la Verrerie and Jeanne set about furnishing it in a manner which quickly dissipated the money they had.

Neither was anxious now. Jeanne was so confident that her plan would succeed; her husband had been so accustomed to debts that a few more meant little to him.

The news spread through the neighbourhood that a Comte and Comtesse had temporarily taken the house in the Rue Neuve-Saint-Gilles, and there was a certain amount of curiosity concerning them, so that when Jeanne issued invitations to several people who had come to call on her and some whom she had not even met but had heard spoken of with respect by the callers, there was a large gathering to celebrate their settling into the new home.

Jeanne was resplendent in a dress which she had copied from the Queen's when she had last seen her. She was glad now of her training in dressmaking; with her imitation jewellery and her fine muslin gown (the Queen had set simple rustic fashions since her preoccupation with Petit Trianon and the model country village she had set up there) she might have been at a court levee rather than hostess in the Rue Neuve-Saint-Gilles.

She dominated the company. It was one of her greatest successes. She sat at the head of her table and talked.

"Oh, but Mesdames, Messieurs, you know how it is. One falls on evil times. In my youth, of course, it was different. I was brought up to expect luxury, I tell you *luxury*. But I am sure that I shall not long be forced to live in penury. I go to court often."

Her guests were impressed.

"The Queen has promised me that my case shall have early attention. . . ."

It was not strange that whenever the Queen's name was mentioned there was a rising of interest in any company for she was the most discussed person in Paris, and although there were a few who supported her and thought her charming, there were many who hated her. During times of famine—and there had been too many of them in the last years—and during times of uneasiness in the government, talk of deficits and the need for even more taxation, there must be someone to blame for the apprehension which seemed to be touching every person in France. Who could better serve as scapegoat than Marie Antoinette, the story of whose extravagances was discussed throughout France, who created scandals by the fortunes she showered on her favourites, whose passionate love of jewels and all finery was proverbial; and who was not even a Frenchwoman, but a native of that country which was no friend to France—Austria.

"The Queen . . . you know her?"

"Now," cried Jeanne archly, "do not expect me to listen to a word against Her Majesty. When you know her you discover her to be the most delightful of women. So kind! So sympathetic! Oh, I must admit she has her faults. Which of us has not? But I have always found her kindness itself."

"You are on friendly terms, Madame la Comtesse?"

"Our friendship is fast growing." Jeanne laughed. "Her Majesty keeps it something of a secret at present. To tell the truth she is a little afraid of La Polignac. That woman has the temper of a fiend. And you know—or perhaps you do not—how difficult the Queen finds it to throw aside those whom she has once favoured."

"I suppose you go often to Versailles, Madame la Comtesse."

"Often. For I am severely scolded if I do not."

Several pairs of eager eyes were on her. The favourites of the Queen dispensed great favours. It was well known that if one wanted a position at court one must plead for it through the Queen's favourites who, once she understood that they wanted it, would do all in her power to persuade the King or his ministers to grant it.

This Comtesse de la Motte-Valois was indeed an important acquisition to the circle.

Jeanne was so excited that she could almost convince herself that what she boasted of was true.

One of her guests talked privately with her during the evening.

"I have long sought a position for my son in the King's Guards," he said. "There have been times when I have imagined I was near obtaining it, but so far nothing has come of it."

"Ah Monsieur, you cannot tell me anything about the ways of the court."

"Madame la Comtesse, since you are on such terms with the Queen you would be able to do in a week what I have failed to do in months."

Jeanne waved her hands and shook her head. "No, no, Monsieur. I cannot do these things. I will explain to you. Even though I have the Queen's friendship I cannot ask favours all the time. What I could do is use my influence in other quarters. There are so many who are anxious to please those whom the Queen befriends. But so often in these cases it is a matter of dropping a little gift here and there . . . you understand me?"

"Ah, Madame la Comtesse, I understand full well, and I should be ready to give as much as I could and what seemed moderate for my son's advancement."

She hesitated. "Oh no . . . no . . . I like not these financial arrangements between friends."

"Madame, it would be the greatest service. . . ."

"But . . . you know how it is . . . the captain must be recompensed or he will declare the newcomer to be unworthy. Then perhaps there are others who will need a little sweetening. Oh no . . . no. I could drop that word in the right quarter but I do not care to be the go-between in these mercenary transactions."

"Madame, if you were such a go-between you would win my eternal gratitude."

"Oh . . . well . . . I will speak to my husband. Come and see me . . . tomorrow night, and I will give you a definite answer."

When the guests had gone, Jeanne told her husband of this conversation.

"Do you not see," she said, "we begin to make our fortunes. Our first gathering, and here is one who is ready to pay me well for my services at court. There will be others. Did you not know that Rose Bertin made two fortunes—one out of her dressmaking, another out of the favours she has been able to sell?"

"There is this difference," said de la Motte. "Rose Bertin truly has the Queen in her pocket."

"Do not allow a little thing like that to disturb you. What does it matter? These people think that I am the Queen's good friend. The great Cagliostro said once that it is what people think true rather than the actual truth, which can make most stir in the world."

De la Motte's brows were wrinkled. "I can see that it will work . . . for a while. But in the end they must discover that you can do nothing for them."

"We will think only of the next few weeks," said Jeanne firmly. "Let us live through those, and pay our debts so that we are given fresh credit. Then we will consider the future. Do not be disturbed, husband. There are many ideas teeming in this head of mine."

"They are excellent ideas, I doubt not," was the answer. "Yet I trust they will not destroy us both."

*   *   *

It was a busy household in the Rue Neuve-Saint-Gilles. Jeanne had engaged a large staff and each week some luxurious piece of furniture was added to grace her reception rooms. De la Motte had suggested that they set up card tables in one of the rooms, and Jeanne congratulated him on the profit these brought. There was now a little income from faro, basset and other games. It was not however large enough to meet their expenses, and Jeanne was certain that only by living more ostentatiously could they hope to do so.

Frequently she visited Versailles and waited to see the Queen pass through the apartments on her way to Mass or to dine. Her quick dressmaker's eyes would take in each detail of the dress the Queen was wearing, so that she would be able to explain it exactly. She picked up gossip about the royal family so that she could tell it as though she had it straight from the Queen or the Princesse de Lamballe. She was always careful to wait in the crowd, heavily cloaked and masked, lest any of her friends should see her there among the common people.

She was living dangerously, and she now began to realize that this was what she had always wanted to do.

She longed for the day when she would be able to have her own carriage, emblazoned with the golden lilies; in the meantime she contented herself by engaging lackeys and maidservants.

She was now such a busy hostess that she found she needed a secretary; and soon after she made this known among her friends a young man presented himself at the house one morning and asked for an interview.

He came into her presence like a courtier, bowed low over her hand and, lifting his somewhat bold eyes, told her that he had heard she needed a scribe and that he would give ten years of his life if he might serve her.

She was a little disconcerted by his manners, but his bold dark eyes were admiring and he attracted her immediately.

"It is true," she said, "that I need a secretary. Can you write well?"

"Madame la Comtesse," he cried, "allow me to give you proof."

"Do, by all means, as I certainly require an example of your proficiency before I employ you."

He sat down at her escritoire and with bold impudence he wrote a letter to her.

"Dear Madame la Comtesse, Having heard that you needed a secretary I came here with a mild hope in my heart that you would employ me. I have seen you, and

H

henceforth I have an urgent desire to serve you. Yours in admiration and absolute obedience, Rétaux de Villette."

He handed the letter to her; she read it and smiled.

"You have a good round hand," she said.

"Or spidery hand, or a backward scrawl ... anything you desire I can give you."

He had turned to the desk. He wrote: "Monsieur de Villette, I have read your letter and I hasten to tell you that I am as eager to employ you as you are to be employed by me. Your mistress, Jeanne de la Motte-Valois, Comtesse."

She stared at the letter. "It is almost exactly like my handwriting," she gasped.

"Not quite correct, I fear. You will forgive the errors, Madame. I have as yet had so little opportunity of studying your handwriting. If I had that opportunity, I can assure you it would be exact."

He was giving her his bold stare, and she was excited by more than his extraordinary gift with a pen.

"I think," she said, "that you can be of some use to me."

*   *   *

The party was at its height and Jeanne watched her guests with satisfaction. La Motte was not present, having been recalled to his duties. He had sworn that as soon as possible he would be back in the Rue Neuve-Saint-Gilles.

There were times when Jeanne missed him, when she wondered how they could continue in the way they were living, when she reasoned that surely they must sooner or later be discovered in their deceit. Then she would tell herself that whatever happened she would find a way out, and wondered why a woman of her ingenuity should fret because she lacked a man's arm to lean on.

Now she went from guest to guest, dropping words of comfort here and there. No, she had not been able to get a satisfactory answer yet from the court official. The cupidity of these people was past belief. It seemed that nobody could do anything nowadays for anyone else without asking payment!

She passed on to another. She was growing a little alarmed about that man who was trying to buy a place for his son in the King's Guards. That affair had gone on too long. Was he faintly suspicious?

Suspicion must not be allowed to enter this establishment. Once it did, the rot could easily set in.

But they all seemed happy enough, all subservient enough.

She went over to the old officer who was a near neighbour and liked to come to her gatherings. There was no hope of getting money out of him. He was far too old to seek favours for himself and had no son to scheme for, but he gave tone to the parties.

She listened to his grumbles about the state of the world.

"What has come over Frenchmen today? That is what I ask you, Comtesse. It is all English now. Everything that comes from across the water is to be admired. All the young men are wearing English fashions. English coats with triple capes . . . hair straight and unpowdered. Hideous! And we are told—'Oh, but it is the fashion. It is English.' Why should not Frenchmen be Frenchmen, eh? Madame, tell me that!"

"Oh, they are all for the fashions, you know. They must follow them, however hideous they are."

"And the English know nothing of cut and style and fashion. Do you know, they are even drinking punch here now. I saw the word written on a window only yesterday. Punch *à l'Anglais*. And if it is not punch it is *le thé*. You sit at a table, Madame, and there is bread with butter and rolls—and served at eight o'clock, when we may have dined at six. But because the English dine at two and are ready at eight for *le thé*, we must have it also. 'Oh, but it is English, Monsieur!' What is France coming to? Tell me that, Madame."

"Who can say?" replied Jeanne, who was not really listening. She was watching that guest—the man who wished his son to have a place in the King's Guards. Had she seen a glint in his eyes? She was sorry de la Motte was not here tonight. She was afraid there would be a crisis, and although she wanted to rely on herself at such times, she felt very uneasy.

"This punch ... it is not bad," went on her companion. "And the best place to get it is at Regny's. You know Regny. He used to sell lemonade before we had to follow the English and drink punch."

She smiled soothingly and, excusing herself, went over to the card tables where there was a great deal of hilarity; but she could not rid herself of her apprehension.

She moved nearer to one of the tables where her new secretary was sitting. She had allowed him to join the parties, for she had discovered that he was as dexterous with the cards as with his pen.

A snatch of conversation came to her. "Oh, everyone must have his carriage now ... be he ever so humble, and starve himself to do so. Grocers, my dear, have their cabriolets now. One cannot move for them in the streets. Any man who has ten thousand francs a year will use a third of it to keep his carriage."

"I have had to rid myself of mine. Since I have been trying to get my son a place at court I find it beyond my means."

Jeanne's heart was beating faster. Was the rot setting in?

"Ah Monsieur, but what value you will get for that money!" It was Rétaux, the bold secretary, speaking. "Once your son has his place, it will be a coupé for your wife, as well as a carriage for yourself and a cabriolet for your butler. A friend of mine was in similar circumstances. He stinted himself for months but eventually, through Madame's good graces, he achieved his desires. Imagine his gratitude, Monsieur. He laughs now to think of his impatience."

The secretary had caught her eyes upon him. It was not exactly a wink he gave her, but it was something very like it.

She was aware of him throughout the evening. He seemed to win constantly at the tables.

When her guests had gone, she was relieved. She sensed that the first phase of success was over. No matter what she or her secretary said, people would not go on paying for ever for something which they did not receive. Each day brought fresh debts. The card tables, while useful, did not make enough money to meet all expenses. She had to think of a fresh line of action soon.

So deep in thought had she been that she did not notice the secretary at her side.

"A successful party, Madame," he said.

She nodded.

"But then, all Madame's parties are successful!"

"Good night," she said.

He bowed once more.

When she went to her bedroom she found that he was close behind her. She opened her door, and was about to shut it when he laid his hand on it.

"Forgive me, Madame, for speaking of such a matter at such a time. Madame is so occupied during the day."

"What is it?"

"There are certain accounts which must be settled without delay. Creditors can be unpleasant creatures."

"We will discuss it tomorrow."

She would have shut the door, but he had placed his foot inside the room preventing her from doing so.

"Monsieur Secretary, you are insolent," she exclaimed.

He forced her back, entered the room and closed the door.

"Servants," he whispered conspiratorially, "have such long ears!"

"I said that you are insolent," she repeated.

"Ah Madame, but then you are so charming, and I am so interested in your little games."

"But . . . how dare you!"

"Lured on by Madame's beauty," he said, taking her by the shoulders.

"You will leave this house tomorrow."

He shook his head. "What! When I can be so useful? Why, Madame la *Comtesse*, you are such a wise woman, you would not allow one to depart who knows as much as I do."

"I do not understand you."

"Then I am amazed. Madame is so clever. The little trips to Versailles . . . the accounts of what goes on there . . . Ah, amazing! Madame, your secretary admires you beyond all women."

With that he took her into his arms and kissed her full on the mouth. She felt her senses respond. She had been attracted by the rogue as soon as he entered the house.

"With Monsieur le *mari* absent. . . ." he murmured.

She made a feeble pretence of anger, but he merely laughed, and in a few seconds she was laughing with him.

"You are a rogue," she said. "I was aware of it the moment I saw you."

"Ah, Madame," he said, "you and I, with perhaps the kind husband in our wake, will travel far . . . together."

*   *   *

She was awake when he was sleeping beside her.

It was not yet light, but soon it would be. Then he must

be dismissed and sent back to his own room with all speed.

She laughed to herself, remembering last night's encounter. Both of them had struggled for supremacy then as they would, she sensed, in their future relationship.

She was amused and exhilarated.

She told herself that she had intended this should happen, during the first days he had spent in her house. He was clever. He would be useful.

She was a woman who liked men, but she would not be such a fool as to let one dominate her.

"No, my dear Rétaux," she murmured to herself, "you have quickly made your way into my bed, but do not imagine I am a woman to let such a thing interfere with our daytime relationship. You shall remain the secretary. I shall stay in command."

IV

BARONNE D'OLIVA

(*The Joker*)

JEANNE WAS HURRYING HOME TO THE RUE SAINT-NEUVE-Gilles. It was nearly seven in the evening and dusk was falling. This was one of the most dangerous hours to be abroad in the streets of Paris. The noise and bustle which had filled them an hour before had completely died down and, although it would be revived again later, at this time when the daylight was fading and the Watch not yet on duty, all wise people were behind closed doors.

Jeanne, who had been visiting friends, had stayed longer than she had intended to, and she was surprised, now that she was out in the streets, to find that it was so late.

She was picking her steps carefully as she hurried along, walking on tip-toe that she might not spoil her stockings with the mud of the streets, when she was suddenly aware of footsteps behind her and realized that she was being followed.

Jeanne was not a nervous woman by any means, but she had heard many stories of the robberies which had taken place in the streets of Paris, and there had been many instances when the robbers, not content with taking a victim's purse, would take his—or her—life as well.

The street lighting was poor. Even the modern reflectors could not change that, for according to custom they were hung out from the walls on brackets and dazzled at a distance but gave little light to the surroundings. Moreover, the lamplighters were not all honest and some only half-filled the lamps, selling the rest of the oil for their own benefit.

When Jeanne quickened her steps, those behind her quickened also. She squelched through the mud, that mud of Paris, surely the worst in the world, consisting of refuse from the houses and pieces of metal which came from the carriage wheels; the whole having a sulphureous effect so that it could ruin clothes onto which it was splashed.

She began to run.

"Madame de la Motte-Valois!" The voice was gentle, and there was laughter in it; and recognizing it, she stopped.

He came and stood beside her. He was wrapped in his long cloak and wore the hat which shaded his face—the one he had worn when she had last seen him.

"Monsieur le Comte, I thought you were a robber."

"That is why I was so eager to put an end to your fears. I wished to speak to you."

"Then," she cried angrily, for her heart was still racing with fear and she was annoyed that he should have noticed it, "why did you not call on me in a respectable manner?"

"I wished to speak to you alone. And so . . . that is why I am here now. Let us go into a café. We will drink a glass of punch together. You like the new English drink?"

"I wish to go home," she said.

"Come," replied Cagliostro, laying his hand on her arm. "This way."

"How did you know that you would find me in the streets at this hour?"

Cagliostro laughed. "How do I know these things? Ah! That is a question I am often asked."

They turned into one of those cafés which had been called lemonade sellers and now specialized in *punch à l'Anglais*, and he led her to a table in a dark corner which made it clear that he wanted privacy.

Punch was brought to them.

"Well?" said Jeanne impatiently, striving all the time

to keep up the pretence that she stood in no awe of this man.

"Your affairs," said Cagliostro, "are in an unhappy state."

"What do you mean by that?"

"You are a woman of intelligence. Need we waste time discussing the obvious?"

"You have heard gossip?" said Jeanne uneasily.

"My dear Comtesse, do you think I need to listen to gossip? You cannot go on selling something which does not exist. You must think of something else."

"What?" she demanded.

"There you will need a little more ingenuity than that, which, my dear Madame, you have shown in the past. Your friends must see some results if they are to continue to buy what you offer. For what have you to offer? Promises. One can live for a while on promises, but not for ever."

"One must live," she murmured.

"Indeed one must live. But you, my dear Comtesse, concern yourself with the goats, when the milch-cow stands patiently by."

"I do not understand you."

"So many do not. Did you ever hear of a woman named Madame Goupil?"

"No, I did not."

"Some years ago she was a friend of the Cardinal de Rohan . . . a *great* friend. He has always been obsessed by the Queen, and this woman made him believe that she was on such terms with the Queen that she could help to restore him to favour."

Jeanne caught her breath.

"For what purpose?"

"To please him . . . and she was of course paid handsomely for her services."

"For how long?"

"The woman was a fool. She could have played her game more cleverly. She was discovered and the matter hushed up. You can understand that a man in the position of the Cardinal would not want the world to know he had been duped. There are some, less eminent, who would be enraged and would not hesitate to bring to justice those who had used them ill."

'I see," said Jeanne slowly.

"Talking of these matters, there was another lady ... oddly enough she was Madame de la Motte. She went farther than Madame Goupil. She bought jewels and articles of value in the name of the Queen, pretending that she was a lady of the court."

"She was discovered?"

"Yes, I fear she was not as clever as her namesake. But then of course she lacked the magic name 'de Valois'. She received a light sentence. Those concerned in scandals of this nature do not care that they should be bruited abroad. They are invariably hushed up. The woman was of course a fool to allow herself to be caught. But it was an ingenious idea."

"Why do you tell me this?" asked Jeanne.

"Because I have felt an interest in you. Moreover, Madame de Boulainvilliers recommended you to me; and now, alas, poor lady, she is no longer here to watch over you."

"Monsieur le Comte, you are a man of deep knowledge. You see into the future. Tell me this: What does the future hold for me?"

He pushed back his hat and gave her the benefit of those prominent dark eyes.

"The future," he said, "is in our own hands. Therefore it is for you to make yours as you will."

"You mean that ... anything I want can be mine?"

"If you go the right way to get it."

"It is not true. I tried hard to get an audience with the Queen. None could have tried harder. What was the result? Miserable failure!"

"Did you try hard enough?"

"I tell you I haunted Versailles. I fainted three times. . . ."

"Some tasks involve great difficulties. There is need for ingenuity. Make up your mind what you want from life . . . go out to get it; and it will be yours."

"You are telling me to . . . to . . . defraud the Cardinal?"

"I have told you nothing. What you do is in your hands. Who knows, if you believe you can help the Cardinal to win the Queen's favour you may do it. Have faith, Madame. All that happens in reality must first be as a dream. Fact is the materialization of dreams. Come, drink your punch and I will escort you to your house. At this hour the streets of Paris are no place in which a lady should be alone."

*   *   *

When Jeanne reached the house in the Rue Neuve-Saint-Gilles she found both her husband and Rétaux de Villette anxiously waiting for her. They were alarmed by her late return and were on the point of coming out to look for her.

She laughed inwardly at their concern. It had not, she knew, grown out of their affection for her. Yet she felt more pleased to consider the real reason. They were, neither of them, scrupulous; they were both looking for an easy way of life; they were two lazy men and, like most indolent people, they often had to do a great deal more work in their efforts to do nothing than they would if they had settled down to an honest livelihood and lived within their means. Their concern meant that they regarded Jeanne as their leader. They must have been wondering what would happen to them if she had been murdered.

"Well?" she looked from one to the other.

"We were alarmed," said de la Motte.

He knew, of course, of the relationship between her and Rétaux. It was typical of him that he should feel no resentment. He only shrugged his shoulders and implied: It is inevitable. Moreover he was not displeased, for he realized that Rétaux the secretary was a very cunning man, and in their circumstances three heads were better than two.

"A most extraordinary encounter," cried Jeanne. "Come to my bedroom and I will tell you all about it. I believe we are on the verge of something really important. It is imperative that what I say shall be for no ears but our own."

They followed her to the bedroom, and she told of her meeting with Cagliostro.

"Have you ever heard of two women named Goupil and de la Motte? There was trouble because the first duped Cardinal de Rohan into believing that she could restore him to the Queen's favour, and the second obtained all sorts of goods by pretending she did so on the Queen's instructions."

"I remember the second woman," said Rétaux. "I recalled it when I came here first, because of the name. She served a term in the Bastille."

"Cagliostro said she was a fool."

"Cagliostro! What is his game?"

Jeanne shrugged her shoulders. "Whoever understood Cagliostro's game would be a magician himself. Why did he tell me this? Do you know, it was almost as though he were suggesting that, instead of making my promises to our humble friends, I turn my attention to the Cardinal."

"I thought he was the Cardinal's great friend and adviser," said de la Motte.

"It is all very mysterious," said Jeanne. "Cagliostro is undoubtedly the Cardinal's friend. His prosperity depends on that of the Cardinal."

"Then why," demanded Rétaux, "would he suggest you should defraud the man?"

Jeanne turned to the two men. "Do you believe his claims to see into the future?"

Rétaux shrugged; de la Motte lifted his hands in a gesture of doubt.

"There is something strange about so much that is happening," said Jeanne. "I wonder why Madame de Boulainvilliers, who had always been so highly moral, should suddenly bring me to the notice of the Cardinal. She knew the sort of man he is."

"The sort of woman you are . . ." mused de la Motte.

Jeanne ignored that. "It is strange. But I feel this Cagliostro has some superhuman power. He hints that, if I believe I can bring a great change into the Cardinal's life, I can do so. He said something about imagining what you want vividly and striving to get it will bring it to you, because fact is only the materialization of a dream."

"It's beyond me," said de la Motte.

"He suggests that, having failed to get an audience with the Queen you should go to the Cardinal and tell him you have had one?" asked Rétaux.

Jeanne nodded.

"He would not," went on the secretary, "be so ready to believe you as these guests of yours are, and even they are becoming a little restive."

"If only you had some sort of proof . . ." began de la Motte.

"A kerchief . . . or some trinket the Queen has given me . . ." suggested Jeanne.

"You could easily have acquired the trinket through some other source," put in Rétaux. "You should have something which has clearly come from the Queen."

"What could that be?"

"Something in her handwriting perhaps?"

Jeanne and her husband were looking at Rétaux.

"Could it possibly be done?" breathed Jeanne.

"It would be simple. We have seen that handwriting on certain documents. Rose Bertin will show you notes she has had from the Queen. One only has to pay a little court to Queen Rose. There are other means also."

"And you could . . ." began Jeanne.

Rétaux threw back his head and laughed in their faces.

"Do you doubt it?" he asked.

    *   *   *

Jeanne called on the Cardinal, and when he received her she asked that she should be taken at once to his private chamber.

When they were there Jeanne said: "I have news which I think will delight Your Eminence. I have seen the Queen."

"You have seen . . . Her Majesty? What do you mean by that? The audience has been granted you?"

"That was some weeks ago."

"And you did not tell me at once!"

"I pray you, my lord, do not be annoyed with me. I had my reasons. I had hoped that I should be able to bring some good news to you."

"And do you?"

"My lord, let me tell you from the beginning. At long last I was received by the Queen. She was most gracious. Indeed, what a charming creature she is!"

He smiled reflectively.

"So dainty! One would hardly believe that she is made of flesh and blood. She is like a porcelain figure. She was dressed in pale pink muslin and diamonds. She was so enchanting that I found it difficult to take my eyes from her. She was interested in my story and was a little angry that a noble Valois should have been treated as I have been. She has promised me that she will look into my claim. I have little doubt that ere long I shall cease to suffer these financial embarrassments which now beset me."

"But tell me," cried the Cardinal impatiently. "What did you say to her?"

"I thought of Your Eminence, but I was cautious. I would not have her think that I came as your emissary. That would have been very unwise. I sensed that immediately."

"Yes . . . yes. . . ."

"So on that first occasion I talked only of myself. It was a brief audience, as you can imagine. There were others waiting. I had scarce ten minutes with Her Majesty but—and this is what delighted me—I was told that I might come again."

"And you did so?"

"Yes, my lord, again . . . and again."

The Cardinal caught his breath. "Then she is indeed interested in you. How fortunate you are! But my dear Jeanne, do not stand there. Come and sit beside me. Let me have some refreshment brought for you."

Jeanne smiled inwardly. Already she had changed in his eyes. She was no longer merely a humble mistress; she was an important lady who might bring him his heart's desire. Already she was touched by that glory which was Marie Antoinette's. What a fortunate woman Rose Bertin was! This was the happy glow in which she lived perpetually; and she could enjoy it without a qualm; she had not to pretend or to imagine it so fiercely that it became the truth.

"No, Cardinal, I am too excited to delay. I want to show you something."

She took from her pocket a piece of blue paper which was embossed with the golden lilies, and from which came a faint perfume.

"A note," she said, "from the Queen to her little cousin,

Jeanne de la Motte-Valois. Her Majesty was unable to keep an appointment, so she wrote this little note of apology. It was given to me when I presented myself for the audience. It merely postponed our meeting, and I was delighted to have it. See in what affectionate terms she addresses me."

The Cardinal took the note; his senses swam at the touch. *She* had handled this paper, had written those words. There they were, in a handwriting with which he was vaguely familiar. "Dear cousin," the letter began, and it was signed "Marie Antoinette."

It seemed as though he would not relinquish the paper, and Jeanne firmly took it from him.

"I have not, of course," she said, "forgotten Your Eminence."

"How so?" asked the Cardinal quickly.

"On our third meeting I mentioned your name."

The Cardinal took her by the shoulders and stared at her. "And what said she?" he demanded fiercely.

"At first she was inclined to shrug the subject aside as though it were one of no interest to her, but I pursued the matter. I told her of your sorrow that she should feel displeased with you. I told her of your deep regret for all that had displeased her in the past, and I assured her that you would give twenty years of your life if you might but be restored to her favour."

"Yes, indeed," cried the Cardinal in anguish. "And what was her answer to that?"

"She was pensive for a while. Then she said: 'You have a great opinion of the Cardinal, cousin?' I said that I had, that I knew you were a man who longed to serve her, and that if she could bring herself to overlook past differences she would never regret taking you back into her favour. Then she said she was not sure that you wished to be taken back into favour."

"Holy Mother of God!" murmured the Cardinal.

"I assured her that there was no doubt of this, and then she said: 'If he were to write me a letter, and if you were to bring that letter to me, cousin, I would read it and think about the Cardinal's case.'"

"A letter. . . ."

"A letter. A letter expressing your deep regret at the insults you once uttered against her mother. If you wrote it with the greatest care and gave it to me, I would present it to Her Majesty at the earliest possible moment."

"My dear Jeanne, what can I say to you . . . ?"

"You have been good to me, Cardinal; if there is aught I can do to repay you, rest assured it shall be done."

"A letter," he repeated; and she saw that the phrases were already forming in his mind.

"Have a care with the wording, Monseigneur. Make it humble. That would touch her most. She admitted that she remembered you from the time when you received her on her first coming to France. She says you were a handsome priest, but a bold one. And she smiled as though she liked the boldness."

"You are sure of this?"

"Quite sure. I think she has been so very angry with you because . . . because in the first instance she admired you . . . more than a little."

He drew Jeanne into his arms and kissed her passionately.

"Nay," said Jeanne, laughing. "You would only be giving half your thoughts to me. Write the letter now. Then I will seize the very first opportunity of presenting it to Her Majesty."

He nodded. "You are right; I will do that. I can think of nothing else."

She stretched herself on his couch and watched him as he bent over his writing-table. He made several attempts and discarded them all. She was sure that while he wrote he forgot her presence.

Humiliating that he should forget vital Jeanne for a dream? Perhaps. But in that humiliation was the foundation of all the good which was coming to her out of this affair.

The milch-cow, she thought.

And lying back on the couch, listening to the Cardinal's sighs and the scratching of his pen, she remembered her first meeting with this man, the strange behaviour of Madame de Boulainvilliers, the coming of Rétaux, the forger. Life was forming into a neat pattern as though some master-hand were designing it and moving figures into position—herself, de la Motte, Rétaux, the Cardinal—guiding their actions.

It was a strange idea. Who was the architect of their lives?

Was it Cagliostro?

The letter was written. He came to the couch and bent over her. She put her arms about his neck. She wanted him to make love to her. She was the benefactress now; that fact added a different flavour to their love-making, and she wanted to savour it.

His thoughts were far away, she knew; they were with another woman. No matter. She now felt the weight of humiliation lifted from her.

"Jeanne," he said afterwards, "you are in need of money."

She laughed lightly. "What is a little hardship now? I feel sure I shall soon come into my own."

"There is no need to suffer in the meantime."

He opened a drawer and took a purse from it.

"I shall be able to repay you ere long."

"Repay me!" He shook his head. "You are bringing me that which I greatly desire. It is I who shall be in your debt, Jeanne, if you accomplish this."

She took the purse and, weighing it in her hands as she

left his mansion, she thought what good advice that was which she had received from Cagliostro. How much more profitable to milk the great Cardinal than the petty seekers after office who came as guests to the house in the Rue Neuve-Saint-Gilles.

*   *   *

In the city of Lyons, Cagliostro lived as he had in Strasbourg. In the streets people gathered to watch him pass; they waited outside his house all day hoping to be admitted and cured. It was said that he was a greater man than Franz Anton Mesmer, the Austrian physician who a few years ago had created such a stir in Paris. It was a great honour to have such a man in the city of Lyons.

Lorenza preferred Lyons to Paris. In the capital cities of the world she was always obsessed by foreboding. Perhaps it was because of what had happened in London. She believed, however, that Alessandro's ambitions grew bigger in big cities.

She was disturbed therefore when Cagliostro came to her and told her that he was about to set out for Paris.

"Do not be alarmed," he said. "It is merely a short visit. You shall stay here in peace while I am away."

"May I not come with you?"

"No. I go in disguise. I want none to know where I am."

"Why this secrecy, Alessandro?"

"There are matters which are difficult to explain."

"You are going to the Cardinal again?"

"You know, do you not, that he is my *alter ego*."

"He has sent for you?"

"Let us say that I know he needs me."

"You mean that, though no messenger has come from the Cardinal, you know this?"

"No messenger has come from the Cardinal," he said. "Ask me no more. Smile and be brave, my love. I shall soon be back with you. Rest assured that I shall look forward to my return no less than you do."

He set out that day, leaving the house by a back door, wearing his black cloak and big hat, so that he looked like an ordinary man of medium height, and not in the least like the glittering Cagliostro.

He guessed why he had this command. The strings were being jerked in Paris, and the puppets beginning to dance. The man in the crowd this morning, while showing him an arm which he declared had been paralysed for years, had whispered the instructions to him.

"Oh, my lord . . . I cannot move it. For years it has been a dead weight by my side. . . ." The man had lowered his head and was staring at his arm as Cagliostro bent closer to look at it. "Go to the Cardinal," whispered the man. "Assure him that he is on the right road. At once. Delay might be dangerous." Then raising his voice—"Oh, my lord . . . I have suffered much from this useless arm."

It had been one of his most spectacular miracles. The man raised his arm that all might see. He had cried: "I am saved . . . I am saved! The saints preserve great Cagliostro." And turning to the Comte he had mumbled his thanks adding: "Without a day's delay."

And so here was Cagliostro on the road to Paris, thinking of the Cardinal who longed to play a great part in French politics and who had been selected to do so by those who wished to destroy the monarchy. He should play a great part in French politics but it would not be the one he so arrogantly imagined himself playing.

*　　　　*　　　　*

As soon as he arrived in Paris, Cagliostro presented himself at the Cardinal's palace.

He was embraced warmly. "You could not have come at a more appropriate time," cried de Rohan.

"I know it, my friend. We are on the verge of great events."

"I daily expect an answer from the Queen."

"I know."

"But of course you know it. Do you not know all!"

"You felt you needed me at your side."

"How did you know that?"

"It is not easy to explain in words."

"It is the woman . . . Jeanne de la Motte-Valois."

"She has secured audience of the Queen," stated Cagliostro.

"And she has spoken of me to Her Majesty, and the Queen is inclined to be lenient."

"It is good news."

"Which you already knew. There is one thing, my dear friend; I have certain misgivings."

"And it is to set them right that you sent out your plea to me, to leave everything and come to you."

"It must have been so. Though I knew that you were with your wise men and did not wish to be disturbed."

"There has been a mingling of our souls," said Cagliostro. "It would not have been possible for you to need me as you do now, and I not know it."

"It is a great blessing that this should be so. Master, I am uncertain whether to put my whole trust in the woman."

"What reason have you for doubting her?" Cagliostro held up a white hand. "I know it. You think of another. Her name was Goupil. Is that not so?"

"I have ceased to marvel at your omniscience," said the Cardinal. "I *had* been thinking of Madame Goupil."

"She was a pretty woman, was she not? And you made her your mistress."

"She tricked me," said the Cardinal angrily. "It was humiliating. She assured me that she was on terms of intimacy with the Queen. I discovered she was a complete fraud."

"And so suspicion of all others was born. You believe that Jeanne de la Motte-Valois is another Goupil?"

"Oh ... I cannot say. I am uncertain. It is for this reason that I want your reassurance."

"It is for this reason that I travelled in all haste to Paris. It is for this reason I come in secrecy."

"Cagliostro, you *are* divine. I swear I would not move a step without you. Tell me this: Should I trust Jeanne de la Motte-Valois?"

Cagliostro was silent for a while. He began to pace up and down the room. Then he said: "If I could give you a direct answer to all the questions you ask me, I should not be here beside you in this material form. I am here thus, in this earthly stage, because, much as I have learned— in comparison with the knowledge of ordinary men—I have still much to learn. You see me before you, Cardinal, a student in the mysteries of the universe. I do not pretend to know all. There are some people whose minds are as easy for me to read as a book. But a book can only be read if it is open. There are some people who shut their minds to me. Jeanne's I read sometimes; at others it remains shut."

The Cardinal looked dismayed, and Cagliostro was afraid that he had spoken too frankly. He went on quickly: "I can however call upon outside forces and discover whether you are walking towards success or disaster. Will you allow me to do this and then, if you can, abide by what I tell you?"

"Ah, Master," cried the Cardinal, "if I could only trust everybody as I trust you!"

"Come," said Cagliostro, "lie on your couch."

The Cardinal obeyed, and Cagliostro laid his hands on de Rohan's forehead. Then he stood back, his hands curved in the familiar gesture.

After many minutes he spoke.

"Come, rise, my lord Cardinal. I have seen beyond this sphere in which we live, and I tell you this, that you are on the verge of great events. That which is about to happen to you will be the means of your name being linked for ever with that of the Queen."

The Cardinal leaped to his feet; he took Cagliostro in his arms and kissed his cheeks.

"Beloved Master," he said, "you bring so much goodness into my life. I pray you, rest here awhile. I would have you with me when the reply comes from the Queen."

"I will stay," said Cagliostro. "But I pray you, arrange it so that my presence here is not suspected."

"It is my greatest pleasure to respect your smallest wish," answered the Cardinal.

*   *   *

When Jeanne arrived at the Cardinal's palace, and she was brought immediately to his private chamber, she was surprised to see Cagliostro there with de Rohan.

"Monsieur le Comte?" she cried.

"A brief visit," he explained, and he noticed that Jeanne was trembling. He smiled at her reassuringly.

"I ... I had expected to find His Eminence alone," she stammered.

"Do not be afraid," said de Rohan gently. "The Master naturally knows everything."

Everything? wondered Jeanne. How good was Rétaux's forgery?

"You have brought me something?" the Cardinal asked her.

She brought a note from her pocket and held it out to him. It was written on gilt-edged paper which was embossed with the fleur-de-lis.

The Cardinal's hands were trembling.

Cagliostro strode to his side and, taking the note, said: "I will read it to you." He read:

" 'I am delighted to discover that I may cease to blame you. I cannot yet grant you the audience for which you ask. When circumstances permit this I will let you know. In the meantime I ask you to be discreet.' "

It was not addressed to anyone, nor was it signed; but it had an extraordinary effect on the Cardinal. His eyes were alight, his face flushed; he looked ten years younger; he was like a man who is about to achieve a desire for which he has longed and worked all his life.

He almost snatched the paper from Cagliostro. He stared at it; his lips moved as he read it, assuring himself that he had heard correctly. He repeated the phrases over and over again.

"It is the end," he murmured, "the end of my exile from court."

Then he remembered Jeanne and Cagliostro.

"My friends," he said, "my dear, dear friends. Never shall I forget this day and all that you have both done to make it possible."

He embraced them; then he read the letter through again.

Jeanne found that the black eyes of Cagliostro were fixed upon her. She shifted uneasily beneath that gaze, for she could not be sure of how much of the truth Cagliostro was aware.

*   *   *

Cagliostro called at the house in the Rue Neuve-Saint-Gilles. He was delighted to find Jeanne at home.

"Such a pleasure," he said. "I wished to see you before I left Paris."

Jeanne was a little nervous. She was not at all sure of the man. She believed he knew the letter to be a forgery, and she could not understand why he did not expose her.

"That is an honour, Master," she said. "Allow me to send for wine."

"No, thanks. It is such a short visit. I cannot stay." He smiled at her. "It was quite touching yesterday. The Cardinal was so delighted with . . . the note."

Jeanne said brazenly: "It was gracious of the Queen to send it."

"Gracious indeed," murmured Cagliostro. "But I wonder. . . ."

"Yes?" said Jeanne uneasily.

"Will our dear Cardinal be so happy if nothing further comes of this?"

"Nothing further?" said Jeanne sharply.

"Oh . . . His Eminence is in the hands of the light-hearted. It might well be that this little affair can go no farther."

"You mean. . . ."

"I mean that if the Queen does not see him soon he is unlikely to remain so happy, merely with letters."

"I . . . I shall do my utmost to persuade the Queen to see him."

"You will do your utmost. Of course you will. But . . . you will need to succeed—to bring about the meeting." He laughed lightly. "Ah, now I remember. It was for this reason I came." He drew a glove from his pocket. "Yours, Madame, I believe. You left it behind." Cagliostro looked shocked suddenly. "But I had two gloves, and now there is only one. I must have dropped one on my way. How tiresome!"

"It is of no consequence," said Jeanne rising. "It was good of you to try to return them."

"But it is of the greatest consequence, and I am deter-mined to pay for my carelessness."

"My dear Comte, I pray you forget the gloves."

"I shall do no such thing. I have a carriage at the door. We will go and buy a new pair immediately."

"It is quite unnecessary, my dear Comte."

Cagliostro had come to her and taken her arm. His black eyes seemed to burn into hers. "On the contrary," he said, "I repeat it is of the utmost consequence."

She felt bewildered, but at the same time she knew that she would be very unwise to disobey.

"Your goodness overwhelms me, Comte," she murmured. "I will put on my cloak and bonnet if you will wait awhile."

He bowed.

Jeanne returned in a few minutes, dressed for the streets; she had succeeded in hiding her apprehension.

"Come," said Cagliostro, "I intend to buy you the handomest pair of gloves you ever set eyes on."

He gave orders to his coachman, and they rumbled through the streets.

Before a shop in which gloves and hats were sold they pulled up, and Cagliostro alighted and helped Jeanne out of the carriage.

As they entered the shop they were smilingly received by the owner who bowed obsequiously; and Jeanne wondered what the man would have thought had he known that the sombrely clad gentleman was the great Cagliostro.

However, they appeared to be prosperous, and the man enjoyed seeing such a fine carriage drawn up outside his shop.

"I want gloves for the lady," said Cagliostro. "Is Mademoiselle Leguay free? If not we will wait for her."

"Monsieur, Madame," said the man, "Mademoiselle Leguay *shall* be free." Then he called: "Marie! Come here at once."

Jeanne was startled at the sight of the girl. She was so

pretty and dainty. She wore her fair hair piled on her head, and her eyes were very blue. She moved with grace, and it was her figure which was so startling, because she seemed to glide towards them rather than to walk.

"Marie, gloves for Madame," said the owner of the shop.

Marie curtsyed and said: "Madame, Monsieur, will you please step this way?"

Chairs were set for Jeanne and Cagliostro while the young woman brought out boxes and laid gloves before them.

But it was not the gloves Jeanne studied; it was the girl. Cagliostro was watching her with some amusement.

Jeanne chose a pair—a very expensive pair—which pleased both Marie and the owner of the shop. They were wrapped up and Jeanne took them with her.

As they drove back to the house in Rue Neuve-Saint-Gilles, Cagliostro said: "A charming creature, was she not?"

"Very pretty," said Jeanne.

"These girls ... they cannot live on what they earn in shops. At least if they tried to they could not have the pretty things they wish for. There have to be other ways. And can we blame them? They are handling beautiful things all day. They long to wear them, and there are many ready to provide them."

"That girl looked so innocent."

"She has a perpetual look of innocence. I doubt not she will retain it until the end of her days. It is that fairness of skin and lightness of colouring."

"It is hard to believe that she is not an innocent young girl."

"I have seen her in the Palais Royal at night with a friend." Cagliostro was looking at Jeanne. "I am surprised that you do not mention the resemblance."

Jeanne was silent. Her heart had suddenly begun to beat with such fury that she felt her companion must notice.

"They tease her about her in the shop," went on Cagliostro. "They call her The Austrian Woman."

"I did notice the resemblance," said Jeanne. "It is not so much the face as the figure and the er . . . the movement."

"If she were dressed in the Queen's finery, I feel sure she could ride through the streets of Paris and none know it was not the Queen they were looking at."

"It is possible," said Jeanne lightly.

They had reached the house. "I pray you, come in," she said.

"It is with great regret I must decline your invitation. A pressure of work, you understand."

"I understand," said Jeanne; and as she went into the house, clutching her new gloves, she noticed that her heart was still racing as madly as it had when Cagliostro had first spoken of the remarkable resemblance.

*   *   *

Jeanne brought another of those scented notes to the Cardinal.

She found him gloomy, and even the note could not cheer him.

"It is so strange," he said. "I saw the Queen today. I was officiating at Mass, and she was as close to me as you are now, yet she gave no sign that she knew I was there."

"She is very anxious that at present none should know how she feels towards you."

"I understand that, but a glance would have sufficed to reassure me. I did not want a word—merely a look. It would have been impossible for anyone to intercept it. Yet she looked beyond me as though I did not exist."

"She begs you to be patient for a while."

"How long must I be patient? It is several weeks now since we began exchanging notes. Yet she has not shown me by a glance that our relationship has changed at all."

"When I next see her, I will tell her how much distress her apparent coldness has caused you."

"Oh, I beg of you do not make it sound like a reproach. I doubt not she has her reasons."

"Nevertheless I will ask her to reassure you."

"Thank you, Jeanne."

He read the note again. It was warmer in tone than usual and it delighted him so much that he almost forgot the Queen's indifference in public.

When Jeanne left him she went straight home and called de la Motte and Rétaux to her bedroom.

"We shall have to do something very soon," she said. "He grows suspicious. How long do you think we can go on supplying him with her letters, when she treats him with complete indifference whenever he is in her presence?"

Rétaux shrugged his shoulders. "That is your affair," he said. "I am merely the scribe."

"Something will have to be done," Jeanne insisted.

"Well, it couldn't last for ever. We knew that," said de la Motte.

"Stop such talk," said Jeanne. "I tell you it has scarcely begun." They looked at her expectantly, and she went on: "I have a plan. I am going to ask the Cardinal for money . . . a great deal of money. I am going to ask for it in the name of the Queen. If we could get a really large sum of money we could all disappear from Paris, and that would be the end of our little affair with the Cardinal. It will have to end some time. Why not in a blaze of glory?"

"What sort of money?" asked Rétaux eagerly.

"Say, sixty thousand livres."

"That would be twenty thousand each," mused Rétaux.

She did not contradict him; he was going to be useful for some time yet.

"He would never hand over such a sum unless he had something more than letters," declared de la Motte.

"It's true," Jeanne agreed. "And the first hint of suspicion has begun to creep in. If only the Queen would give him one little smile we could go on for many more weeks. But we are going to give him more than letters."

"How shall we do that?" asked de la Motte.

"We are going to pay Mademoiselle Leguay to help us."

"Mademoiselle who?" cried de la Motte.

"I said Mademoiselle Marie Nicole Leguay."

"I have never heard of the woman," said de la Motte.

"But I have just mentioned her. And in the next few weeks I think we are all going to know her very well."

*   *   *

Marie Nicole Leguay twisted and turned in front of the mirror as she tried on the hat she was making. It was a wonderful hat. Fit for the Queen, said her fellow milliners, and Marie, wearing it, looked the living image of Her Majesty.

"Of course," she was told, "you have to hold your head higher. You have to look down your nose at us common people."

Marie strutted about the work-room, trying to look haughty.

"There was a gentleman came into the shop only this morning," said one of the girls, "and the first thing he said was 'Where's the little Queen?'"

Marie giggled. She was pleased with life. It was pleasant to have respectable work, a trade at her finger-tips. She could make hats and she had a way with customers too, so that often she was called out into the shop to sell gloves and the hats which were made in the work-rooms.

Life was hard and it was difficult to keep warm in winter and have enough to eat all the year round and to keep up with the rent of her little room not far from the Palais Royal. But Marie had quickly discovered means of augmenting her tiny wage, and in these fields she was even more successful than she was at the shop.

Indeed the shop opened the way to so many opportunities, and if she had not a previous engagement Marie went to the Palais Royal in order to find a friend.

"Marie! Marie! Come out quickly."

The voice came from the shop and it was a call which made the girls look at each other and giggle. Another of Marie's admirers. They were constantly coming into the shop ostensibly to buy gloves, but actually to have a word with Marie. Their employer was delighted.

Marie took the hat from her head, tidied her hair and went out to the shop.

"A gentleman wishes you to show him gloves for a lady," said Marie's employer; and Marie went forward to where an elegant young officer was sitting in the chair which was reserved for the best customers.

He caught his breath when he looked at her.

He wanted a pair of gloves, he said, for an elegant lady. Would Mademoiselle Marie help him to choose them?

"With the greatest pleasure, Monsieur."

He studied her while she served him, but said little.

When Marie returned to her companions they swarmed about her.

"But he was elegant. Clearly a gentleman. Did he ask you to meet him?"

Marie shook her head. "No, he just stared and stared. That was all."

"Yet he asked for you. I have it. Someone told him that you were the living image of the Queen, and he came to see if it were true."

"I wonder if he thought it was true," said Marie.

*   *   *

Marie could scarcely wait to reach the Palais Royal,

that paradise where a shop-girl could walk beneath the trees and dream that she was a young lady with a mansion in the Faubourg Saint German or Saint Honoré.

Here congregated all sorts of people. Intellectuals sat at the tables drinking their wine or coffee and talked of the state of the world; gamblers placed their stakes on this that and the other; those who found fault with the world as it was, those who wished it to remain untouched, argued with each other; those who had a new plan for a new world stood on boxes and harangued the passers-by.

The Duc d'Orléans had passed over the Palais Royal to his son the Duc de Chartres because he was unable to cope with the upkeep of such a costly establishment, and Chartres had hit upon the idea of turning the place into something which was not quite a pleasure garden and not quite a club, but entirely profitable to the Duke. The ground floor of the great palace had been made into shops, a great many of them cafés. There were a hundred and eighty of these in the palace, and there were booths and tents which had been set up in the gardens. Here in the Palais Royal it was possible to buy most things; the shops showed a dazzling variety of goods; and it was by night that the Palais Royal took on that quality which lured Parisians from all quarters to enjoy its delights.

Here under the trees the prostitutes paraded, looking for clients, appearing charming in the artificial lights which shone in the Palais Royal from dusk until eleven. Here those men who were determined to make revolution in France met, and the humblest was smiled on by the Duc de Chartres, who was often seen mingling with the men and women who frequented his estate. He cared not, it was said, whether a man was a duke or a shopkeeper. The Duc de Chartres—royal as he was, cousin of the King—had declared that in his opinion all men should be equal.

To Marie the Palais Royal was a happy hunting-ground.

K

There she found her gentlemen friends who would talk to her of the positions they held in the royal households, even though she often knew them to be merchants or even servants of such; they would all discover sooner or later her extraordinary resemblance to the Queen; it was, Marie was sure, the secret of her success.

As she left the shop that night a man stepped out from the shadows and followed her. Marie was accustomed to being followed, so she was not alarmed.

She made her way to the Palais Royal, and she was conscious that all the time the man was close behind her. She sat down on one of the seats under the trees. The lamp which had been fixed there shone on her young face and the muslin gown which, she had been told by the second-hand clothes woman in the Place de Grève last Monday, was an exact copy of one which the Queen had been seen wearing at Petit Trianon only a few weeks ago.

The man who had followed her sat beside her.

"Mademoiselle," he said, "you will forgive the impertinence?"

She started, for she realized at once that it was he who that day had come into the shop to buy gloves.

"I guessed you were making for this place," he went on. "I am glad. It is easy to talk here. You are very charming, Mademoiselle."

"Thank you. I suppose you are thinking that I am a little like someone."

"The resemblance is remarkable. I shall tell Her Majesty when next we meet."

"Oh!" cried Marie, putting her hand to her mouth. She was imagining the Queen's sending for her, saying "You shall make my hats in future." She saw herself wearing the Queen's cast-off clothes, an important person at Versailles. Why not? All Paris knew what had happened to Rose Bertin.

"She will be very interested," said the man.

"You . . . you know the Queen well?"

He did not answer, but his laugh was significant, and Marie was sure that she was in the presence of a nobleman.

"I . . . I should like to talk to her," said Marie. "I'd like to see her close up . . . you know . . . so that I could see if I really am all that like her."

"In appearance there is a resemblance. But that is all."

"Why . . . what do you mean . . . ?"

"Mademoiselle Marie, you must be aware that you speak with the accents of the streets. However you were dressed, once you opened your mouth everybody would know that you were not the Queen."

"Oh," said Marie deflated.

"Then you have not the same grace. You do not hold yourself as a queen but as a shop-girl."

This was very different from the compliments Marie was accustomed to receive from gentlemen who followed her into the Palais Royal.

"Now," went on her companion, "look at that woman walking there. You see how she carries herself? She is of the nobility; it is apparent in every movement." Marie obeyed and looked. "Now look at those women, extravagantly dressed, a-glitter with jewels which may or may not be real—who can say in this light? But they are of the gutter. You see what I mean?"

"Well . . . not really, but. . . ."

"Ah, Mademoiselle, you have a great deal to learn."

"Suppose I could walk like a lady and talk like one, do you suppose . . . ?"

"If you could walk like the Queen and talk like the Queen, as well as look like the Queen, a glorious future would certainly await you."

"I'm talking to a noble gentleman, I believe."

"You are talking to the Comte de la Motte-Valois."

"Oh—er!" gasped Marie.

He laughed. "Do not be overawed. You interest me."

"I know. It's because I look like her. It interests a lot of them."

"There are many things I could teach you. Would you be willing to learn?"

"Well . . . if I could."

"Tell me, where do you live?"

"I couldn't take you there . . . not a gentleman like you. It's in the Rue de Jour in the Quartier St. Eustache."

He nodded.

She went on: "It's not my fancy. I tried for a place in the Île de Saint Louis. But . . . they wouldn't have me."

"Île de Saint Louis! It is a prim provincial town in the heart of Paris. I think I should almost prefer your attic."

"Oh no, you wouldn't. I couldn't take you there. Not a comte!"

"We will meet here in the Palais Royal."

"Is that all right for you . . . ?"

"You mistake me, Mademoiselle. I do not ask what most of your friends ask. My first task is to see if it is possible to make you resemble Her Majesty in more than looks."

"Well, I never!" Marie exclaimed.

De la Motte said: "We will meet every evening here at this spot, when I will give you a short lesson. I will teach you how to control your mouth when you speak, to speak more slowly and make sure that you consider each word before you say it, to hold yourself upright, and not use vulgar expressions; and when you walk, to imagine that you are carrying a crown on your head. Would you like to try this?"

"Oh . . . er . . . yes, I think I would."

"Very well then. We will begin the first lesson."

"Yes, but what's it all about? What are you . . . after like?"

He patted her hand. "You will see, Mademoiselle; and then I do not think you will have anything to regret."

Marie was excited. They drank coffee together and he made her work hard. It was the strangest evening of Marie's life, and she was sorry when just before eleven he insisted that they leave so that they should not be in the gardens when the lights were extinguished.

He escorted her as far as she would let him, but she could not allow a comte to accompany her in that maze of streets.

She met him again the next night, and the lessons continued.

"Here, Marie," said her friends, "what's come over you? This is the work-room, this is, not the Palace of Versailles!"

She merely laughed. When she spoke now, she did so with caution; she held her head high as though it supported a crown.

"I swear Marie's dreaming half the time," said her friends. "Being told she looks like the Queen has gone to her head."

*   *   *

Two weeks had passed since Marie had first met the strange comte who had undertaken her education. He had told her that he no longer thought of her as Mademoiselle Leguay. She should have a title bestowed upon her. She was now Baronne d'Oliva.

"Baronne d'Oliva," she had repeated when he told her. "But can I be that? Don't the King have to make you it?"

"I give you the title," he said. "Oliva. You can turn those letters about and make them Valoi; and the Valois were once kings as great as the Bourbons."

"It's ever so clever," said Marie.

And it was wonderful to think of herself as a baronne.

"Do you know," she told him, "it makes it easier for me. It makes me remember more. When I'm going to talk like I used to I can say to myself: 'Now then . . . is that the Baronne d'Oliva!' "

"Remember it then," she was told. "Remember what you owe to your title."

She came to their usual meeting-place under one of the trees in the Palais Royal where he was waiting for her.

When he rose, took her hand and kissed it with a courtly gesture, Marie was thrilled. During their acquaintance she had not seen any of her gentlemen friends, and she was finding it difficult to make ends meet in her little attic; but she did not seem to be interested in gentlemen, or the benefits they could bestow; she was so intrigued by her teacher and the hints he threw out of all the good that would come to her if she learned her lessons.

She had mentioned him to some of her friends at the shop for it had been impossible to keep the secret from them. When her gentlemen came in and wanted to make assignations with the little queen she had to refuse, and the girls said she was foolish to do that, so she simply had to tell them of what was happening.

They too were awed.

"I know what it is," said one girl, "this comte has fallen in love with you. It is clear that a comte cannot marry a shop-girl, so he is going to make a lady of you."

"What of her *dot*?" demanded another.

"Oh, he is so rich he can afford to ignore that. He is going to make her exactly like the Queen and take her to court. What a sensation!"

They were as excited by Marie's prospects as she was.

During the afternoon a lady came into the shop and asked for Marie.

As soon as Marie saw her she felt her to be vaguely familiar; and she remembered, while she was serving her, that the lady had come in with a gentleman who had bought a pair of gloves for her, and they had asked that Marie should serve them.

The lady was saying: "Mademoiselle Leguay, you are acquainted with Monsieur le Comte de la Motte-Valois?"

"But . . . yes, Madame." Marie was frightened; she believed that her story was falling into a conventional pattern and that this lady was a relative of her comte, come to tell her she must see him no more.

But she was mistaken. "Do not be afraid," said the lady. "You should in fact be delighted. Would you like to earn fifteen thousand livres?"

"Fifteen thousand livres, Madame!" Marie was startled; she had never in the whole of her life thought of possessing such a sum.

"It is a great deal of money," said the lady, "and it can be earned in a very short time."

"But, Madame, I pray you tell me how I can earn this money."

"I come from one whom you resemble in a small way."

Marie's mouth fell open; she had never looked less like Marie Antoinette.

The lady was looking at her with faint distaste and Marie hastily shut her mouth and held her head as the Comte had so often instructed her to do. Then the lady seemed relieved.

"When you leave the shop this evening," she went on, "you will find a carriage outside. In it the Comte de la Motte-Valois will be waiting. He will bring you to Versailles. You may be required to stay there for a day or so. Have no fear. You will lose nothing; on the other hand you will gain a good deal, and you will have the satisfaction of knowing that you are performing a service for your Queen."

Marie was bewildered. The lady chose her gloves and left the shop.

All that day Marie was in a daze but, when she left in the evening, there was the carriage waiting for her; the door was opened for her by the coachman and inside was her friend the Comte de la Motte-Valois.

*   *   *

In Jeanne's lodging at Versailles she, with Rétaux, eagerly awaited the coming of the Comte and Marie.

Jeanne was so restless she could not keep still. Rétaux was watching her with amusement. He was pleased with life. Jeanne was a clever woman, and his premonition that once he walked in step with her he would be in clover was proving to be true.

Sixty thousand livres! he was thinking. And they would not stop at sixty thousand livres. After all, if this girl could play the part there was no reason why they should not extract many more payments of sixty thousand livres from the gullible Cardinal.

"It cannot go wrong," Jeanne kept saying as though to reassure herself. "The girl is quite stupid, but she cannot fail, can she?"

"Be at peace," growled Rétaux. "It's all to the good that the girl is stupid. A fool will suit our purpose better than a wise woman."

"How long they are! I hope all is well."

Jeanne went to look at the dress and the hat which she had made herself. They were exact copies of those which the Queen had worn in a recent painting.

"Her looks are perfect," murmured Jeanne. "But those sudden lapses of hers clearly show she comes from the Bièvre district. What if he asks a surprise question?"

Rétaux was reassuring. "Well, then you just whip her away. You hiss: 'Someone is coming'. It will be perfectly all right."

"I wish it were over."

"It's not like you to be nervous."

"We've never done anything like this before."

"Listen! The carriage. Here they are."

Jeanne steeled herself as de la Motte brought the girl into the apartment. Then she rose and went to them, smiling at Marie in a reassuring fashion, for the girl looked bewildered.

"There is nothing to be afraid of," said Jeanne. "You should consider instead how fortunate you are. And all because you bear a resemblance to the Queen—a matter which is pure luck and no credit to you."

"Please," said Marie, "please, Madame, will you tell me what I have to do?"

"Of course I will. But, Madame la Baronne d'Oliva, you must not tremble so. You have all this evening and tomorrow in which to learn your part. Come, and I will show you the dress you are to wear . . . and the hat. I'll warrant you never saw the like."

She drew Marie into the bedroom, where the gown and hat lay on the bed. Marie gasped at the sight of them and forgot her fear for a few seconds.

"We'll try them on," suggested Jeanne. "It may be necessary to make a few alterations. That my maid will do."

When Marie put on the muslin gown, the transformation of her appearance was astonishing. She was beautiful now.

"Now the hat. Of course your hair is wrong and we shall have to do something about that. Never mind. We have the pomade and powder waiting for you. However, put it on and let me look at you."

It was a graceful hat of straw and ribbons, and most becoming.

Jeanne looked at the girl through half-closed eyes. Perhaps, she thought . . . if the light were dim enough. The light would have to be dim. And the girl must not say more than a sentence. All de la Motte's training had not been able to wipe out that tang of the streets.

"Please tell me what I've got to do," begged Marie.

"It is very simple. All you have to do is take a rose and a letter which I shall give you, and at dusk go with us to the park of Versailles. There you will meet a gentleman. He will kiss your hand and you will give him the rose and the letter, saying: 'You know what this means'."

"You know what this means," repeated Marie in a monotone.

"You shall practise saying it with us so that you get the tone and accent exactly right."

"And that is all?"

"All. But you must do it very carefully. The Queen will be watching you."

"Watching *me*!"

"Yes, it is a test. If you do this to her satisfaction, there is no knowing what good may come to you. Do not forget, although it is so simple, it is of the utmost importance. Now! Come and show them how well you look in your hat and gown."

Jeanne led her to the room where the men were waiting.

"That's . . . very good," said de la Motte.

"Excellent!" cried Rétaux, leering at the girl.

"But she is *gauche*. She will have to learn to stand and speak better than she does at the moment."

"Look here," said Marie, "I don't think I want to do it."

De la Motte went to her and put his arm about her shoulders. "Now, Baronne, be sensible. Remember you are no longer a shop-girl, a *habituée* of the Palais Royal. You are a baronne, Baronne d'Oliva."

"All right," muttered Marie.

She assured herself that they were testing her in some way, and that if she could play the part well she would marry the Comte and be a lady of the court, for even though she did earn the better part of her living in the

Palais Royal, she had heard that most of the great ladies at court earned favours in a similar fashion.

She spent the evening walking about the apartment as though she were a queen and saying over and over again those words "You know what this means," in what seemed to her a hundred different ways and none of them right.

She was at length given her supper and allowed to go to bed. It was a more luxurious bed than the one to which she was accustomed, but she was too worried to enjoy it, and every time she was on the point of going to sleep she would wake up and find herself murmuring "You know what this means."

*　　　*　　　*

The next day Jeanne left Versailles for Paris and went to the Cardinal's house.

He was eagerly awaiting her.

"Yes?" he cried as soon as he had conducted her to his private apartment.

"All is well. It is to be tonight."

De Rohan clasped his hands in rapture. "My dear Jeanne, what can I say to you!"

"It is of no consequence what you say to me. It is what you say to Her Majesty which is all-important."

"So she will meet me . . . this very night. At last, after all these years of waiting. . . ."

"I beg of Your Eminence, listen carefully. You will come with only one servant; and let it be one whom you can trust."

"It shall be Planta. I trust him as no other."

"The meeting will take place in the Bosquet de Vénus. It will be safer there. You know the spot below the high terrace wall and the Hundred Steps."

"I know it well."

"It will be a dark night as there is no moon."

"There should be a glorious full moon on this night of nights," cried the Cardinal.

"Do not say that. Had there been, Her Majesty would never have risked meeting you."

"No, of course not. I must be thankful for the moonless night."

"Between eleven and midnight then. You may have to wait awhile. It is not easy, as you can imagine, for Her Majesty to slip away."

"I will wait all night if necessary."

"Then . . . all is clear. I shall be with Her Majesty in the Bosquet de Vénus between eleven and midnight. Till then, Eminence, adieu."

"Jeanne, what can I do to repay you? Allow me to . . ."

She shook her head. "You have been good to me, my lord, and most happily do I perform this service for you. There should be no talk of payment between . . . friends."

He kissed her hand as though she were the Queen herself.

Jeanne smiled secretly; but she did not allow herself more than a few minutes to enjoy this triumph. All her thoughts must be for tonight. So much depended on that meeting. Sixty thousand livres to begin with . . . a fortune without doubt.

She took her dignified leave of the Cardinal, knowing that he was as impatient for the night as she was.

*   *   *

Jeanne herself dressed the girl's hair. Already she was in the long white robe, and a sheet was about her shoulders while Jeanne and her trusted maid worked on her.

Rosalie was deft, and had a good knowledge of hair-dressing. They pomaded the long beautiful hair until it stood straight up and stiff from the somewhat vapid little face. They then proceeded to drape it over a cushion stuffed with horsehair, securing it with pins, seven or eight inches in length, until it stood high above the girl's head. They curled it and powdered it and, when they had finished, Marie could scarcely believe that it was herself whom she glimpsed in the mirror. Now with the dress, the hair style and big hat which they set on her hair, she could indeed believe that she was a queen.

"Oh, I do hope the Queen will like me."

"She will if you play your part well," Jeanne assured her. "Do not forget that she will be close to you, watching how you do it."

"Oh . . . will she speak to me?"

"She doubtless will if she is pleased with you."

"But what shall I say to her?"

"You will wait to hear what she has to say to you."

"But what do I call her—just Madame . . . or . . . what?"

"Always say 'Your Majesty'."

"Your Majesty," repeated Marie.

Now that she was ready, she must be inspected by the two men.

"But you are a charming little queen!" cried Rétaux.

Marie looked anxiously at the Comte. "I will take the part of the man whom you will meet," he said. "Now show me how you will act. No . . . for the love of God, do not come towards me. Stand very still. Stand as I have taught you to stand. Show your dignity. That's better. Now. I shall come and you will give me your hand. I kiss it. Then you hand me the rose and the letter—and what do you say?"

"I . . . you . . . you know what that means," stammered Marie.

De la Motte raised his eyes in exasperation. "Try it again, Marie. You must not stumble. That is imperative."

Marie tried again. She stood still. "You know what that means," she cried out hysterically.

Rétaux sniggered; de la Motte sighed. And they must try it all over again.

Then de la Motte said to Rétaux: "It is time you prepared yourself."

*   *   *

It was a little past eleven. The Cardinal, trembling with excitement, waited impatiently in a clump of bushes. Planta was waiting a little distance away. The Cardinal looked up at the dark sky in which a few stars were visible, and he was filled with anxiety lest the Queen should not keep her appointment.

What if she had not forgiven him after all? What if she were laughing at him? What if the whole thing was a hoax? He could not bear it.

"My lord."

He started. He saw a man in the livery of the palace servants close to him.

"You are here on a special mission, my lord," said the servant. "I pray you, follow me."

"With all speed," said de Rohan.

Rétaux in his livery laughed inwardly and asked himself what the amorous Cardinal would say if he knew that he was walking with the writer of those charming little notes he had been receiving.

They moved to the shelter of a clump of trees, for they heard the sound of running footsteps.

"What is that?" asked the Cardinal in a low voice.

"I cannot imagine, my lord. Unless there is some hitch and someone has come to warn us. Hide here, my lord, and I will see if I can discover."

From his hiding-place the Cardinal saw a figure in a dark cloak hurrying towards the man; with relief he recognized Jeanne.

"Where is the Cardinal?" whispered Jeanne.

"I am here." He came out and stood before her.

"It is very unfortunate," said Jeanne. "Her Majesty is annoyed. It is those wretched sisters-in-law of hers. Madame and Madame d'Artois asked her if she would allow them to walk with her this evening at the very moment when she was about to leave."

"And this means . . . ?" cried the Cardinal, despair in his voice.

"It means that she will not be able to spend as much time with you as she wished. She has slipped away from them but they are curious. Oh, if you only knew how curious! Her Majesty will not want the tale of this meeting discussed at Bellevue and the Luxembourg."

"Indeed not!"

"However, follow me. You shall at least *see* Her Majesty. But be very quick. I shall remain on the alert for the coming of Mesdames."

Jeanne turned and hurried towards the thicket; and there in that grove among the pines and cedars the Cardinal saw a sight which filled him with exultation. She was standing beneath a tree and she was beautiful. Her long white gown, simply but exquisitely cut, shone in the semidarkness. He saw her face, shaded by the great hat.

He went forward swiftly. He did not see the hand which was outstretched towards him. He fell to his knees, and slightly lifting the hem of her gown, he kissed it.

"Your Majesty!" he breathed.

Marie was holding out the rose, expecting him to take it as all those who had enacted this scene with her before had done. She dropped the rose at his feet. He picked it up and pressed it to his lips.

She spoke the words very quickly and very quietly as she had been taught: "You know what this means. . . ."

He was staring at her as though stunned. He was murmuring: "Your Majesty . . . This . . . this is the most wonderful moment of my life. This great honour ... All that I have suffered in your displeasure was worth while since it has brought me a moment of such supreme joy ... such unadulterated happiness. . . ."

Marie was frightened. She had no notion how to reply to that sort of thing.

But Jeanne was at hand to rescue her.

"Your Majesty," she cried, "there is not a moment to lose. Madame and Madame d'Artois have followed you here. They are not far off. At any moment. . . ."

Jeanne's hand so firmly gripped Marie's arm that, had she not been so alarmed by the darkness and the strangeness of everything, she would have cried out in protest; as it was, she allowed herself to be led away.

The Cardinal stood staring after her for a few seconds. Then he was aware of the manservant, who had brought him to this spot, standing at his elbow.

"My lord, it would be wise if you left here with all speed."

The Cardinal turned and made haste back to Planta.

Shortly afterwards he was riding back to Paris, a rose in his hand and a song in his heart.

*   *   *

In their lodgings at Versailles the conspirators congratulated themselves.

The plot had worked as well as could be expected and they were sure that there had been no doubt in the Cardinal's mind that he had spoken to the Queen.

Marie asked them if the Queen was pleased with what she had done.

They looked at her as though they were scarcely aware of her. She was astonished. They had taken such pains with her before the adventure.

Into Jeanne's expression there crept a look of distaste.

"Well, my dear," she said, "you did not play your part very well, did you?"

"But I did what you said."

"You dropped the rose. You were told to give it to him. And you gabbled your words."

"So the Queen didn't like what I done?"

"She hoped you would do better."

Marie's mouth showed her disappointment.

"Never mind," said Jeanne. "It is all over. Now we will take down your hair and you can get into your own things."

"Oh, can't I keep my hair like this?"

"No."

"Oh, do let me. Ladies do. I can tie it up at nights and it'll last like this for weeks."

No, thought Jeanne. You are going back to Paris looking exactly like Marie Nicole Leguay of the glove and milliner's shop and the Palais Royal, and you are going to forget your little adventure at Versailles. You will therefore take no reminders with you.

Jeanne's answer was to take out the long pins, remove the horsehair pad and bid the girl wash the powder and pomade out of her hair because, undressed as it was, it was far from becoming. But first let her take off the fine gown and get into her own.

Marie obeyed, and when she had done this she lay on the bed on which she had slept the previous night.

Early in the morning Jeanne aroused her. She gave her coffee and milk and a piece of bread.

"When you have eaten you will return to Paris," she said.

"I was going to be paid a lot of money for what I done," Marie reminded her.

"When you go back to Paris you are to say nothing of what happened here."

"Oh . . . but . . ."

L

"You will tell your friends that you spent the days and nights with a lover."

"You said I would get fifteen thousand livres for doing what I did."

"I was naturally joking. Fifteen thousand livres is a fortune."

Marie looked hurt. "But they'll ask me," she said.

Jeanne said quickly: "I am going to give you four thousand two hundred livres. It is a great deal of money. I'll swear you have never had so much."

Marie nodded in agreement.

"Then you shall have it on condition that you say nothing of what has happened here. You did not go to the park of Versailles and meet a gentleman. You were with a gentleman friend of your own in Paris. Do you hear that? You never left Paris."

"But. . . ."

"If you swear to do what I say you shall have your four thousand two hundred livres. If you do not . . ." Jeanne shrugged.

"I'll say nothing," said Marie.

"If you ever do you will greatly regret it."

"What would happen then?"

"Do not ask. The answer would frighten you. Be a wise girl. You have earned money in strange ways before, I'll be bound. This is just another way of earning money. In this instance part of that money buys your silence. Now, you will be taken back to Paris and left outside the Barrier. You will go into the city and resume your life as though none of this ever happened."

Marie nodded.

She was driven to the Barrier where she alighted from the carriage; and she went back to her lodgings in the Quartier St. Eustache the richer by more than four thousand livres.

She hid the money and went back to the shop.

Her employer was annoyed by her desertion, but because she was the 'Little Queen' who brought good business to the shop he allowed her to return to her job.

Where had she been?

"Oh . . . there was such a nice gentleman."

"The Comte?"

"Not exactly the Comte."

They laughed at her. She seemed bewildered. It had evidently been a startling adventure.

In the evening she went to Palais Royal, but the Comte was not there.

And in a few weeks she would have forgotten that it had ever happened, but for the money she kept hidden in her attic.

*   *   *

Jeanne called on the Cardinal.

As soon as they were alone she said: "I have a message from Her Majesty."

He waited eagerly for her to go on.

"She was disappointed that she could not stay longer with you in the Bosquet de Vénus."

"She said this?"

"Several times. She fears that Mesdames are suspicious. They watch all her movements."

"Those cursed females!" muttered de Rohan.

"But she says you must be patient. Now you know her feelings, she is certain that you will be."

"Tell her that she has but to command me and I will do . . . all . . . all that she asks."

"There is one request I have to make to you . . . on her behalf."

"Then do so, I beg you, with all speed."

"My lord, may I offer an opinion?"

"Certainly."

"I think she does this to test you."

"What is it? Tell me quickly."

"She is in need of money."

"Is that all?"

"A great deal of money. She wants sixty thousand livres immediately."

"You mean the Queen is short of sixty thousand livres!"

"She has so many debts of late. You know how she is watched . . . criticized at every turn. Even the King has been listening to tales of her extravagance. She wishes to help a friend who is in distress and needs the money immediately."

"This is a strange request from the Queen."

"But Monseigneur, I do believe it is meant to test you. Take my advice and give her this money without hesitation. I have a note for you."

She handed him one of the gilt-edged letters, which he read eagerly. "She says that I am to entrust you with what she asks for, and commands me to burn this letter."

"Then she will wish me to take it to her immediately; I have an audience tomorrow."

"Take it tomorrow," said the Cardinal. "And tell her that everything I have . . . my lands . . . my jewels . . . myself . . . all are at her disposal."

"I will tell her this, and I must tell her also that I have seen you burn the letter. She was anxious about others she has sent."

"Tell her she need have no fears, and that her letters are the greatest joys in my life."

"She wishes them destroyed. She is often very much hurt by the evil stories which are circulated about her, and although she trusts you completely, she fears that by some mischance her letters might fall into other hands."

Jeanne then had the pleasure of seeing the letter—and others—burned before her eyes. She felt very much more comfortable when she had witnessed their destruction.

She left the Cardinal's house and made her way at once to the Rue Saint-Neuve-Gilles, where de la Motte and Rétaux were waiting for her.

"It succeeded," she said. "I have the sixty thousand livres."

"Sixty thousand livres, for a little masquerade!" cried de la Motte.

Rétaux was smiling at Jeanne.

"And do not forget," he said, "that this is but the beginning."

*   *   *

V

THE QUEEN'S JEWELLERS
(*The Ace of Diamonds*)

LIFE WAS VERY MERRY IN THE RUE NEUVE-SAINT-GILLES.
Money was flowing freely. Sixty thousand livres was a use-
ful sum, and there had been a further loan from the
Cardinal to the Queen.

They were all aware that this was a state of affairs which
could not be permanent, but Jeanne was certain that when
the occasion arose she would find another means of extract-
ing money from the Cardinal.

Parties were more lavish. The guests were of a higher
social standing than they had originally been. It was understood among them that the Queen had agreed that Jeanne's
claim to some of the Valois estates was justified. Tradesmen
who had been a little hesitant now became eager for the
patronage of the de la Mottes. They could be seen waiting
for audience. More and more people were begging Jeanne
to plead their causes at court. She was not very encourag-
ing. The small amounts she could extract from them now
seemed hardly worth the trouble of working for.

It was true that the Cardinal, having got over the ecstasy
which had followed his adventure in the Bosquet de
Vénus, was at times a little troublesome. He could not
understand why the Queen should continue to treat him
so coldly in public. "Her attitude towards me has not
changed in the slightest degree," he complained.

"You cannot understand," Jeanne persuaded him, "with
what Her Majesty has to contend. She is surrounded by
spies."

"But if she is going to receive me as her friend, should she not begin to show a little warmth towards me?"

"Ah, she does not trust her feelings. She fears that she would show more than a *little* warmth."

This was a reply which gave the Cardinal such acute pleasure that he was silenced for a while.

It was an autumn day some weeks after the adventure in the Bosquet de Vénus when Jeanne, who was beginning to feel a little uneasy as to how she could possibly keep the Cardinal satisfied, was told by one of her guests that a friend of hers had heard of her rise to favour and was longing to meet her.

Jeanne was scarcely listening. Such a request was often made and she had no notion at this time that the meeting was to be the most significant of her life.

"I pray you bring your friend along some time."

"He will be delighted. He feels that you can be of great help to him."

"Oh? Who is he then?"

"He is Monsieur Boehmer."

"Boehmer? I have heard his name."

"Certainly you have. He is on the way to making his fortune since he became *Joaillier-Bijoutier de la Reine*."

"Of course. But he must have been a rich man before he took the position. I'll warrant it cost him dear."

"He is a rich man, but at the moment he is a little worried, and he thinks you can help him. I know, of course, that this will only be of secondary importance to you, but he is ready to pay a handsome commission to any who can help him make a certain sale."

"Commission!" Jeanne's nose wrinkled. "I am not a saleswoman, you know."

"He knows that well. Do not mistake him. But I pray you allow me to bring him to see you."

"Oh well, let him come. You know how helpful I always am . . . when I can be."

"He will be delighted."

*   *   *

Charles Auguste Boehmer, the Queen's jeweller, was delighted when he heard he had received an invitation to the house in Rue Neuve-Saint-Gilles.

"This," he told his partner, Paul Bassenge, "may be the way out of our difficulty."

Paul sighed. Their 'difficulty' had occupied their minds day and night for several years now—in fact ever since the death of Louis Quinze in 1774.

The object of their hopes and fears was a necklace, a necklace which had to be seen to be believed, for it was composed of the finest diamonds they, as shrewd jewellers, had been able to lay their hands on. The diamond necklace to them represented dreams of great riches; it was the crowning lifework of the jewellers. It was to bring them a fortune so that they could, if they desired, spend the rest of their lives in comfort.

It consisted of a string of diamonds, all specially selected for their size and lustre, from which hung pendants of pear-shaped stones surrounded by clusters; from this string hung another, looped and composed of equally fine stones, and from this looped string hung more pear-shaped clusters. Then there was the double string of diamonds with an enormous centre-piece from which hung tassels of dazzling gems.

It had taken years to find stones worthy of the necklace, and there was no doubt in the minds of its creators that there could not be another such in the world. The price asked was one million six hundred thousand livres, and the difficulty in selling such a piece was that, although the whole world admired it and recognized its worth, there were very few people who could have afforded to buy it.

The jewellers had begun their task in great hopes, for at that time Madame du Barry was at the height of her power and the doting old Louis was clearly ready to give her anything she asked; and the somewhat ostentatious design of the necklace was made especially to suit the tastes of Madame du Barry.

Alas for du Barry and for Messieurs Boehmer and Bassenge, the smallpox intervened; Louis was carried off and du Barry banished from the position in which she could expect such gifts.

"One star sets, another rises," said the optimistic Monsieur Boehmer to his partner, Monsieur Bassenge. "It is well known that although the new King has no mistress, he has an extravagant and beautiful wife whose taste for diamonds is obvious."

Thinking of Marie Antoinette, the jewellers were able with good hope to continue with the task of making their masterpiece.

The necklace was completed and the occasion arrived— as they knew it must—when it might be shown to the Queen.

Here was the first rumble of disaster. After all those years of waiting, which had caused distress and embarrassment to them both, the Queen had presented the King with an heir. The King would wish to give the Queen a little token of gratitude. What more suitable than the diamond necklace, which none could fail to notice and admire?

But the Queen's passion for diamonds had faded a little. She had fallen in love with her little house, Petit Trianon, and she enjoyed the simple life there. To live the simple life the Queen must dress accordingly. So fashion changed. Muslin and cambric took the place of brocades and satins; and diamonds did not go well with the simple fashion.

The Queen did not want diamonds. She advised the King
that the money would better be spent on men-o'-war.

The jewellers could scarcely believe their ears. They left
the royal presence in a daze.

"We are ruined!" cried Bassenge.

"Unless we can sell the diamond necklace in some other
court," replied his partner.

They were unfortunate. They went first to the King
and Queen of the two Sicilies. The necklace was beautiful—
but oh, the price! The two Sicilies were not France, they
must know.

And so they travelled from court to court, always
meeting with the same answer. Bassenge was in despair,
for it had been necessary to borrow heavily to buy the
stones with which to make the necklace. For such a project
long credit was extended, but all creditors knew now that
the necklace was completed. Why then did they not see
the Queen wearing it?

The two wretched jewellers began to realize that they
had staked too much on one project. It was becoming more
and more clear that if they could not sell the necklace to
the Queen of France they would be obliged to break it
up and sell the stones separately. Four years of work and
dreams of fortune would thus be as though they had never
existed. Moreover, they would not be able to get back the
high prices they had paid for the stones, for in their endeavour to match them they had bought recklessly.

They must make a last desperate attempt to get the
Queen to change her mind.

And now they had heard of this Comtesse Jeanne de la
Motte-Valois who seemed to be on as excellent terms with
Marie Antoinette as was La Polignac. It was said in court
circles that the friendship between the Queen and Polignac
was fading. Could it be that the Comtesse was taking
her place?

It was very likely. In that case the woman should be able to persuade the Queen.

"And would she?" asked Bassenge.

"For a big enough commission she certainly would," Boehmer reassured him.

So with fresh hope the jeweller set out for the apartments in the Rue Neuve-Saint-Gilles.

*   *   *

Monsieur Boehmer did not play basset, nor faro, and as soon as she had had a word with those of her guests who merited her attention, Jeanne invited him to her private room.

"I heard, Monsieur Boehmer," she said, "that you wished to see me very particularly."

"It . . . it is indeed kind of you to receive me." The jeweller was so anxious and excited that he stammered. "I believe *you*, Madame, and you alone, can help me. I am in a very difficult position."

Jeanne inclined her head.

"It may be, Madame, that you have heard of the diamond necklace?"

"Why yes, I believe I have."

"There is no other necklace like it in the world. It was made for Madame du Barry. She was delighted with the work. But as you know, with the death of Louis Quinze . . ." The jeweller spread his hands.

"That must have been rather awkward for you, Monsieur Boehmer. But there are others who like diamonds besides Madame du Barry."

"I had thought of Her Majesty. In fact my partner and I had no doubt of Her Majesty. We completed the necklace and . . . you can imagine our chagrin and . . . our anxiety . . . when she declined to buy it."

"I do not see how I can help you in this, Monsieur. I could not afford to buy your necklace."

"But, Madame, you have great influence with the Queen."

"Her Majesty is most gracious to me, it is true."

"It has occurred to my partner and myself that a little friendly persuasion. . . ."

"I see that you wish me to use my influence with the Queen."

"I assure you, Madame, that we are ready to pay a very high commission to anyone who can bring about the sale of the necklace."

"I understand," said Jeanne.

"We would keep this matter of the commission secret . . . if Madame had the slightest desire that we should do so. You could rely, Madame, on the utmost discretion. . . ."

"I am sure of that."

"Then, Madame . . . ?"

"I like to help people. I am wondering if it is possible . . . I have never seen the necklace. It would be difficult for me to talk of it without having seen it and. . . ."

"Madame, allow me to show it to you. I will bring it to you in person . . . tomorrow morning. You understand, after dark one would not care to walk about, carrying such an object. If any heard that I carried it, God alone knows what schemes might be put in motion to take it from me."

"Show it to me," said Jeanne. "Yes, bring it to me in the morning and show it to me. If I saw it and admired it, I should find it easier to mention it to Her Majesty."

"I will do so."

"I understand what anxieties must have been yours, Monsieur Boehmer. You have my sympathy. I promise you that no one but my husband and my secretary shall know that you are bringing the necklace here."

"Madame, you are kind beyond belief. If it gives you any satisfaction, know this: my partner and I will sleep a little easier this night."

"Oh, please do not have too high hopes. I can only try; I cannot be sure of success."

"Madame, men in the position of myself and my partner cling fast to hope."

*   *   *

Jeanne was thoughtful. The commission would be useful, but how could she possibly obtain it?

Rétaux and de la Motte were full of mad schemes, but she must restrain them. There must be no highway robbery. That might be traced to them. She shuddered to think of the consequences of such folly.

They had come along the road to fortune audaciously but shrewdly, she believed. But she could see no way of getting that commission on the diamond necklace.

Early in the morning a visitor called at the house.

It was Cagliostro, sombrely dressed, and incognito.

"I heard of your grand establishment," he said, "and I could not come near to Paris without calling on you to congratulate you."

"That is good of you, Comte."

"And it is wonderful to know that the Cardinal is in such good spirits."

"You have called on the Cardinal?"

"No. I am paying but a fleeting visit. I know that he is a very happy man though, a very hopeful man. I know of course that he had a very pleasant adventure in the Bosquet de Vénus."

"He told you of this?"

Cagliostro smiled. "Suffice it that I know. Also that he has been called upon to offer a loan of sixty thousand livres which he has been delighted to do." Cagliostro's smile was sardonic. "The Cardinal is happy; you are prosperous. Nothing could more delight one who is so interested in the welfare of you both."

Jeanne fidgeted uneasily.

Why was it that Cagliostro had placed himself in the background of her life? she was asking herself. Why did he always seem to appear like some good—or bad—fairy at crucial moments?

"You had an interesting visitor last night," he said.

"I have had many interesting visitors, Comte."

"I was thinking of the jeweller, Boehmer, Comtesse."

"You find him interesting?"

"Not so much the man as his predicament. He has made the most fabulous piece of jewellery in the world. I've no doubt it is the masterpiece he claims it to be. Imagine! The expense, the time . . . everything that goes into such a work, and then to find no one wants to buy it. The poor man and his partner are well nigh distracted. Madame du Barry we can be sure is enjoying the joke." He put the tips of his fingers together and stared at them. "Speaking of jewellery," he went on, "I am reminded of a certain Madame Cahouet de Villers. Did you ever hear of the creature?"

"No. I do not recall the name."

"A foolish woman. She was imprisoned at Sainte-Pélagie. She had a short spell there."

"For what offence?"

"She forged the Queen's signature." He laughed. He was watching Jeanne closely. "Silly woman. Her forgery need never have been discovered."

"Why did she forge the Queen's signature? For what purpose?"

"She stated that the Queen had commanded her to buy jewels. You can imagine the tale. The Queen wanted certain jewels but did not wish it to be known that she was buying them. As you know, Marie Antoinette is a sensitive lady. She is disturbed by these stories of her extravagance. You can see how easy it was for the jewellers to accept this story. The stupid woman betrayed herself by being careless. It is interesting to speculate that but for her stupidity she could have made a pleasant little fortune for herself."

Jeanne felt the excitement grip her. She forgot that she had been warning herself against this strange man.

"Another Madame Goupil, it would seem," she said, trying to speak lightly.

"Oh, *she* was more clever. *She* first became the mistress of our friend the Cardinal. She knew that by involving him in her fraud she was to some extent playing for safety. The Cardinal is a proud man. If he were involved in any unsavoury matter he would certainly do all in his power to hush it up. Madame Goupil knew this. That was why there was no Sainte-Pélagie in her case."

"Let me fill your glass, Comte."

"Thank you."

He surveyed her over it, his dark eyes holding hers for what she felt must have been a long time.

"To your continued success," he said. "I see before you, Madame, a career which will make you famous in the history of France."

"Are you speaking as a courtier or as a prophet, Comte?"

He laughed lightly and drained his glass.

"Madame," he said, "as I told you on our first meeting, flattery is for fools. You are no fool."

*   *   *

In a small room in the house on the Rue Neuve-Saint-Gilles, Monsieur Boehmer opened the case and placed it on the table.

Four pairs of eyes gazed at the most dazzling piece of jewellery they had ever seen.

Jeanne caught her breath; lights of cupidity shone in the eyes of de la Motte and Rétaux de Villette;

there was only pride and infinite hope in those of the jeweller.

"Magnificent!" breathed Rétaux.

"Unique!" cried de la Motte.

"Oh, yes," said Monsieur Boehmer, "it is a masterpiece. But I very much fear that it may lead me to bankruptcy."

"We must do all in our power to prevent that happening," said Jeanne.

"Madame, how kind you are!"

"I can promise nothing," said Jeanne quickly; "you understand that, Monsieur. I can only say that I have seen the most perfect and beautiful necklace in the world, and I know of only one person fit to possess it."

"If only you would!"

"I will, depend on it.'

"Madame, the commission . . ."

"Oh, do not let us talk of such a sordid subject in the presence of such a work of art, Monsieur."

Rétaux was looking at her with shining eyes. "Madame can be very persuasive," he murmured.

"You know," said de la Motte, "how Her Majesty listens to all you say to her."

"Monsieur," cried Jeanne, growing alarmed by those looks of wild cupidity which she saw in her men's faces, "they are raising your hopes too high. Shut the case. Take your necklace away. I promise you this: I will do all in my power. But it is an important matter and I cannot promise you certain success."

"You will do your best, Madame. That is all I hoped for. I am sure the Queen loves you for your kindness, and that a persuasive word from you will mean a great deal."

With that he closed the case and rose to leave. They accompanied him to his carriage, and then returned to the house.

Rétaux was murmuring: "To think that in that carriage rides one million six hundred thousand livres!"

"If we had the necklace, our fortunes would be made," mused de la Motte. "No more lies, no more subterfuge. We could disappear from Paris . . . from France, and live in peace and plenty for the rest of our natural lives."

They noticed that Jeanne was not speaking, and they looked at each other speculatively. They were remembering that all their schemes had been first suggested by Jeanne. She was their leader. They must not forget that, merely because she was the wife of one and the mistress of the other.

At last she spoke. "I want to think. You understand this matter needs much careful thought. It will be the most difficult, the most complicated we ever undertook."

"Of what are you thinking?" demanded Rétaux.

"I hardly know yet. It is something which has been put in my mind by the Comte de Cagliostro. A stray remark of his. I cannot see it clearly yet. I must think . . . I must see it from all angles. Until I do, I will say nothing."

"Come, tell us," they pleaded. "We could doubtless help."

But she would say nothing; and all that day and night she was haunted by the diamond necklace. When she thought of it she did not see the glittering stones. She saw one million six hundred thousand livres—a fortune.

*   *   *

Cardinal de Rohan was in Strasbourg. As Archbishop of Strasbourg he could not stay indefinitely in Paris, however anxious he was to remain there. Life had become almost unbearably frustrating, and at the same time more exciting than it had ever been.

There was so much that he desired, and so much of it seemed within his grasp. She had actually met him

M

clandestinely in the Bosquet de Vénus. Surely she could not
have said more clearly that she was willing that he should
become her lover?

A Queen of France to meet her lover in the park at
midnight! What a situation! And how tender she must
feel towards him, thus to risk her reputation. Had the
enchanting creature given a thought to what might have
happened had they been discovered together?

Clearly she had, for she had made such excellent arrangements through good Madame de la Motte-Valois; and it
was all the more delightful to know this, for did it not show
how much she was ready to risk for his sake?

Yet progress since then had been disappointingly slow.
He had her delightful notes of course, but almost always
they contained excuses, pleas for his patience. Only a little
longer and all would be well. That was the theme of all
those notes.

But how long before she would receive him at court?
And what harm could it do for her to show him a little
favour? Was she afraid of showing her affection for him?
Well, what was a little more scandal? There had already
been scandals with the Swede, Fersen, her own brother-in-
law the Comte d'Artois, the Comte de Vaudreuil and the
Duc de Lauzun. What if Paris began to whisper that the
new friendship between the Queen and the Cardinal de
Rohan was of a tender nature? She should not allow another
rumour to disturb her.

But she would not receive him, and when they met in
public she seemed scarcely aware of his existence.

And here he was, fretting for her and for power, longing
to step into an office of state, to slip on the giant's robes
discarded by Richelieu and Mazarin.

In time of course all France, the whole world, would
mention the name of de Rohan with those other states-
men-cardinals. But why not now?

He wished that Cagliostro were with him. Being in Strasbourg he remembered their first meeting in the street, and those long illuminating conversations which had followed. It was at times like this that he needed Cagliostro. He wanted the magician's advice and help.

Letters! Of what use were letters? Letters from the Queen, letters from Cagliostro. He wanted them both close to him—the Queen in his arms that he might be her lover in more than imagination, Cagliostro at his elbow that he might be his guide and counsellor.

One of his pages was at the door.

"Monseigneur, a messenger from Paris. He brings a letter."

"Then let me have it."

"Monseigneur, he says he has express orders to put it into no other hands than those of Your Eminence."

"Then bring him to me at once."

He took the letter. He knew the writing, and he was consumed with eagerness. He shut himself in his very private chamber and broke the seal.

He smelt the perfumed paper; he exulted at the well-remembered hand as he read:

"The time we desire has not yet arrived, but I am asking you to cut short your stay in Strasbourg and come back to Paris. I wish you to undertake some secret negotiations of personal interest to me and which I would not confide to any but you. Madame de la Motte-Valois will explain, if you will return at once and present yourself to her."

Secret negotiations! Was it a matter of politics? Was this how matters were conducted between Anne of Austria and Mazarin?

He called for his servants who came hurrying to learn his bidding.

"Have my carriage made ready," he said. "I leave at once for Paris."

*   *   *

Jeanne was waiting for him. She knew exactly how long
he would take to reach her, for she calculated that he
would leave Strasbourg with all speed and, as soon as he
arrived in Paris, present himself at the Rue Neuve-Saint-
Gilles.

She was right.

"Monseigneur," she cried in great relief as he bent
over her hand.

"Madame la Comtesse, I have received a letter."

"I know all about it. I have my instructions. I pray you,
come at once to my private chamber."

When they were there she said: "This concerns a
certain diamond necklace. It is the property of Messieurs
Boehmer and Bassenge. It is the finest in the world."

"You are talking of *the* diamond necklace?"

"You know of its existence then?"

"My dear Comtesse, who has not heard of the diamond
necklace and the trouble its makers have taken in order to
rid themselves of it?"

"They will do so now. The Queen wishes to buy it."

"It will look enchanting on her neck."

"She is determined to have it. You are aware though
that of late she has been somewhat short of money."

"The King offered to buy it for her once."

"That was long ago, at the time of the Dauphin's birth.
Things have changed. There are economies at court.
The Queen wants to buy the necklace without the know-
ledge of the King."

De Rohan looked startled.

"The King is so ... " Jeanne lifted her shoulders. "As
you know, he has no eye for beauty. All he cares for is
his locks. He has wasted time and money on them, God
knows! He grudges the Queen her diamond necklace.
But she is determined to have it; and that is where you
come in."

"I?"

"You look startled, Cardinal. I pray you do not. The Queen merely asks you to arrange the negotiations for her. She does not know how to arrange these matters with the jewellers and, as a mark of trust, she asks you to do it for her. I told Her Majesty that you would be delighted. Was I wrong?"

"Why . . . no. If it is Her Majesty's command, most eagerly will I do this."

"She will be delighted when I tell her. She said: 'It is something I would ask of no one else. But knowing the Cardinal's devotion, I do not hesitate'."

De Rohan exulted in those words, but he could not rid himself of a certain anxiety. One million six hundred thousand livres, which he knew to be the price of the necklace, was a great deal of money even by his reckoning. He could not quickly raise such a sum. He was relieved therefore to know that she did not intend him to supply the money, merely to arrange the transaction. Those little sums of money which he had already advanced had not been repaid. He could not of course suggest payment, and he was prepared to forget, as he suspected she was. Greater sums than those were paid for positions at court.

"Tell me what the Queen has said to you on this matter of the necklace."

"That the matter is to be a secret between you. She wants you to arrange for four payments on the necklace to extend over two years. The first of these payments she will meet on August the first of this year, 1785."

"It is a most strange transaction," said the Cardinal. "I have never before heard the like."

"There has never before been such a diamond necklace," said Jeanne; and she added softly: "nor such a cardinal, nor such a queen."

"Do you think that the Queen would grant me an

audience so that I might discuss this matter with her in detail?"

Jeanne's heart was leaping about in a manner which she sought vainly to control.

"I am certain that as yet she is unready to meet you."

The Cardinal looked at her sharply. "What makes you so certain of this?"

"She has told me clearly that she dare not speak to you in public, and that it is too dangerous for you to meet in secret; that in the Bosquet de Vénus she believes she may have been seen. You know that, when you were speaking with her, Madame and Madame d'Artois were only a short distance from you. Thank God I was at hand to warn you in time."

"But, there have been no rumours of the Queen's meeting with a stranger in the Bosquet?"

"That does not mean that there have not been suspicions."

"Yet, often a mere suspicion will give rise to a rumour."

"Let us be thankful that the secret of that meeting appears to have been kept. May I go to the Queen and tell her that you will do her this service?"

"The Queen already knows that I will serve her with my life and my honour."

"I told her she could count on this."

"And what did she say to that?"

"She kissed me, and she wept a little. She said: 'I know that the Cardinal is one of the few people in this country whom I can trust. May God preserve him and bring near that day when I may speak openly with him and not through secret notes and your kind offices, dear cousin'."

"She said that. . . ." murmured the Cardinal.

"The time cannot be long now. But, Monseigneur, I beg of you be patient a little longer. I shall see the Queen tomorrow, and I shall tell her that all is well."

*　　　*　　　*

Messieurs Boehmer and Bassenge presented themselves at the house in Rue Neuve-Saint-Gilles.

They were speaking in jerks. They were too nervous for coherence.

"Did you think it possible. . . ."

"Why else should she have sent. . . ."

"If it is as I pray it may be, this will be the end of all our troubles."

"In future we will not undertake such enterprises. . . ."

"Once let us get free of this, once let us settle our commitments. . . ."

"Madame de la Motte is ready to receive you, Messieurs."

She held out her hands to them and as soon as the door was closed she smiled.

"You can see," she said, "that I have good news."

"Madame!"

Boehmer was on his knees kissing the hem of her gown, for all the world, she thought grimly, as though I were Marie Antoinette—or some little drab representing myself as such—and this plump jeweller a foolish cardinal! Bassenge kissed her hand with tears in his eyes.

"Perhaps," said Jeanne, looking from one to the other, "it is too early to rejoice. There will have to be special terms of payment."

They smiled. "Of course. Of course. That makes no obstacles, Madame. Once our creditors know that we have sold the necklace and that the Queen has bought it, they will be ready to await the Queen's pleasure as far as payment is concerned."

"Ah, that is another matter. The Queen wishes that the

fact that she has bought the necklace shall remain a secret. She wishes you to let the news leak out that you have sold it to the Sultan of Constantinople."

"But if the Queen buys the necklace, does she not want to wear it? And when she wears that necklace, Madame, no one will be unaware of it. There is not such another in the world."

"The Queen longs to possess the necklace. She longs to wear it, yes. But at the moment there are difficulties. You understand? The King wishes to curb her extravagances. She does not wish him to know . . . only for a few months . . . that she has bought the necklace. When the first payment is made, then doubtless she will wear it. You should not concern yourself with such matters. I thought your one concern was to sell it."

"It is, Madame, it is," said Boehmer hastily; "and I cannot tell you how grateful we are for your services in this matter."

Jeanne bowed her head a little haughtily.

"Well then, she has appointed a certain gentleman of very high rank to deal with you. Only he, you and myself are in this secret. You must make sure that it is kept. If it leaked out that the Queen was buying the diamond necklace, I have no doubt whatever that the whole transaction would fall through."

The jewellers were trembling at the thought.

"Therefore," said Jeanne, "I would most strongly advise you to keep this matter secret and do all that the Queen asks. The sooner the rumour that the necklace has been sold to the Sultan of Constantinople reaches her ears, the better pleased she will be. Now I have the pleasure of telling you that the nobleman whom she has appointed to see this matter through will very shortly be calling upon you to see the necklace and arrange the terms."

*   *   *

The jewellers were eager to see the man whom the Queen had appointed to deal with this very secret transaction.

The whole matter was being conducted in a manner which did seem a little strange. Usually they would take their articles of jewellery to the Palace of Versailles, wait for an audience, carry them to the Queen, and she would try them on surrounded by her friends who would comment and advise.

However, as Madame de la Motte-Valois had hinted, they would be wise in this case to ask no questions. All that concerned them was that they sell the necklace and extricate themselves from their financial predicament. When the Cardinal de Rohan called on them, they could not believe that *he* had come in connection with the necklace, and he smiled with amusement as he convinced them of this.

He knew what they were thinking. The Cardinal de Rohan! But the Queen is no friend to him! She even dislikes him! The affair was getting stranger and stranger.

"There are many things happening in France of which you, my sons, are ignorant," the Cardinal told them benignly.

He was impressed by the grandeur of the necklace, and it gave him great pleasure to explain that he had the Queen's confidence in this matter and had been instructed by her to discuss the terms of payment for the necklace.

"There shall be four instalments of four hundred thousand livres each, and the first will be paid to you by Her Majesty on August 1st of this year 1785. Are you agreeable to these terms?"

"We accept them most gratefully," said Boehmer.

"There will of course," put in the cautious Bassenge, "be a contract . . . a written contract."

"Of course," said the Cardinal, "if you wish it, I feel sure Her Majesty will see reason in that."

"Then, my lord Cardinal, let the contract be drawn up, and as soon as it is in our possession we shall be delighted to hand the necklace to you."

"It shall be done," said the Cardinal.

*　　　　*　　　　*

As the Cardinal went thoughtfully back to his Paris mansion, the Hôtel de Strasbourg, he found that it was impossible to continue in his mood of exultation. He had a strange feeling that he had been living in a crazy dream and that, although he had not yet awakened, he was suddenly aware that he had been dreaming.

It was a strange feeling, and it gave him twinges of alarm although he was not quite sure why he should be alarmed.

There were times—was it in his sleep?—when everything that was happening to him seemed extraordinary—more than extraordinary—unreal. Did it begin when the Comte de Cagliostro came into his life, when he had made diamonds and gold in the attic at Saverne? Now he was asked to accept equally strange happenings. The meeting in the Bosquet de Vénus . . . it too was like a dream. The Queen had stood there and spoken so softly that he could not be quite sure what she said. And this was the haughty arrogant Austrian woman who, when in the course of his duties he found himself in her presence, treated him as though he were beneath her notice.

It was small wonder that he felt alarmed.

He sent for Jeanne and when she came to him, inwardly apprehensive, outwardly calm, he said to her: "I have prepared the contract, but I have been thinking a great deal about this matter and there are certain facets which seem to me quite extraordinary. I am sure Her Majesty will understand my trepidation when I explain that I feel that, since she is buying the necklace, her signature should be on the contract."

Jeanne was relieved. It was only a signature he wanted. Very well, let Rétaux earn his portion of the prize.

"Why, my lord," cried Jeanne, "I am sure Her Majesty will understand fully. Give me the contract and I will take it to her with all speed. I am sure she will sign it, as you wish it to be signed. She will immediately see your point of view."

Jeanne hurried away with the contract, but when she had gone, the Cardinal's uneasiness persisted.

He sent for one of his servants, and said to him: "Prepare at once to leave for Lyons. I want you to take a message to the Comte de Cagliostro."

*   *   *

As soon as Cagliostro received the Cardinal's message, he set out for Paris. This time he came undisguised and went straight to a splendid suite of rooms in the Palais Royal. He then presented himself to the Cardinal.

"My good friend," cried de Rohan, "I knew I could rely on you."

"I recognized your *cri de coeur*," Cagliostro told him.

"I am a little uneasy."

"Concerning your affair with the Queen and the good Madame de la Motte-Valois?"

"Everything is so strange. In August we had our meeting in the Bosquet de Vénus; it was very brief, but during it I was given to understand that the Queen was ready to risk a good deal to see me. It is now January. Five months have passed. Yet when I meet her during the course of my duties she is as cold towards me as she ever was; and I am becoming worried."

Cagliostro began to pace up and down the apartment.

"A love affair with a little modiste . . . a little lady of the

Palais Royal, or the charming wife of a friend ... these are conducted with speed which is understandable. There is the hope of pleasure, the realization of pleasure and the decline of pleasure. But a love affair with a queen, Cardinal ... that could be high politics."

"I remind myself of this. But five months, and not a word spoken to me!"

"You have her letters."

"Letters are well enough, but what harm could there be in a smile, a look of promise?"

"She is closely watched. Every move she makes is observed."

"Yet she is renowned for her indiscretions. Why should she suddenly become so discreet?"

"Could it not be that she now sees before her something which halts her love of frivolity? Might it not be that her very ability to be discreet proclaims the strength of her feeling for you?"

"Master, this is so?"

"It would appear that it may well be."

"I knew you would bring me comfort. Yet ... my uneasiness persists. I can say this, Comte: I have never before been involved in such a strange affair."

"May I repeat that you have never before been involved with a queen?"

"I feel great events moving towards me. I want you to look into the future for me. I want you to reassure me, to tell me that all is well and that I am travelling along the right road. Will you do this?"

Cagliostro laid his hands on the Cardinal's shoulders. "It is for this reason that I have come to Paris," he said.

*   *   *

In the Cardinal's small and most intimate chamber he and Cagliostro were alone.

The heavy curtains were drawn and the sounds of Paris shut out; many candles shone from all parts of the room.

At Cagliostro's bidding the Cardinal reclined on a couch. Cagliostro himself, in the impressive costume of Grand Cophte of Egypt, stood in the centre of the room, his arms upraised, as he muttered incantations.

The Cardinal was only half aware of Cagliostro. He seemed to be sailing through time as effortlessly as he would pass along the road from Paris to Versailles in his elegant carriage. He saw what appeared to be the great Cardinal Richelieu in conference with Louis XIII; but it was another man whom he saw—himself, Cardinal de Rohan. It was he who declaimed against the Protestants, declaring that they should never become a political power in France; it was he who was determined to bring about the humiliation of the House of Austria. On and on he went, passing lightly through time. He saw the young Mazarin, protégé of Richelieu; he saw Richelieu recommend his successor to Louis XIII; he saw the death of Richelieu, yet he, de Rohan, lived on in Mazarin. He saw the crushing of the Fronde; he sensed the immense favour bestowed on this man by the Queen, mother of the young King Louis Quatorze, and it seemed that it was not at Mazarin and Anne of Austria that he looked, but at himself and Marie Antoinette.

During that long night there would be times when he appeared to wake from his dream, and then he would find the dark eyes of Cagliostro fixed upon him as, standing there, his arms outstretched, a strange figure in the Egyptian costume, he continued to murmur words which were beyond the Cardinal's understanding.

In the early morning de Rohan came out of his dream. Most of the candles had guttered out. Cagliostro had thrown off the Egyptian gown and was in his familiar scarlet embroidered waistcoat.

"Our labours are over," said the Cophte of Egypt with a smile.

"And your verdict?"

"This I have learned during my night's vigil," said Cagliostro. "Those negotiations in which you are now concerned are worthy of you, my Prince. The Queen of France needs your help. I have been in communication with forces which inform me that in days to come your name will be linked with that of the Queen. You have been chosen, my lord Cardinal, to walk beside the Queen of France along a certain road, and in these negotiations you are helping to bring about a happy state for this great country."

The Cardinal rose from the couch and embraced Cagliostro.

"I knew I could rely on your help," he said. "I shall now go on with a good heart in this matter to which I am committed. I shall no longer question the strangeness of all that is happening. You have consulted greater powers than are known to any other man alive; and, my dear friend and counsellor, you have soothed my fears."

"Fate has brought us together," said Cagliostro.

The Cardinal sank to his knees and, taking Cagliostro's hand, raised it to his lips.

Poor fool! thought Cagliostro. And this is a Prince of France! I have not lied to him; but this frail man reads into my words what he wishes to read; and so he discovers not the advice I give but the advice he wants to find.

But in this he does not blaze a trail but follows a well-worn road.

*　　　　*　　　　*

In Jeanne's apartments at Versailles they were waiting, she, de la Motte and Rétaux.

The suspense was almost unbearable.

Jeanne was pacing up and down the room. "Until it is actually in our hands I shall not rest," she said.

De la Motte laid a hand on her shoulder.

"Do not excite yourself so, Jeanne. All goes well."

"I tell you, until he is here. . . ."

"At any moment now he will be with us."

Jeanne went to the window and looked down on the street below. These lodgings were in the very shadow of the palace, and sometimes even Jeanne believed that the whole plot was too fantastic to be real.

Everything had gone easily so far. Could it continue? Had they had luck? Or was it due to that common sense on which Jeanne prided herself?

Sometimes it seemed so easy that there came to her the feeling that some mighty hand was guiding them in the way they were to go.

First there had been the alarm about the contract, when she had thought the Cardinal was going to refuse to go further; and she had been in trepidation lest he should write to the Queen—telling her that he needed more authority before continuing with the negotiations—and the letter should reach her.

But no. That trouble had blown over. Rétaux had merely taken his pen and written at the bottom of the contract: "Approved, Marie Antoinette de France." And when the Cardinal had looked at it, kissed the signature and declared that he was ready to go ahead, he had taken it to the jewellers.

Rétaux had his uses.

Now he was dressed in the uniform of one of the King's lackeys and when the Cardinal arrived he would be in another room to reappear a few minutes later as though he had come from the Palace of Versailles. The note purporting to come from the Queen was ready and waiting in his hand, that note which commanded that the necklace be handed to the bearer, who would convey it at once to the Queen.

There could be no hitch now. But what if the jewellers had decided to consult the Queen? No! They would not do that; they had been so solemnly assured that the negotiation was a secret one and only to be conducted through the Cardinal and Jeanne de la Motte-Valois. Everything *must* be all right. It could not conceivably go wrong.

"He is here," cried de la Motte. Rétaux hurried from the room; Jeanne stood in readiness; and within a few seconds the Cardinal was announced.

To Jeanne's great relief she saw that he carried the necklace case.

"You have it?" said Jeanne in a whisper.

"I have only this day collected it from the jewellers. I came here with all speed in accordance with Her Majesty's instructions."

Jeanne took the case. Her fingers were trembling but, if anyone noticed, they would not have been surprised. She held that which was tantamount to one million six hundred thousand livres in her hands.

There it lay, the unique necklace, the most dazzling piece of jewellery in Europe.

In my hands, thought Jeanne. In my hands at last!

There was a sound from without. Jeanne hastily shut the case as she bade a servant enter.

"Yes, Rosalie?"

"Madame," said the woman in the doorway, and her voice held an awe-stricken note: "There is a messenger here who comes from the Queen."

"Then bring him to me at once," said Jeanne.

Rétaux came into the room; he bowed to Jeanne, to the Cardinal and to de la Motte.

"I have a note here from Her Majesty the Queen."

He handed it to Jeanne, who said to him: "Will you please wait outside the door?"

Rétaux bowed and retired.

Jeanne then said: "The Queen is asking that this man be given the necklace and told to take it immediately to her personally."

De Rohan read the note. It was in the same handwriting as those little notes he had been receiving for so many months, and it was signed "Marie Antoinette de France".

Jeanne put a wrapping about the case, sealed it and then said to de la Motte: "Call in the messenger."

Rétaux came in.

"I pray you, take this package with all speed to Her Majesty," said Jeanne. "Give it to no other. She is waiting for it."

"Thank you, Madame."

The Cardinal, Jeanne and de la Motte all watched him as he went out.

"I recognized him," said the Cardinal; and Jeanne was frozen with momentary terror.

"He is the man who was in the Bosquet de Vénus," resumed the Cardinal. "I should know his face anywhere."

"It is Her Majesty's very personal footman, a man she uses when she needs someone whom she can thoroughly trust." She turned to the Cardinal. "Ah, Monseigneur, you will soon reap your reward. Once the necklace is in the Queen's hands she will hesitate no longer. She has implied this. Moreover, my lord, who could look at such a masterpiece and not think, every time she did so, of the one who had made it possible for her to possess it!"

"My hopes are high," said the Cardinal.

"With good reason," agreed Jeanne.

She was glad when the Cardinal took his leave. She wanted to join Rétaux who, in accordance with their

N

careful plan, had not left the lodgings but had hidden himself in one of the smaller rooms of the apartment.

Jeanne could scarcely wait to open that case again and lay her hands on those glittering stones.

*   *   *

Jeanne and de la Motte hurried to the small room where Rétaux was waiting for them.

Silently they looked at each other. In those first moments they were too excited for speech. So Jeanne drew the curtains and lighted two candles.

On a small table lay the case. They opened it. In this small, dark room the diamonds seemed more dazzling than ever.

For some seconds they continued to stare at it—the diamond necklace which represented to them wealth, prosperity, freedom from want, escape to affluence.

Jeanne, the natural leader, the instigator of the plot laid her hands reverently on the gems. Then she laughed suddenly.

"Let us waste no time. There must no more be a diamond necklace . . . only diamonds. This work of breaking up the necklace will take us some little time, so let us go to it with all speed. Having done that, we shall have the task of disposing of the diamonds." She laughed again; it was laughter of triumph not unmixed with hysteria. Then she was suddenly calm. "We have done it," she cried. "My companions, we have the necklace. The rest is child's play. Now to . . . fortune."

Rétaux laid his tools before him, and they all sat down at the table.

VI

THE QUEEN
(*Cards on the Table*)

THEY WERE NOW RICH. THE DISPOSAL OF A VERY FEW OF those superb diamonds had made them that, and a great fortune still lay in their hands.

Those which they had offered for sale had been snatched up with eagerness by certain Paris jewellers who realized that they were being offered at about half their worth.

Jeanne bought a mansion in Bar-sur-Aube, and twenty-four carts carried out of Paris the treasures she had amassed in a few weeks. For a little while she, de la Motte and Rétaux gave themselves up to a life of luxury in the country. They could not resist flaunting their wealth. They had so longed for it, they could not restrain themselves from enjoying it now that it had come.

Jeanne's most cherished possession was her carriage—the symbol of her affluence. She rode about the country, and people stood by the roadside to curtsy and bow as she passed; the four English mares who drew it were admired by all who saw them, and those country folk were agog at the magnificent liveries of her lackeys. Those in the neighbourhood sought positions in her mansion, and there was much gossip of the splendour they saw there. The little town of Bar-sur-Aube had never witnessed magnificence like this; but most glorious of all was the berline, light grey outside, upholstered in white satin, and embossed with the arms of the House of Valois, beneath which were engraved the words: "From the King, my ancestor, I derive my blood, my name and the lilies."

They were blatantly and ostentatiously content in their affluence. At all times of the day and night Jeanne appeared in the most magnificent gowns; de la Motte could indulge his passion for gambling, and during those weeks in the new house at Bar-sur-Aube they lived as extravagantly as the Queen. They had engaged a retinue of servants; they gave banquets at which the most elaborate foods were served. Rétaux had ceased to be regarded as a secretary and was living as an equal in this *ménage à trois*.

It was Jeanne who called a halt. They had enjoyed many weeks on the sale of a few stones, but they had the rest of them to dispose of.

In the country mansion she called a conference, and once more the three conspirators sat round a table in a very private room to discuss the future.

The necklace had been procured in February; the first payment was due in August.

"Six months," said Jeanne, "in which to do our business."

"And afterwards?" asked de la Motte.

"We will decide then how we are to act. All we need concern ourselves with at the moment is translating diamonds into money and keeping our foolish Cardinal contented."

"I'd rather attempt the first than the latter," put in Rétaux with a grimace.

"Then that is well," answered Jeanne tartly, "for it is all you will be called upon to do."

De la Motte said anxiously: "But, Jeanne, I'm thinking of what is going to happen when the first payment is due."

"In the progress of our affairs," said Jeanne, "we have succeeded by dealing with each difficulty as it presents itself, and not by long planning ahead. The circumstances change, and how can we decide to do such and such a thing when we do not know what may have happened by a certain time?"

"You have been right so far," admitted her husband.

"Then leave the planning to me. Rétaux, we should now turn more of the stones into money. Take a few, but not too many, to Paris. Sell them to the Jews there, and when you have disposed of say half a dozen, take another half-dozen to Amsterdam and see what you can get for them there."

Rétaux nodded. The stones were selected, and he set out for Paris next day.

*   *   *

Rétaux handed the stone to the jeweller, who studied it intently.

"It is a fine stone, is it not?" asked Rétaux.

"I do not deny it."

"It is yours for twenty thousand livres."

The jeweller continued to study the stone.

"Oh come," said Rétaux, "I am a man in a hurry. I'll take eighteen thousand for it."

"Very well, I'll take it," said the jeweller.

Rétaux left with the money in his pockets. He was doing well, and by the end of the week he proposed to leave for Holland.

When he had left the shop the jeweller showed the diamond to his partner.

"A fine stone, eh? What would you think I paid for it? Mind you, I've made a bargain."

"Eighty thousand livres?"

"Eighteen thousand."

"Impossible!"

"I could scarcely believe my ears when the fellow suggested that figure."

"There is only one thing for honest men to do. It's clearly stolen property. Pass me my hat. I will go at once to the police."

*   *   *

Madame la Comtesse was preparing to receive her guests—her flunkeys in silver lace and scarlet brocade at their posts; in her kitchens the cooks were busy; and in an hour the finest carriages of the country-side would be at her door—when a visitor arrived from Paris. His business was official, he declared, and he asked that he might be taken immediately to the presence of the Comtesse.

Jeanne looked at the man coldly. "I am very busy," she said. "Tell me your business as quickly as you can."

"I am an agent of the police, Madame."

Jeanne's fingers tightened on her fan, but she did not allow herself to betray the terrible fear which beset her.

"But . . . I do not understand; what do you want of me?"

"I am afraid there has been a robbery . . . a very big robbery . . . and some valuable diamonds have been stolen."

Jeanne felt dizzy with horror but she managed to say haughtily: "And what concern of mine can this possibly be?"

"Madame, we have arrested a man, and he has mentioned your name."

"I . . . I am quite bewildered."

"He has said that he is disposing of the jewels on your behalf."

Rétaux! It could be no one else, and he had been arrested!

Jeanne thought quickly. Then she said: "Is there any crime in disposing of one's jewels?"

"But no, Madame."

"Then why should you arrest a servant of mine because he disposes of jewels for me?"

The agent was embarrassed. "We did not believe his story, Madame. That is why I have been sent to you here to confirm it."

"Why did you not believe his story?"

"Because, Madame, he has disposed of jewels of great magnificence for a fraction of their value, and it is this—forgive me, Madame—which has aroused the suspicions of an honest jeweller, for most people who wish to sell their jewels ask a price commensurate with their value."

Jeanne said: "Monsieur, I understand. You must release this man at once. His story is true. He is disposing of the jewels on my behalf." She looked ruefully about the room. "The upkeep of a place like this . . . it is ruinous . . . ruinous. . . . Families such as mine are not in the same position as they once were, you understand, and it is necessary sometimes to sell old treasures. I had no idea that the jewels which I wished to sell were so valuable. They were given to my great great-grandmother by King Henri Deux. They have been in the family for years, but in these expensive times. . . ."

"You must accept our abject apologies for what has happened, Madame de la Motte-Valois."

"Do not mention that. You were but doing your duty. I think my husband and I should return to Paris. My servant will be terrified. Poor man, to be treated thus for doing a service for his mistress! But you, Monsieur, must not be upset. You must stay here for the night. The journey back to Paris is too arduous to undertake immediately. We shall entertain you here and my husband and I will return to Paris with you. My servant must not remain in captivity a day longer than is necessary."

"Madame, you are indeed kind."

Jeanne lifted her hand. "I should not be so foolish as to blame you for doing what is your duty."

The *agent de police* was entertained lavishly. Jeanne insisted on bestowing a gift on him—a few livres would make a difference to the man. Not a bribe. Oh no, certainly not. There was no need of a bribe. But a gift, royally given by a descendant of kings.

Madame de la Motte-Valois was indeed a royal lady. One recognized them at once, the agent was thinking.

But to the quiet of her own room Jeanne summoned her husband.

"We must take this as a warning," she said. "It is no longer safe to dispose of the jewels in Paris. As soon as Rétaux is free he must take a portion of those which remain to Holland, and you must be prepared to travel to London immediately with the rest."

She scarcely slept at all that night. When she dozed she would awake in sudden terror. The arrival of the *agent de police* had temporarily terrified her. But, when she contemplated how shrewdly she had dealt with him, she exulted in her cleverness which she felt sure amounted to genius.

It seemed to her that she could not make a false step. Whatever difficulties arose she would overcome them.

De la Motte and Rétaux de Villette might ask themselves what was going to happen when August came. She was not perturbed. She relied on her shrewdness and her intuition to show her what she must do when the time came.

*   *   *

Spring was passing. Rétaux was in Holland, and de la Motte was preparing to set out for London; the necklace was now completely broken up; and Jeanne awoke every morning to a sense of deep satisfaction.

There was one who was far from satisfied.

The Cardinal de Rohan asked Jeanne to call on him at his Paris residence.

"It seems incredible," he said, "that .his can go on. I have seen the Queen many times since the necklace was taken to her. She was not once wearing it."

"She dare not wear it," said Jeanne. "The necklace

could not possibly be unnoticed, and the King is still against her buying more jewels. Sometimes she puts it on in private. She delights in it. She murmured once: 'And to think that but for my dear Cardinal I should not possess this lovely thing!' It is a symbol, Monseigneur, of your devotion to her and her delight in it. But at the moment it must remain a secret symbol."

"This I understand to some extent," said de Rohan, "but she gives me no sign. Her manner has not changed at all."

"She is aware of the spies about her."

"But this cannot go on. Soon it will be a year since she came to meet me in the park of Versailles. Almost a year! Think of that."

Jeanne was thinking of it. In August it would be a year. She was not greatly looking forward to the 1st August, when the first payment on the necklace would be due.

The Cardinal went on: "I cannot endure this waiting. There must be a sign from her."

"I will tell Her Majesty what you say," promised Jeanne.

When she left him she felt exasperated. It was annoying to have to think of the man. He had served his purpose and she wished now to forget him; she wanted to give all her time to enjoying the great fortune which had miraculously come to her, and planning for the even greater fortune she would have.

She still visited Versailles when she was occupying her lodgings there. She still appeared masked, that none might recognize her. Yet now that she was able to pay these visits in her fine garments she was admitted, as all well-dressed people were, to the Œil-de-Bœuf in the great gallery. There she would see the Queen pass by, note the gowns she was wearing and listen to the comments.

She was wondering how she was going to satisfy the Cardinal, when the Queen, resplendent in satin and lace, ablaze with jewels, passed by on her way to Mass.

She was smiling and, as she passed the Œil-de-Bœuf, she lifted an exquisite hand as though in acknowledgment of the homage of the people there.

"The Queen is gracious today," said Jeanne to her neighbour.

"Oh that . . ." was the answer. "It's a habit. She always lifts her hand in that way as an acknowledgment to the people in the Œil-de-Bœuf."

"Always?" said Jeanne.

"I've been here several times and never known her not do so. It has become a habit."

Jeanne smiled.

How good was Providence, good fortune, fate, whatever it was called. Every time Jeanne was in a difficulty, some means of extricating herself was, it seemed by chance, thrown to her.

*   *   *

The Cardinal waited in the Œil-de-Bœuf. At any moment she would pass through. She would turn, and their eyes would meet, and she would give a signal . . . the sign that he so desperately needed.

It would mean: Have patience. Do not despair. Do not think because I have not yet been able to receive you that I do not think of you. Soon all will be well, as I have told you in my letters. For the time being rest content with those, and as soon as it is possible all that you desire shall be yours.

So he waited, waited desperately, his eyes fixed on the door through which the Queen would come.

On the edge of the crowd in the Œil-de-Bœuf a shrouded figure waited with equal anxiety. She always did it. It was a habit. But what if she failed to do it today?

"The Queen! She comes!" The murmur went through the Œil-de-Bœuf. And there she was, smiling and gracious, very beautiful in her exquisite gown, wearing her enchanting head-dress, diamonds glittering on her person.

The Cardinal thought of the great necklace and wondered fleetingly how it would look on that graceful neck. He was aware of a faint flicker of surprise as he gazed at her. She was so dainty, and everything about her seemed to reflect that daintiness. What he remembered of the necklace was an over-elaborate piece of jewellery which would surely seem in bad taste on such an exquisite creature. Ideal it might be for Madame du Barry for whom it was originally intended. But for graceful, dainty, exquisite Marie Antoinette, surely not!

Yet, thought the besotted Cardinal, it was possible that she transformed everything when she put it on!

Now! She was approaching the Œil-de-Bœuf. She turned her head and looked, it seemed to the Cardinal, straight into his eyes. He felt a shiver of ecstasy run through him as the slender arm was raised in a gesture of salute.

The Queen passed on. The Cardinal's glistening eyes followed her.

Jeanne quickly left the crowd, exulting.

Once more she had succeeded.

*   *   *

The Queen's gesture made the Cardinal happy for some little time. He sought every opportunity for being in her company; yet not once did she show that she was aware of him.

On one occasion, when he was quite close to her, he looked at her appealingly, but he saw that haughty arrogance slip down over her smiling face and she looked through him implying, as she knew so well how to, that she despised him and that the only way in which she could tolerate him near her was to pretend that he did not exist.

This was disconcerting. It was inconsistent after the charming recognition which had come to him in the Œil-de-Bœuf. She was carrying her precautions too far.

He found that he could not rest, and had not Cagliostro told him that he was pursuing a course which would link his name with that of the Queen in the history of France, he would have been seriously perturbed.

As it was he decided to precipitate matters.

He called on the jewellers.

"You have, I doubt not," he said, "heard from the Queen that she is delighted with the necklace?"

"We have heard nothing, Eminence."

The Cardinal was surprised. He said: "I trust that you have expressed your gratitude that she has bought the necklace."

"Monseigneur, we have done no such thing," said Boehmer. "We understood from Madame de la Motte-Valois that the whole matter was to be conducted in secrecy, and that we were not to communicate with Her Majesty."

"You should have sent a letter, thanking her for taking the necklace," said the Cardinal. "Please do so without delay."

"We will, Eminence."

When the Cardinal had gone the jewellers discussed the matter.

"It is of course the usual procedure," said Bassenge.

"What harm could it do?" asked Boehmer. "I will write the letter at once, and seek the first opportunity of delivering it."

He wrote it and read it to Bassenge, who declared it to be adequate.

Boehmer was about to seal it when he paused.

"I think," he said, "that on second thoughts I will

show it to Madame de la Motte-Valois. As she is now in Paris I could easily do that."

"There's no harm in that," said Bassenge.

*   *   *

When Jeanne read the letter which the jeweller presented to her, her alarm made her furious.

"But did I not tell you that the matter is to be a strict secret?"

"We know that, Madame, but surely it would remain a secret if this letter were delivered into the Queen's hands."

Jeanne was silent for a few seconds. She was visualizing what would have happened if she had been in the country and the letter *had* been delivered to the Queen.

"Her Majesty has expressly asked that all matters concerning the necklace should pass through *my* hands . . . or the Cardinal's. Surely, Monsieur Boehmer, if you value your appointment as the Queen's jeweller you should respect her wishes."

"I bought my appointment, Madame," said Boehmer. "I doubt whether even the Queen could dislodge me from it."

"She could buy fewer jewels," said Jeanne grimly.

"Well, of course we wish to please Her Majesty. But I have had no letter from her about the necklace, and because it is a piece of such unusual beauty and value it seems strange. The Cardinal suggested that I had failed in good manners by not expressing my thanks."

"I see," said Jeanne, all her anger against the jeweller now diverted to the Cardinal. "I will try to meet your wishes. Give me the letter, and I will see that it is placed in the hands of the Queen."

"I am grateful to you, Madame."

Jeanne felt exultation mingling with her horror. Once

again she had come near to disaster, and once again she had avoided it.

*   *   *

June was passing. One more month and it would be necessary to have some brilliant plan ready. The simplest thing would be to leave France, just to slip away and meet Rétaux and de la Motte, perhaps in London or even farther away, and live in opulent obscurity for the rest of their lives.

That was a solution but Jeanne could not bear to leave her beautiful mansion at Bar-sur-Aube. It represented the realization of a dream. And how could she bear to part with her handsome berline on which was embossed that magic motto: *Rege ab avo sanguinem, nomen, et lilia.*

There must be a better plan than that. There must be some way of staying in France and enjoying her fortune. She had had so much luck, ever since she had started to plan, that she would not believe she could not command the way events would go.

She was going to postpone the day of discovery as long as possible. But she was remembering some words of Cagliostro—and how often did she remember Cagliostro's words!—which were to the effect that Madame Goupil had been wise in robbing the Cardinal, for he had not allowed her to be prosecuted since to do so would expose his own folly. What greater folly would be exposed if the part he had played in this affair were made known!

There was the trump card. If there were no other way out she would simply tell the jewellers that the Queen's signature on the contract had been forged, and the Cardinal was so deeply involved that he would be obliged, for the sake of his reputation, to pay the money so that the matter might be hushed up.

In the meantime she would go on trying to delay exposure, and she hit on a plan which she thought would certainly involve a great deal of argument and so postpone the payment to a date later than the 1st August.

She went to see the jewellers, Boehmer and Bassenge.

"I have grave news for you," she told them.

They looked grim.

"The Queen has been considering the necklace," she said, "and she feels that the price you have asked is far too great."

"But, Madame," moaned Boehmer, "Her Majesty must surely realize that in the necklace she has the finest stones in the world."

Jeanne shrugged her shoulders. "She declares that the price is too high."

"Well, what does her Majesty suggest?"

Jeanne watched them closely. "Unless," she said firmly, "the price is reduced by two hundred thousand livres she will be obliged to send the necklace back to you."

Boehmer wrung his hands in anguish; Bassenge buried his face in his hands. Jeanne watched them sardonically. That will give them something to think about, she told herself grimly. Now there will be haggling which I must make last for many months.

"There is no need to hurry your decision, my friends," she told them. "Think about it. But the Queen is adamant. Either that reduction or the necklace is returned to you."

*   *   *

When she had left them the jewellers looked at each other and grimaced.

"A blow," said Bassenge.

"Indeed yes. But there is nothing we can do but accept."

"Nothing whatever!"

"And waste no time about it. It might well be that the suggestion has been made in the hope of delaying payment."

"And that is one thing which we cannot afford—the delay of payment."

"All these bills must be met in August. Even at the reduced price we are safe enough."

"Safe indeed! There was a pretty profit on the necklace."

"And so there should be! Think of the effort that went into its making."

"Ah, what a risk! But never mind. It is over now."

"There is one thing that worries me somewhat. She has never been seen wearing it and there has been no denial of the story that it was sold to the Sultan of Constantinople."

The jewellers were silent for a while. Then Boehmer said: "Have you ever known any sale to be quite so mysterious as this one?"

"Never."

"I suggest that I write to the Queen about it. Why should I not? I shall be calling at the palace to deliver those diamond epaulets and shoe buckles which she is giving to the Duc d'Angoulême for his birthday. I will write a letter telling her that we accept the new terms and deliver it at the same time."

"And you think it is wise to do this . . . not, as usual, through Madame de la Motte-Valois?"

"I think," said Boehmer, "that in this very big transaction the time has come when we should have a word direct from the Queen. I will write the letter immediately. The diamond epaulets will be ready in a day or so."

He sat down and wrote:

"Your Majesty, it is with the utmost gratification that we venture to think that this latest arrangement, which has been put before us and to which we have immediately and respectfully agreed, will assure Your Majesty of our great desire to serve you; and it gives us great satisfaction that the most beautiful diamond necklace that has ever been made is in the possession of the greatest and best of Queens."

Bassenge read it over his shoulder. "And you do not think that you should first show this to Madame de la Motte-Valois?"

Boehmer looked into his partner's eyes, and Bassenge became aware of a certain uneasiness which was communicated to him.

"No," said Boehmer firmly. "This I shall deliver with my own hands."

*   *   *

The Queen was busy when the epaulets and buckles for the Duc d'Angoulême's birthday were brought to her with a letter from the jeweller. Her thoughts were entirely occupied with a production of *Le Barbier de Séville* which was to be performed at her own theatre at Petit Trianon. She herself was to play Rosine to Artois' Barber, and she could spare no thought for anything but her costumes and the learning of her lines.

Thus it was when the jewels and the letter were brought to her.

She glanced casually at the jewels. They were charming and Angoulême would be delighted with them. She wondered vaguely what the jeweller was writing about, read the letter and re-read it.

"... the most beautiful necklace that has ever been made is in the possession of the greatest and best of Queens. ..."

She had no idea what the man meant.

She called to one of her women, Madame de Campan. "Read this," she said, "and tell me: Do you think Boehmer has gone mad? What does this mean?"

Madame de Campan read the letter. "I have no idea, Your Majesty."

"Is he still thinking about that diamond necklace of his, of which we heard so much at one time?"

o

"It cannot be so, Your Majesty, for he sold that to the Sultan of Constantinople."

"Oh, yes, I remember. But this is strange. Go after him and bring him back. We will hear what he has to say."

Madame de Campan hurried away to do the Queen's bidding, but in a little while she returned to explain that the jeweller had left the palace.

The Queen's mind had gone back to her costumes, and she was repeating her lines to herself. She had already forgotten the jeweller.

"Doubtless, if he has anything of importance to say, he will do so in good time," she said. And she held the letter in the flame of a candle.

So once again Jeanne's almost incredible good luck stayed with her.

*   *   *

July was passing and the fateful August 1st had almost arrived. Jeanne had heard from the jewellers that they had accepted the new terms, and she knew they were eagerly awaiting payment.

She went to see the Cardinal.

"I have news from Her Majesty."

She saw the eager lights in the man's eyes, and inwardly she laughed at him as the easiest fool in the world to dupe.

"About the payments on the necklace." She saw the eagerness fade from his eyes. "Her Majesty simply cannot meet the first payment. She has given me thirty thousand livres which I have with me, and she wants you to ask Boehmer and Bassenge to take this thirty thousand and wait until October 1st for the rest. Will you go to them and explain?"

"As you know, I am always ready to serve Her Majesty."

*   *   *

Boehmer looked from the Cardinal to Bassenge.

"Thirty thousand!" said Boehmer. "I am afraid that we are obliged to press the Queen for the payment of the full amount."

"You cannot press the Queen for payment!" declared the Cardinal.

"This thirty thousand will not satisfy our creditors," said Bassenge.

"As it is," continued Boehmer, "we have had the utmost difficulty in staving them off for so long."

The Cardinal was distressed. "Do not imagine," he said, "that I cannot appreciate your difficulty. But I do not see how the Queen can be pressed for the payment."

"Her Majesty has a kind heart," said Bassenge. "I feel that if I or my partner had an audience with her and explained the predicament in which we find ourselves, she would understand and pay us. If Your Eminence could explain to her. . . ."

"I cannot explain," said the Cardinal bitterly. "*You* would probably find it easier to obtain an audience than I should."

The jewellers were astonished. In fact the whole affair of the necklace was becoming more and more baffling every day.

"We will accept this thirty thousand livres," said Boehmer, "but we must find some means of bringing our case before the Queen."

*   *   *

Jeanne knew that the end was in sight now. The latest plan had not worked out as she had hoped. It could only be a matter of days before the jewellers obtained their audience with the Queen, and then the whole plot would be exposed.

The jewellers must not lay their story before Marie Antoinette. So Jeanne prepared to play that last card which she held in reserve for the crisis.

She went to see the jewellers.

They received her eagerly, imagining that she had brought a message from the Queen, and they were confident that once the Queen understood how they were placed she would pay them what she owed.

Jeanne faced them squarely.

"Well," she said, "how stands this matter of the necklace?"

"We have had only the thirty thousand livres," said Boehmer. "We must have the rest, and I am seeking an early opportunity of putting my case to the Queen."

"That will do you no good."

"It is the only course left to us; and the Queen, who has had the necklace, must pay for it."

"The point is," said Jeanne brazenly, "that the Queen has never had the necklace."

"What do you say?"

"The signatures on the documents were forged. If you want your money back, there is only one way to get it. You must go at once to the Cardinal de Rohan. He will give it to you. He must. He could not risk being involved in a fraud of this nature."

The jewellers stared at her. "But, Madame, you yourself . . ." began Boehmer.

Jeanne lifted her shoulders as though by such a gesture she put herself aloof from this affair of the necklace. "Take my advice," she said. "Tell the Cardinal that you know the signatures to be forged. He will pay you. He will not dare refuse."

"This cannot be true!" cried Bassenge.

"We are going mad . . . *mad!*" declared Boehmer.

Jeanne was watching them closely. "To whom did you hand the necklace?" she asked.

"Madame, you know. It was to the Cardinal on the orders of the Queen."

Jeanne nodded slowly. "On the *forged* orders of the Queen," she said.

"But you yourself assured us . . ." began the bewildered Boehmer. "Are you telling us that you and the Cardinal are guilty of this . . . this deception which must surely be the biggest fraud ever attempted!"

Jeanne stepped back a pace or two. "Do not attempt to solve this complicated matter," she said sharply. "You have no time to waste if you wish to save your money. Go at once to the Cardinal. Tell him how you have been duped. He will pay you. After all, he is as deeply involved in this as I am—more deeply involved. Did you not hand the necklace to him? He will pay you. He must. He dare not be involved in a fraud of this nature. He is rich and can pay, in four easy instalments."

Bassenge was plucking at Boehmer's arm. "We *must* go to the Cardinal," he said.

Boehmer continued to gaze at Jeanne, and Bassenge went on: "We have been cruelly deceived. But let us hear what the Cardinal has to say. There is no time to lose. Come . . . without delay."

Jeanne nodded briskly and hurried out of their shop. She was going to leave Paris at once for Bar-sur-Aube, and there in the country she was going to try to forget this unpleasant matter of the necklace.

But when she had gone Boehmer said: "There is only one person who should hear of this. We have already trusted the Cardinal and Madame de la Motte-Valois too blindly."

"You mean?"

"I must find a means of approaching the Queen."

*   *   *

Boehmer presented himself at Versailles, to be told that there could be no audience with the Queen as she was at

Petit Trianon; she was busy with the rehearsals and had given orders that no one was to visit her there.

"Then," said Boehmer distractedly, "allow me to see Madame de Campan."

"Madame de Campan is staying with her father-in-law at Crespy."

Boehmer returned to his partner and told him that he was going to set out for Crespy immediately. He knew Madame de Campan, who was one of the Queen's most intimate ladies, and since he could not see the Queen he must see her.

When he arrived at Crespy, Madame de Campan was giving a dinner party. She received the jeweller graciously and bade him join her guests, but it was clear to her that he had a great deal on his mind, and she took an early opportunity of talking to him in private.

"I am in great distress," he told her.

She looked at him in alarm, remembering the strange note he had written to the Queen. He looked so bewildered that she began to believe that he really was suffering from some delusion.

"You wrote a letter to the Queen a few weeks ago," she said.

"I have had no answer to it."

"The Queen does not wish to buy any more diamonds."

"I was referring to the necklace."

"The Queen does not want a necklace."

"But, Madame. . . . I must have the money owing to me."

"Your account has been paid in full."

"Madame de Campan, you are wrong. The first instalment was to have been paid on the first of this month, and all I have had is thirty thousand livres."

"I do not know what you are talking about."

"The necklace . . . my great diamond necklace."

"That necklace of yours! The one you sold to the Sultan?"

"Madame, it was not sold to the Sultan. That was a story which was put about because the Queen did not wish it to be known that she had bought the necklace."

"I am of the Queen's intimate circle. I have never seen her with the necklace."

"It is a secret as yet. The Cardinal de Rohan made the arrangements."

"The Cardinal de Rohan! The Queen dislikes him heartily. She has refused to speak to him since he slandered her mother. You have been robbed, Monsieur Boehmer."

"No," said Boehmer anxiously, "it is you who have been deceived. The Queen has given the Cardinal thirty thousand livres as part of the first payment. But I must have the rest. If I do not get it this month I shall be bankrupt."

"I am sure," said Madame de Campan, "that the Queen has never had the necklace."

"Madame de Campan," said the jeweller earnestly, "I confess to you that I am very worried. Please tell me what I should do."

She said: "I will call my father-in-law, and we will tell him the whole story."

When Monsieur de Campan had listened to what Boehmer had to say he looked very grave.

"It sounds an incredible story," he said. "You are to blame for entering into such a secret transaction without the King's knowledge. You should now go to the Baron de Breteuil, tell him everything, and he, as Minister of the King's Household, will know best what should be done."

Boehmer, frantic with anxiety, left Crespy and returned to Paris. He did not go to de Breteuil, for he had determined that he would no longer be fobbed off by those who surrounded the Queen. He would present his case to her and to no other.

Therefore he went to Petit Trianon; but the Queen declared she wanted no jewels and had no time to waste discussing them.

*   *   *

The Queen sent for Madame de Campan, to come at once to Petit Trianon; her help was needed with the production.

When Madame de Campan arrived, the Queen kissed her and cried: "But my dear Henriette, you look *distrait*! What has happened to you in the country?"

"There is something about which I must talk to Your Majesty immediately."

"First I wish you to hear my lines . . ."

"Madame, forgive me . . . I am indeed *distrait*. . . . I could not listen to them."

"My dear Henriette, you had better tell me all about it."

"The jeweller Boehmer visited me at Crespy."

"Boehmer! So he is persecuting *you*."

"He is greatly distressed. He says that you bought the diamond necklace."

"Oh, that diamond necklace! I grew so tired of it. I was delighted when he sold it to the Sultan. And now he *says* that I bought it. Clearly he must be mad."

"I do not think he is mad, Madame. I think that there has been a terrible fraud practised on Boehmer, and that these . . . these scoundrels have had the temerity to involve Your Majesty."

"He is certainly mad, Henriette. I remember there was that letter which I could not understand. That referred to the necklace."

"He says that the Cardinal de Rohan made the purchase in your name."

The Queen laughed. "Oh, then undoubtedly he *is* mad."

"Madame . . . something will have to be done . . . quickly."

"Indeed something must be done," agreed the Queen. "Send for Boehmer and tell him to come to me without delay."

*   *   *

When next Boehmer presented himself at Petit Trianon there was no delay in admitting him to the Queen. She was indeed most eagerly awaiting his arrival.

"What is this mad story I am hearing?" she demanded.

"Your Majesty," said Boehmer, falling to his knees, "it is no mad story." He then began to tell her everything from the beginning, how he had sought to sell her the necklace through the good offices of Madame de la Motte-Valois.

"Who?" exclaimed the Queen.

"Madame de la Motte-Valois, the lady who has your confidence."

"I do not know this woman," cried the Queen. "I have never even heard of her."

The jeweller looked amazed. He said: "Many believe that she has the confidence of Your Majesty; and through her and the Cardinal de Rohan it was arranged that you should buy the necklace and pay for it in four instalments, the first due on the 1st August . . . this August, Madame. . . ."

"Madame de la Motte-Valois!" repeated the Queen. "The Cardinal de Rohan! Monsieur Boehmer, you are indeed mad. Do you not know—you must, the whole court does—that I have not spoken to the Cardinal de Rohan for more than eight years!"

"Your Majesty, there is the contract."

"What contract? Show me."

"I have brought it with me. In this Your Majesty agrees

to pay in four instalments. See, it is signed and approved by you."

Marie Antoinette held out an imperious hand for the contract. She stared at those words "Approved Marie Antoinette de France".

"That is not my writing!" she declared. "Marie Antoinette de France! When should I ever sign myself *de France*! You know I never do."

"Oh, Madame," cried the jeweller, "I see that we have been the victims of one of the biggest frauds that were ever enacted."

"You will leave this contract with me," said the Queen. "I shall lay this matter before the King immediately."

*   *   *

It was a hot August day and the Cardinal de Rohan, a white surplice over his scarlet cassock, was in the Palace of Versailles preparing to officiate at Mass, which the King and Queen would attend.

He was excited, as he always was when he was about to be in the presence of the Queen. He would always wonder whether on this occasion there would be that change in her demeanour for which he longed. A whole year he had brooded since they had met in the Bosquet de Vénus, and she had spoken those few words to him. A whole year! It seemed incredible that he had had to wait so long. He could scarcely believe it possible. And yet the months had slipped by. He might never have undertaken all those difficult negotiations about the necklace, for all the gratitude she showed! Was the exquisite, seemingly light-hearted creature really so much afraid of her enemies?

In the chapel the tapers were lighted; in the galleries and the Œil-de-Bœuf the crowds were assembling. It was a special occasion, for the Assumption of the Holy Virgin was also the Queen's name-day and it was for this reason that there was to be a special ceremony at the palace with the Grand Almoner officiating.

The Cardinal went to the King's Council Room where the notable people of the court were assembling. In a very short time the King and Queen would pass through the gallery on their way to the chapel.

Suddenly a lackey in the uniform of the King's servants came into the chamber.

"The Cardinal de Rohan!" he called.

The Cardinal stepped forward.

"Monseigneur, the King desires your immediate presence in his private apartments."

The Cardinal bowed his head. He was aware of all eyes upon him as he followed the lackey.

When de Rohan entered the King's private apartment he was startled to see that the Queen was there; he felt so moved at the sight of her that he did not immediately notice that Baron de Breteuil, the Minister of the King's Household, and the Comte de Vergennes, the Foreign Minister, were also present.

The King spoke sternly: "Have you bought a diamond necklace from Boehmer, cousin?"

De Rohan hesitated. He looked towards the Queen, who was looking beyond him as though he did not exist.

"Why, yes, Your Majesty."

"What have you done with this necklace?"

Again the Cardinal sought the eyes of the Queen, but still she continued to ignore him.

"I . . . I believed it to have been handed to the Queen," stammered the Cardinal.

"Pray tell me who suggested you should carry out this commission for the Queen."

"Sire, it was the Comtesse de la Motte-Valois who assured me that Her Majesty wished me to undertake the matter."

"I know of no such woman," said the Queen shortly. She turned her haughty gaze on the Cardinal. "I cannot imagine why you should think I would ask *you* to perform such a service for me when I have not spoken to you for eight years. Why should I suddenly ask you to do this thing?"

"But . . ." began the Cardinal, panic taking possession of him as he remembered that tender scene in the Bosquet de Vénus, "Your Majesty . . . I had a letter from . . . letters from you . . . commands."

"I have sent you no letters," said the Queen.

"I begin to understand," said the Cardinal. "I have been the dupe of scoundrels." He turned to the King. "Sire, there is nothing I can do but pay for the necklace. But I must assure Your Majesties that I am innocent of any fraud. I have here the letter purporting to come from the Queen, in which she commands me to take over the necklace from the jewellers."

The King held out his hand for the letter. He studied it for some seconds. "This is not the Queen's writing," he said. "This is not her signature."

"Sire, I have been duped."

"You," cried the Queen, who had gone over to the King and was studying the paper, "you, a Prince of France, feel no suspicion when you see the signature 'Marie Antoinette de France'! Surely you know that, had the letter been from me, it would have been signed only with my Christian names!"

The King laid a restraining hand on the Queen's arm. He said: "Our cousin is overcome by shame and chagrin." He smiled his slow kindly smile at his kinsman. "It would seem to me, cousin, that you have been in the hands of clever swindlers. Do not think that we want to prove you guilty. But the Queen's name, it seems, has been mentioned in connection with this most unhappy business, and her honour is very precious to me. I must have a full explanation of the whole matter. I see that you are deeply distressed, and that you find it difficult to answer our questions. I want you now to go into my ante-room where you will find pen and paper, and there write an account of this unhappy affair. I think you will find that easier than answering questions."

The Cardinal bowed his head. "Thank you, Sire," he said.

He left them and, sitting before the table in the small room, he tried to recall everything that had happened, leading up to this day of shame.

*   *   *

He could not collect his thoughts. He could not understand what had happened to him.

"Marie Antoinette de France," he murmured to himself. "Why did I not see it then? How could I have been such a fool!"

Cagliostro had told him that the negotiations would be successful. He had approved of the relationship with Madame de la Motte-Valois. What did it mean? Why was it that, since Cagliostro and Madame de la Motte-Valois had come into his life, he seemed to have lived in a trance so that he could receive a letter signed 'Marie Antoinette de France' and believe the Queen had signed that letter?

He still felt as though he were living in that trance. How could he tell the truth? How could he tell the King: I planned to become the Queen's lover and rule France with her!

When he had finished writing he feared the account he gave on paper was as jumbled as that which he had tried to give when they had questioned him.

*   *   *

In the Galerie and the Œil-de-Bœuf, there was a great deal of whispering. What was happening? Why did not the King and Queen come to Mass? What had happened to the Cardinal de Rohan? The minutes were slipping by. Clearly something serious was afoot.

At last the door leading to the King's apartments was opened and the Cardinal de Rohan, still wearing his surplice over his cassock, stepped out; but something had changed the proud Cardinal. His face was as white as his surplice, and he looked like a sleep-walker. He was coming slowly through the Œil-de-Bœuf to the Galerie des Glaces when the Baron de Breteuil appeared.

He stood in the doorway for some seconds while the Cardinal began to walk slowly through the press of people.

Then the voice of de Breteuil rang out: "Arrest the Cardinal de Rohan."

*   *   *

Meanwhile Jeanne was staying in her mansion at Bar-sur-Aube. She felt contented. The affair of the necklace was over, she believed, as far as she was concerned; the Cardinal would now realize that he had been duped. And whom could he blame for that but himself? He would pay the jewellers the sum they desired, in order to save his face; and she hoped they would never meet again. Rétaux was in Holland; her husband was in England; and she had plenty of money which the sale of certain of the stones had brought her; moreover the remainder were out of the country and no one could lay his hands on them now.

All she need do was play the grand lady, drive about the country in her berline, entertain her friends and stay out of Paris until the affair had blown over.

She gave a party; she went among her guests, courted and flattered—rich Madame la Comtesse who was a member of the royal family of France and a shining ornament of the neighbourhood.

She retired late and slept well. But in the early hours of the morning, hearing a commotion below, she started out of her sleep, asking herself what was happening. It must be de la Motte, arrived from England. She threw on a robe and, when she opened her door, she saw strange men on the staircase.

One of these cried as soon as he saw her: "You are Madame de la Motte-Valois?"

"I am," she said haughtily. "And what are you doing in my house?"

"Your servant let us in, Madame. But do not blame him. We come in the name of the King."

"For what purpose?"

"We must ask you to return with us to Paris, Madame."

"But this is absurd. I prefer to stay here in the country. On what grounds do you make this suggestion?"

"We are arresting you, Madame, in the name of the King."

"On what charge?"

"On being concerned in the theft of a diamond necklace."

"A diamond necklace! Listen to me. There has been a mistake. You must go to the Cardinal de Rohan. . . ."

"Madame, the Cardinal has been arrested."

She was silent.

The fool! she was thinking. Did he not see that he could bring only harm to himself and to her? The man must be mad. He had not acted as she had expected that he should. Did he not understand that the only possible course for him was to pay up and keep quiet? What now? she asked herself in sudden panic. What now?

She looked about her for a way of escape. Why had she been such a fool as to stay in France? Rétaux was safe. De la Motte was safe. Only she . . . she was left behind!

The *agent de police* smiled grimly. "There is no escape, Madame," he said. "I pray you, dress quickly. We have orders that you are to be brought to Paris with all speed to answer this charge."

*   *   *

Jeanne's spirits sank as she was taken to that grey fortress with its eight pointed towers, of which every Parisian had heard horrifying tales. Often she had looked at it, looming over the crowded Faubourg, and shuddered. And now she, the Comtesse de la Motte-Valois, at the very pinnacle of success, was finding herself a prisoner in the dreaded Bastille.

But immediately her busy mind was twisting and turning in an endeavour to discover a means of release for herself. How could she do this? Only by making her captors believe that she had been the dupe of someone. But when she considered all that had happened—which the Cardinal had probably betrayed—this seemed an impossibility.

She was taken to a small room in the prison where she was subjected to questions; and as these were fired at her, she realized with horror that the Cardinal had told all, and that she was going to find it almost impossible to extricate herself from this alarming situation. She felt that her safest plan was to deny everything.

"It is all lies . . . lies," she declared again and again.

But she had been living in great style from recently acquired wealth, had she not?

She had.

Then how had she suddenly acquired that wealth?

She hesitated for a while; then she said slowly: "The Cardinal de Rohan was a very generous lover."

In that moment she had a flash of inspiration. The Cardinal had acted as a fool because he was under the influence of Cagliostro. What if they proved that she had acted criminally? What if she too had been under the influence of that man?

She turned her blue eyes on her questioners. "It is true," she said, "that both the Cardinal and myself have done some strange things, but they did not seem strange to us at the time. We but obeyed the Comte."

"What Comte?"

"The Comte de Cagliostro."

Her questioners exchanged glances.

That night Cagliostro and his wife were lodged in the Bastille.

*　　　　　*　　　　　*

Cagliostro walked up and down his cell. He smiled gently at his wife. Poor Lorenza! She was so frightened.

"There is nothing to fear," he said. "I promise you we shall not remain here long. We shall soon be free."

"But why are we here, Alessandro?"

"Do not trouble yourself with reasons. Soon we shall be free."

"But _you_ know why we are here."

He nodded, and he stared beyond her as though she were not there, and he saw a scene other than this prison cell in the Bastille.

He had done his work well and he could imagine the exultation there would be throughout the Lodges of Europe. Events had followed the course along which they had been subtly guided. The wretched woman La Motte and her creatures, the foolish Cardinal, the impulsive Queen and the short-sighted King—yes and even he, Cagliostro—had all danced to the piping.

And now all the world knew—or would soon know—of the existence of the most elaborate diamond necklace that had ever been made; they would remember it in the stormy years to come as a _cause célèbre_; there was going to be a

P

trial in which the Cardinal, Madame de la Motte-Valois, himself and other minor characters would be brought to the notice of the people of France, who were already turning sullen eyes towards the throne.

This was more than a rumble of thunder; it was more like the beginning of an earthquake. The Queen was a foolish woman to have made of this a public show. How much better to have considered it behind the walls of the private apartments, to have paid the jeweller, and to have said to the criminals: "Go your way in peace." But that was not what the High Masters wanted.

From that day, when he had sworn his oaths to the Illuminati, they had hoped for something such as this. In dominating de Rohan, that lover of the Queen, he had prepared him for just such a situation as this, and when the time had come, had helped to lead him to it. Could the Grand Masters have foreseen such a situation? Had they merely seized each opportunity as it came along?

The flimsy foundations of the throne were shaken by this affair of the necklace, shaken so severely that they could not recover.

For himself? He had not a qualm. He was too valuable. His friends the Grand Masters, who had brought the King and Queen to this dangerous pass, would not desert such a useful agent as the Comte de Cagliostro.

*   *   *

VII

THE PRISONERS

(*The Reckoning*)

IT WAS A SUNNY MAY DAY AND PARIS WAS CROWDED WITH excited sightseers. They filled Dauphine Square at the rear of the Palais de Justice; they jostled each other in the narrow streets about Notre Dame and the Hôtel Dieu. They clustered about the statue of Henri Quatre at the Pont Neuf and many eyes were raised to that figure of France's best loved King on that day.

"How different is Louis XVI from his great ancestor!" they said to one another.

"Oh, but it is not Louis who is to blame for the state of France today. It is the Austrian woman who is responsible."

"But would great Henri have allowed himself to be led by a woman?"

There was much murmuring in the crowds that day, the day when all had come to hear the result of the trial; and, in the minds of most, the guilty party was not the Cardinal de Rohan, nor the de la Mottes, but the Austrian woman, Marie Antoinette.

Never in the history of France had the pamphleteers been so busy; never had there been such excitement in Palais Royal, that hot-bed of revolution. The Duc d' Orléans (who until last year, when his father died had been the Duc de Chartres) was watching the rising excitement with an eagerness he could not hide. As he strolled through the gardens, stopping to talk with all classes with that ease of manner which was winning for him the title of Philippe-Égalité, he scattered the seeds of revolution to come. He had friends among those men who stood on platforms asking the people if they were content to starve while the Austrian woman squandered money on diamonds or became involved in frauds to possess them. Those who produced songs which the people could sing, who wrote placards which were hung on the trees—those also were his friends.

There were crowds in the Palais Royal that day; and throughout the capital there was tension, that ominous, waiting silence before the storm.

It was nine months since the participators in the affair had been arrested, and during those months not for a single day had the people, not only of Paris but of the whole country, been allowed to forget the affair of the diamond necklace.

All those who had taken part, with the exception of de la Motte—who had had the good fortune to be in England at the time of the exposure and the good sense to stay there—were now lodged in the Bastille. Rétaux de Villette had been brought from Holland and was now awaiting sentence with the rest. Marie Nicole Leguay, who had since her adventure in the Bosquet de Vénus called herself Baronne d'Oliva, had also been brought to the Bastille. This was of great interest to the people who had heard varying accounts of the story. But the most interesting factor in the case was that the Queen was involved and that a prince of the royal house was held for trial.

Through the streets of Paris on that May day strolled the retainers of the great families of Rohan, Soubise and Lorraine, kinsmen of the Cardinal. They were all dressed in mourning, and their expressions were solemn and shamed. This was excitement such as the Parisians loved. It implied that these great families were plunged in mourning, not because of any infamy connected with their famous relative—they refused to consider that he might be guilty

—but on account of the shame and insult under which they were suffering since a member of their great houses had been arrested like a common felon and subjected to humiliation.

It was the duty of these people to spread abroad two rumours: one was that the Cardinal was innocent, knew nothing whatever of the diamond necklace and had been imprisoned on the Queen's orders because she had always hated him; the other was that the Queen herself was guilty of fraud and that the Cardinal was chivalrously protecting her.

Whatever these people believed, all the rumours pointed to one culprit: The Queen.

There were to be forty-six judges, for the Queen had insisted that the affair of the diamond necklace should be judged by the *Parlement de Paris*.

Those who wished her well had sought to dissuade her from this action, for thus would the case achieve the utmost publicity. She would be well advised, she was told by her true friends, to hush up this great scandal; but the Queen had been humiliated in a hundred ways during the last years; she had been accused of adultery and passing off her bastards as true heirs of France. Rashly she believed that if she could prove herself completely innocent in this affair she would triumph over her calumniators for all time.

Therefore she chose the most public form of trial. She was determined that the Cardinal de Rohan should be exposed in all his villainy, for she, more than anyone in France, believed him guilty; she hated him more than she hated any other; and her hatred blinded her vision so that she determined to revenge herself on this man who, she considered, had now insulted her as he had once insulted her mother.

In the streets, pamphlets were being sold by the hundred. Messages were being sent to every country in Europe. The important question was not: Who stole the diamond necklace? so much as: Did the Queen meet the Cardinal de Rohan at midnight in the Park of Versailles? The crown of France was being brought to ridicule and humiliation, and those who cried 'Liberty' had never before felt so hopeful.

Into the *grande chambre* marched the judges.

The most sensational trial of the century had begun.

*   *   *

And in the *grande chambre* the judges debated.

For sixteen hours they talked together. They discussed the evidence from all angles. They reviewed the whole story from beginning to end. They considered each person who had taken part in this extraordinary adventure.

Was it possible that the Cardinal de Rohan, a man of culture and education, a member of the royal house, could have been so duped? Could he have read notes signed 'Marie Antoinette de France' and believed them to have come from the Queen? Yet for what reason could he have gone to such lengths? To put himself in possession of a diamond necklace? It was true it was the most expensive necklace that had ever been made, but was a cardinal and wealthy prince going to involve himself in such a fraud for the sake of one million six hundred thousand livres?

Now the de la Motte family were another proposition. They had been near starvation. Such people would be ready to do a great deal for one million six hundred thousand livres. Moreover, the woman de la Motte was proved to be a cheat. She had declared that she was a friend of the Queen, and all the ladies at court could testify that she had never been in the Queen's company.

The man Rétaux de Villette—an ordinary rogue who could write a fluent hand and give a fair imitation of any he tried to copy: It was easy enough to understand that man's actions.

The jewellers, Boehmer and Bassenge, had contradicted themselves over and over again. They did not seem to be sure whether the Cardinal or the woman de la Motte had approached them. But the great Baudard de Saint-James, from whom they had borrowed money in order to make the necklace, gave them his full support. Saint-James was a member of Egyptian Masonry and a friend of many of the Freemasons who, through influential juggling in certain quarters, were the judges in this case. The jewellers, Saint-James had hinted, must be exonerated from all complicity.

As for the young woman who called herself Baronne d'Oliva, she had done nothing but wear a white dress and stand in the Bosquet de Vénus at midnight. She had impersonated the Queen, but she had thought she had done this at the Queen's command. A simple woman, a poor girl who was accustomed to hiring herself for any purpose, and she had given her evidence with straightforward innocence. She had merely looked upon her part in this as a professional engagement. She was in any case unimportant to the affair.

And Cagliostro: It was unthinkable that he should have been involved. Paris, the judges' bench, the whole court, was thronged with those who were determined that the founder of the new Lodge of Egyptian Masonry should go free—he and the Cardinal together.

There would have to be culprits. The guilt should fall mainly on three people—the de la Mottes and the Queen.

The judges were ready to give their verdict.

*   *   *

The atmosphere inside the *grande chambre* was tense; that in the streets no less so.

The news was out. The Cardinal and Cagliostro were acquitted without a stain on their characters. The Baronne d'Oliva was also acquitted. Rétaux de Villette, the forger, was employed as a secretary by Madame de la Motte-Valois and was therefore acting on the instructions of his employer; he was guilty of forging the Queen's signature and should be banished from France for as long as he lived. The Comte de la Motte, at present in England, was to be sent to the galleys. His wife, Jeanne de la Motte, was to be publicly flogged, branded on the shoulder as *Voleuse*, sent for life to the Salpêtrière, and to have all her goods confiscated.

*   *   *

As the Cardinal and Cagliostro left the courtroom, the crowds surged round them.

"Vive le Cardinal!" cried the people, led by those who had been instructed to do so.

"Vive le Comte de Cagliostro!"

This was victory, thought Cagliostro, victory for the Grand Masters, victory for the secret societies who had worked for this end.

The Cardinal, against whom the Queen had wished to bring a charge of *lèse-majesté* because he had based his defence on the supposition that she was a light woman who would meet a lover at midnight in the Bosquet de Vénus, was dismissed by the judges as a man who had committed no misdemeanour. No misdemeanour! And he had insulted the Queen. Guiltless he might have been in the theft of jewels; but guilty he had been in his theft of the Queen's honour. So raged the Queen. Her enemies knew this and exulted.

The Grand Masters had wished Cagliostro to dominate the Cardinal on account of his passion for the Queen, hoping to lure her to some indiscretion, but they could not have hoped for success such as this until Jeanne de la Motte-Valois had appeared with all her wily schemes. Surely, thought Cagliostro as he acknowledged the greeting of the crowd, this was a *cause célèbre* which would resound through the world, which would reverberate so violently through France that the flimsy throne must begin that rocking which would end in its fall.

*   *   *

Jeanne lay on the floor of her cell dazed with horror, telling herself that this was a nightmare; it could not in truth be happening to her. She felt as though the four walls of her cell were stifling her; the carvings, made by other prisoners, leered at her. This was the end of her grand adventure.

She had been lying thus since she had been brought here. She had no idea how many hours had passed when she heard footsteps outside her cell, and four men entered.

"Prepare yourself for a short journey," she was told.

"Whither are you taking me?" she demanded.

"To the Palais de Justice, where your sentence will be read aloud to you."

She stood up almost eagerly. Out into the streets! Surely there would be some means of escape. Perhaps Rétaux would have devised something. Perhaps he had some plan for her escape so that he might take her into exile with him.

It was five o'clock in the morning and Paris was not yet astir, so there were very few people to see her taken to the steps of the Palais de Justice. She was frightened by those quiet streets. It would have been easier to have effected an escape in the crowds. She looked frantically about her; there were one or two people coming from *les Halles* on the way to the various smaller markets of the town, wheeling their goods on barrows; some of the bakers of Gonesse were already arriving, as they did twice a week, with their loads of bread which they must sell to the Parisians, as they would not be allowed to take their loaves back through the Barriers; a coffee-woman, hoping to catch the early workers, stood at one corner, her tin urn on her back, her earthenware cups rattling as she croaked out that she had *café-au-lait* at two sous the cup.

No sign of Rétaux, and she was surrounded by thirteen guards.

At the steps of the Palais de Justice they halted, and the sentence was read to her.

Flogged! Branded! It was more than she could endure. Mists of anger enveloped her; she screamed like a wild creature and threw herself at her guards. But all her fury could not save her.

They would have discreetly bared her back, but she fought them, and her bodice was torn from her shoulders; she was held firmly while the lash was applied.

With each stroke she sent forth a piercing scream, and very soon windows were thrown open and people came running into the streets to see what was amiss.

Dishevelled, eyes wild, Jeanne kicked, scratched, bit and spat at her tormentors.

And when she saw the branding-iron she let out a great cry of fear. She, a member of the Royal House of Valois to be so treated! Curses and threats came from her livid lips; but the guards ignored them; and still the crowds gathered.

The hot iron was so close to her face that she could feel its heat on her flesh. On her shoulder! Where it.could be seen! She, Jeanne de la Motte-Valois, to spend the rest of her life with that tell-tale V branded on her as though she were an animal!

"Get away from me," she screamed, "or it will be the worse for you."

"It would be better to remain still," she was warned.

The iron was poised above her shoulder; she wrenched herself away sharply, so that she turned in the arms of her captors, and the iron descended on her bare breast. With a howl of agony Jeanne dug her teeth into the hand which held the iron. It fell clattering on to the stones; and Jeanne, overcome by pain and horror, fell fainting beside it.

For a while the crowd was silent and motionless; all eyes were on the woman stretched out on the ground, bare to the waist, and with the inflamed patch on her bosom.

A man moved closer to a group of women.

"Well," he said, "there had to be a culprit."

The women turned and looked at him eagerly. He was well dressed, his voice cultured; he looked like an official of the court.

"You do not think, Monsieur, that she was guilty?"

The man laughed lightly. "They could not bring the guilty one to the steps of the Palais de Justice. They dared not brand *her* white shoulder . . . not with a V nor with A. . . ."

"The Queen . . ." whispered one of the women.

Another said: "Oh, what a wicked thing it is that one woman should suffer for the sins of another!"

Jeanne's jailors lifted her unconscious body into a cart which began making its way to the Salpêtrière.

A little group followed. The man was with them; he talked quietly but earnestly of the injustice and disgrace to France, when one woman should suffer for another's sins.

And all that day, when men and women gathered together to discuss what had happened outside the Palais de Justice, there was always someone to whisper of injustice and to hint or to murmur against the Queen.

*   *   *

When Jeanne returned to consciousness she found that she was lying on the floor in a room which she shared with many other women. The atmosphere was close, the stench horrible. It was this, she realized, which had brought her back to consciousness. The burning pain in her breast made her groan.

She was aware of a lull in the noise when she opened her eyes; and she realized that all in that room were watching her intently.

"She's coming round."

"She looks half dead."

Jeanne moved uneasily; the sackcloth had stuck to her bleeding shoulders; she moaned faintly.

"Feeling all right, eh?" said a woman beside her, and a grinning face from which black hair sprang out like serpents bent over her.

"Let's have a look at her V," said another.

Rough hands were laid on her, and the upper part of her body exposed. She cried out in anger, but she was weak against so many.

Another woman slipped her sackcloth off her shoulder and disclosed a blistered wound in which could be distinguished a V.

"You should have kept still," said this woman. "It wouldn't have hurt so much. See how clean mine is. Trouble is, the least little thing and you're stripped and accused. A nice thing, to go around with all your life."

"But she's a Comtesse . . . ! Who'd have thought we'd have the company of Comtesses, eh?"

They all laughed.

"What really happened?" asked someone. "Tell us all about the necklace."

"Yes. Where is it? Did the Queen really have it?"

"What goings-on, eh! Bosquet de Vénus in moonlight. Lovely! They say cardinals make good lovers."

"Not that you'll ever try one."

"Why shouldn't I! I've as much chance as you."

Jeanne lay back, closing her eyes. "Let me alone . . ."

she moaned. "Give me a little rest. Later ... later I will tell you all about it. ..."

She sank back on to the evil-smelling floor. She heard someone say: "She's a Comtesse. Their skins ain't so tough as ours. They're different."

"Don't you believe it. There's no difference. We're all alike. Comtesses ... cardinals and queens."

Ribald laughter filled the room and Jeanne felt the nausea sweeping over her again. Gratefully she slipped into unconsciousness.

*　　　　*　　　　*

Life in the cell of lost women was the most horrifying experience of Jeanne's life. During the days she spent there she longed for a way of ending her life. All her belief in her own destiny, in her own skill to get what she wanted, deserted her. The conversation of the women, their manners, everything about them sickened her. There were times when she thought longingly of those days of begging by the roadside, when she wished that she could go back and begin her life again. If she could do that, she would have one determination in view: to keep herself free of the Salpêtrière.

The food sickened her—black bread and lentils without any variations—and it was not until she was almost starving that she could bring herself to eat some of it. She who had cared so much for ostentatious display must become as unkempt and dirty as her fellow prisoners. She hated the sounds of sabots on stones; her sackcloth gown irritated her skin and inflamed the wounds she had received from whipping and branding.

She had come to the very depth of misery, and as the days passed and some of that energy which she had once possessed began to return, she gave her thoughts to one object: escape from this life.

There was only one consolation. She enjoyed talking about her grandeur of the past and the cruel way in which she had been treated.

She could always be sure of an audience, and indeed she was prompted and even threatened if she did not tell the prisoners about the mysterious affair of the diamond necklace.

So she talked; she talked of the Cardinal, whose mistress she had been, of her friendship with the famous Cagliostro, of the Queen's favour.

She told several versions of the affair of the necklace; they differed widely. It did not matter. There had never been such a prisoner in the common cell of the Salpêtrière, and her companions were always ready to listen to her.

*   *   *

It could not go on, that unadulterated misery, that bitter frustration which was making her ill in mind as well as body.

One day she was called from the common cell, and the guard told her that some kind friend had arranged that she should have a room to herself.

The man, she noticed, had ceased to treat her as though she were an animal. Was it respect she saw in his eyes?

"Who has arranged this?" she asked.

"I cannot say. I have my orders. Come this way."

She was taken to a row of cells; there were thirty-six of them in all. A door was unlocked and she was shown into a compartment which was only six feet square. There was a small barred window which looked out on a courtyard, and there was straw on the floor for a bed. It was very small, but after the common cell it seemed like luxury to Jeanne.

That first day and night in her new surroundings, she enjoyed not only solitude but the absence of that acrid smell of dirty human bodies which had permeated every part of the common cell so that there was no escape from it. Even black bread and lentils seemed more tolerable in the privacy of her own little cell.

But to spend one's life in a room six feet square was no very happy prospect, and soon the old bitterness began to return.

*   *   *

She had however passed through the blackest period of her life in the Salpêtrière when she had left the common cell. The very fact that she had been taken from that den to a cell of her own was a clear indication that she had friends.

That thought came to her frequently, and she wondered who was working for her in the world beyond her prison. Could it be that de la Motte had returned secretly to France?

She was soon to realize that it was not her husband but people of very great power, and from that moment of discovery Jeanne began to plan as avidly as she had ever done in the past.

Two days after her removal to her private cell she was told that a visitor had come to the prison and would be admitted to her.

She was startled to see a very elegant lady enter her cell. So splendid was this woman that Jeanne at first thought she was dreaming. She hastily stood up and gave the visitor the only stool in the cell.

The lady took the stool and bade Jeanne sit on the straw. Handing her a parcel, she said: "I have brought some food for you. Unwrap it." Jeanne did so. It contained new bread, chicken and a bottle of wine—food such as Jeanne had not seen since her entry into the Salpêtrière. Her mouth watered, but her desire to know why this grand lady had come to visit her was greater than her hunger.

"You do not know me," said the woman.

Jeanne stared at her. It could not be. But surely she had seen her in the royal party when she, Jeanne, had haunted Versailles.

"Madame d'Orléans," cried Jeanne starting up.

The lady nodded. "I have come to tell you that you are not forgotten," she said.

"Madame, this is kindness itself."

"You have friends beyond these walls," said the Duchesse.

"Friends, Madame? What friends?"

"Those who would have seen another blamed in your place. My husband grieves for your condition, and he asks me to tell you not to despair."

"Madame, what is left to me but despair?" Jeanne opened the sackcloth garment and exposed her breast.

"I have brought an ointment for you. I am assured it is the best available. Apply it each day. It will at least soothe the burning."

"Madame, how can I thank you?"

The Duchesse smiled into Jeanne's eyes and said: "By not despairing, but by being prepared for release."

"I have been condemned for life."

"I know it. You were taken to the common cell, but you are there no longer."

"That seems like a miracle. But how could I escape from here? The King and Queen would never consent to my being given my freedom."

The Duchesse smiled fleetingly. She whispered: "Some might decide otherwise." She put her fingers to her lips. "I can trust your discretion. Not a word of this. Eat all the good things that are sent to you. Keep up your strength and . . . hope."

When the Duchesse had left her, Jeanne knew that her blackest despair was over. She had always been lucky, and even now when she had believed herself to be deserted she found that her luck held.

She thought of her husband—poor ineffectual de la Motte—when there were powerful people in France who, for their own good reasons, were ready to be her friends.

After the visit of the Duchesse, carriages were constantly arriving at the Salpêtrière; parcels of good things were sent in to her; her guards thought that one who had such rich friends outside should be treated with consideration. With each day Jeanne's spirits rose.

Meanwhile in the streets rumour persisted. Why did so many carriages call at the Salpêtrière? At whose instigation? At the Queen's? Her one-time friend who had taken all the blame for her misdemeanours was imprisoned there. Was the Queen's conscience disturbing her? Was it she who sent comforts to her scapegoat?

Everything was done to keep the story of the diamond necklace alive, to arouse the people's indignation for the victim of the Salpêtrière. In the Palais Royal there were many fiery speakers to harangue the people, to play on their sentimentality, on their envy, to flog their self-pity to fury.

Pictures began to appear about the town. There was a woman, hair wild, eyes crazed with pain, and a V branded on her breast; and beside her, hair piled high, cynically smiling, was the Queen, wearing an enormous diamond necklace.

*   *   *

De la Motte had believed that he would be wise to get as far away from France as possible. So he left England, crossed the border and took lodgings with an Italian teacher of languages who lived in Edinburgh.

He was well provided with money; he had enough to live in comfort for the rest of his life, for he had received

Q

a great deal from the sale of some of the diamonds, and he had still a collection which was worth a fortune.

The Italian was alert and very interested in his lodger, who seemed restless and yet stayed on in Edinburgh, who seemed to have plenty of money, and yet chose to live in a humble room in a quiet street.

The Italian paid a visit to South Shields, and when he was there he saw a poster which declared that a certain Comte de la Motte, who might be living in England under an assumed name, was wanted by the Government of France who were prepared to pay ten thousand livres to anyone who could deliver him up. There was a description of the Comte, and it seemed to the Italian that the wanted man was very like his lodger.

He grew excited. Ten thousand livres would free him from want for the rest of his life! He could give up teaching languages and go back to Italy.

He came back to Edinburgh and kept a sharp watch on this man. One night he invited him to drink with him and slipped a sleeping draught into his guest's wine.

When de la Motte was fast in a drugged sleep he searched his room, and in his clothes, sewn into the linings, he could feel what could be diamonds.

He was sure then of his man.

He returned to South Shields and told the authorities there that he intended to earn that ten thousand livres.

"This wanted man is my lodger," he said. "I am convinced that he is the one." He described de la Motte, and it was agreed that the description fitted exactly. Moreover he had felt the diamonds sewn in the man's clothes and had ascertained that in Edinburgh his lodger had disposed of a diamond of great worth to a local jeweller who was delighted with a bargain.

The French Government was informed, and during another visit to South Shields it was arranged that the

Italian should bring his lodger to the town on some pretext and take him to a tavern there where he could be drugged. A ship would be waiting and he would be carried on board and taken to France.

That was all very well, said the Italian, but he had had a great deal of expense to contend with. He must have an advance.

He was paid a thousand livres by the French Government, and the arrangements were made.

Back in Edinburgh, he invited his lodger to a drink.

"It is not good for you to stay in your rooms so much," he said. "I have had a little windfall and I am going to take you to South Shields to stay with some relations of mine who have settled there."

"To South Shields?" said de la Motte. "That is a little sea-side town, is it not?"

"It is an interesting place. You will like it."

"And you will pay my expenses? That is good of you."

"It is nothing. Shall we leave at the end of the week?"

De la Motte did not answer. He stood up suddenly and, going over to the Italian, he laid a hand on his shoulder and gripped it hard.

"Who has paid you to betray me?" he demanded.

The Italian squirmed and stammered: "Signor ... I do not understand. . . ."

De la Motte laughed. "All these visits to South Shields, all this excitement! All this prying in my rooms when you think I do not know. You move things in my room, my friend. The first lot of drugged wine you gave me was successful. I awoke next morning with a foul taste and a headache. Do you think I do not understand these things? You gave me another dose. And I did not take it. You thought you felt diamonds in my clothes. You took out my doublet. You unstitched and stitched it up again. I knew of these things. Now tell me, why do you want me to go to

South Shields? And tell me quickly who is behind this." He released the Italian so that he fell back against his chair. He held out his hands and laughed at them. "They are big enough to go round that skinny throat of yours and squeeze . . . and squeeze . . ."

"Signor . . . I swear to you . . ."

"Who is behind this? You had better tell me quickly."

"Well, Signor . . . it was a paper I saw in South Shields. A man named Comte de la Motte is wanted by the French police."

"And you think I am this man?"

The Italian nodded helplessly.

"And you are offered a reward?"

"Ten thousand livres, Signor. It is a great deal of money to a poor man."

"They have paid you something, in advance?"

"One thousand livres, Signor."

"Good," said de la Motte. "We will share it. And, my friend, as you value your life, there will be no more drugged wine, no more peeping and prying, no more visits to South Shields."

The little Italian gasped out that it should be as his illustrious lodger wished.

Five hundred livres, he pondered. It was not ten thousand; but he would not come too badly out of the affair.

So the French Government were cheated of the man they sought, and de la Motte continued to live in obscure comfort in the old city of Edinburgh.

*   *   *

Cardinal de Rohan rode out of Paris.

The King and Queen, incensed by the verdict which had declared the Cardinal acquitted without a stain on his character, determined not to let the man escape unscathed.

The Queen was furious, the King bewildered. It was as

though the judges had chosen to ignore this great insult to royalty. A man who believed it possible to enter into clandestine correspondence with the Queen of France, to meet her in the Bosquet de Vénus alone at midnight and to help her buy a necklace without the King's consent, was hideously guilty of *lèse-majesté* and should have been sentenced to imprisonment in the Bastille.

Yet he had been allowed to leave the court, a free man, to go into the streets accompanied by the cheers of the crowd. It was unendurable.

The Queen wanted the King to use a *lettre-de-cachet*, and so put an end to the Cardinal's liberty; but Louis was uncertain as he ever was. The judges had been set up to give judgment, and they had given it.

However, to placate the Queen, he deprived de Rohan of his position of Grand Almoner and sent word to him that his presence was not required at court, and it was the King's pleasure that he exile himself to his Abbaye de Chaise-Dieu.

Thus the Cardinal was riding out of Paris.

*   *   *

Nor could Louis allow Cagliostro, who many suspected had played a larger part in the affair than had been brought to light, to go unpunished.

He intimated that there was no place in France for the Comte, and the King would be obliged if he would leave at once.

Cagliostro shrugged his shoulders. His work was done, and he and Lorenza rode to Passy where they were entertained by friends. These were the Masons of Lodges who had good reason to be grateful to Cagliostro, and in the mansion which one of them had placed at the disposal of all who had come to this spot to meet Cagliostro before he left France, they talked of the affair of the diamond necklace and predicted that it would be long before that matter was forgotten.

They discussed the progress of their schemes and the distinct blow to the Monarchy of France that affair had been.

It was clear that Cagliostro had done his work to their satisfaction.

He and Lorenza would have wished to linger in this pleasant company, but he did not forget that he had been ordered to leave France, and after a short sojourn he was forced to set out for England.

*　　　　*　　　　*

Jeanne sat in her cell. Before her was the usual plate of black bread and lentils. She stared at it without interest. She had just eaten a leg of chicken which had been brought to her.

The rough sackcloth of her gown, the clatter of her sabots on the stone floor of her cell, no longer irritated her, for she could assure herself that life was about to change.

There were plans afoot. She had not been forgotten. There were evidently some who remembered what was due to a member of the House of Valois.

She was conscious of a feeling of excited anticipation. It had been with her for some time. She had had her visitors that day. They had brought her good things to eat and they had implied that she should hold herself in readiness, although they had not said for what.

She lay down on her straw and tried to sleep, but she felt too excited. She let her fingers stray to that hideous V on her breast, and even that did not inspire her with anger.

And as she lay there the door of her cell was opened and a man entered.

"Madame," he murmured.

She started up. He was dressed in the uniform of the guards but she had not seen him before.

He threw a bundle on the floor and whispered: "Put on these clothes as quickly as you can."

With hands that trembled so much that she found it difficult to obey, Jeanne slipped into breeches, waistcoat, boots, a long blue coat and a round hat which did much to shade her face. She looked like a country wagoner, but she realized exultantly that this was as good a disguise as she could possibly have, for such men were often seen in the grounds carrying loads to and from the prison.

Before she was dressed she was aware of the man fidgeting impatiently at the door of her cell.

"Follow me," he said, "with all speed and in silence."

Then began a hurried walk through the gloomy passages and down spiral staircases, past a guard who did not challenge them, and quite simply out to freedom.

"From now on," said the man who had led her from her prison, "you will be alone. In the pocket of your coat you will find ample money for your needs, and an address in Luxembourg. Listen carefully. Make your way with as much speed as possible, hiring carriages as you go, across France to Luxembourg. There go at once to the address where a woman, whose name is MacMahon, will be waiting for you. She will accompany you to Ostend, and from there you will both make your way to England. Mrs. MacMahon has a house in Haymarket in London. She will take you thither."

"Tell me one thing," said Jeanne. "To whom am I indebted for this help?"

"You will learn in good time," she was told. "Go quickly. There is not a moment to spare."

Jeanne hurried away. She crossed the Seine and, when she had put some distance between herself and her prison, she hired a carriage.

She lay back, listening to the sound of the carriage wheels as they went through the Barrier and out of Paris.

*   *   *

VIII

THE GAME IS OVER

THE FEVERED YEARS WERE PASSING.

More libels, more pamphlets had been let loose after the trial than ever before.

1786. 1787. Events moved swiftly during those years, but there were always many to make sure that the affair of the diamond necklace was not forgotten.

At the end of the year 1788 the Cardinal left Chaise-Dieu for Saverne, and he travelled with the pomp of a prince. People lined the roads to cheer him as he passed. There had been so many stories of the wickedness of the Queen and the chivalry of the Cardinal that they believed them.

The Cardinal had become the hero of the Story of the Diamond Necklace, the Queen the villainess.

Cagliostro had not fared so well. The English had never accepted him with that acclaim which had been accorded him in other countries, and he found himself once more within prison walls. It was clear that England was not the place for him, and as soon as he was free he left that country and made with all speed for Rome, where he planned to form a Lodge of his Egyptian Masonry.

But here he fell foul of the Papal authorities. Lorenza was sent to a convent and he was imprisoned in the fort of San Leone where he was prevailed upon to make many confessions and expose the plans of such societies as the Illuminati.

*　　　　*　　　　*

248

Jeanne meanwhile prospered in England. No sooner had she arrived in that country than she was approached by a publisher who told her he was ready to pay her handsomely for her account of the affair of the diamond necklace. Jeanne was only too ready to provide this. Indeed she gave many accounts; and so great was her pleasure in vilifying the Queen that she wrote several versions of her memoirs. It did not matter that they differed. She was particularly fond of the one in which the Queen commanded her to procure the necklace. In this version there was passionate love between herself and the Queen—for the Queen (wrote Jeanne) a nymphomaniac, was also ardently fond of her own sex. She had procured the necklace as she had recounted, but it had been given to the Queen, who had broken it up and given her many of the diamonds as presents.

In another version Marie Antoinette had been the mistress of de Rohan when he was on his mission in Vienna. The fact that Marie Antoinette was at Versailles at that time was of little importance.

Jeanne's memoirs were voraciously read.

Jeanne had many invitations to dine out. She was in great demand. She had countless stories to tell of the profanity of the Queen of France, and every week she added to her repertoire.

Her husband joined her in London and they lived together in great comfort and luxury, for they had the remainder of the diamonds to provide them with a fortune.

And one day Jeanne received a visitor at her London house. It was the Duc d'Orléans.

He had come, he said, to ask her to repay a debt she owed him. He had rescued her from prison, and now he was going to ask her to do something for him.

"And that is, Monsieur le Duc?"

"Return to Paris," he answered.

"But I have been sentenced to life imprisonment! If I were caught I could be sent back to the Salpêtrière."

"My dear Madame, you do not know what is happening in France. You should have been in Paris on July 14th. You should have seen the storming of the Bastille. It was the beginning of revolution. You would have enjoyed being in the crowd which escorted the royal family from Versailles to Paris in October. No one would want to put you in the Salpêtrière now. All Paris would welcome you. They would applaud you, they would love you, Madame, because they so hate the Queen that they love all her enemies."

"Paris," whispered Jeanne. She thought of Bar-sur-Aube and the berline in which she had once ridden with such pride. She thought of her motto: "From the King, my ancestor, I derive my blood, my name and the lilies."

"You would be safe in the new Paris," said the Duke. "You shall have apartments in the Place Vendôme. Come to Paris. You will have nothing to regret."

"Monsieur le Duc, what do you ask of me?"

"That you write for us . . . that you tell Paris, as you have been telling London, all you know concerning the Queen."

*   *   *

She was a public figure now. There were many people who wanted to re-try the case of the diamond necklace, so that they might put another woman in the dock.

She had succeeded well. Libels had poured from her vitriolic pen. Her masters were pleased with her.

But in her dreams she was unable to escape from her nightmares, and in these she was always in the hands of her enemies. Often she would awake screaming because she had dreamed that the hot branding-iron was about to touch her flesh; at others she would awake in tears of despair because she had dreamed she was lying on the hard floor of the common cell in the Salpêtrière.

Horror was never far from her. It stalked the streets during those days of terror. There was no longer respect for royalty, no longer respect for life.

She had been a witness of the humiliating return of the royal family from Varennes, and when she slept that night she had been haunted by wild faces which she had seen in the crowds, and her dream was that it was she who sat in that carriage, not the Queen, she, Jeanne, who kept her haughty head high and looked neither to right nor to left.

She was as extravagant as ever. She was paid well for her work but she could not forget the old days of affluence. She often thought of Rétaux who had not returned to France, and of her husband who would shortly join her. He would have done so ere this, but there had been trouble in Brussels. De la Motte had met a certain Mr. Grey, a jeweller of London, a man who had bought diamonds from him and had come forward and testified to this; he had engaged him in a duel for his offensiveness in interfering in this matter of the diamond necklace, and the young jeweller had been killed.

Jeanne doubted not that de la Motte would extricate himself and that he would soon join her in Paris.

She had need of him, for in the years during which she had become notorious she had gathered many enemies about her. Even in revolutionary France the King and Queen had their friends, and she knew that there must be many people in Paris at this time who would think it a noble and heroic deed to put an end to the woman who called herself the Comtesse de la Motte-Valois. They hated her for the stories which she had set in circulation—so many stories, many of them so different although they were meant to be an account of one great happening. How could she resist the desire to embroider, to garnish, to represent herself as an angel of virtue, and the Queen as a demon of sensuality and greed? Yet there were occasions when she felt her character was made more attractive by devilry. Nobody minded these diverse accounts, and publishers were clamouring for works from her pen.

Moreover, she was compelled to write them on orders from Palais Royal.

Even so there were debts. Try as she might, she could not live within her income. There had been creditors who threatened her with prosecution if she did not meet her bills. It was one of her nightmares that she would be imprisoned for debt.

Prison! The very word brought her out in a cold sweat.

Thus it was one evening, when her servant came to her to tell her that a man had called.

She said that he might be brought in, and when he came, to her horror she realized that he was a bailiff and that he had come to arrest her for failing to pay a debt of thirty livres.

She had not thirty livres in the house, and when she was told that she must either pay it or go with him she became frantic.

The scar on her breast throbbed as it always did in moments of agitation. There was one thought in her mind now: She must not be taken to prison.

"Excuse me one moment," she said. "I will go and fetch the money for you."

She slipped out of the room and locked him in. Then she hurried to her bedroom and hastily threw her jewellery and a few clothes into a valise.

But the bailiff had a friend in the house—one of the maids—and he called to her to unlock the door, which she promptly did.

"Which is your mistress's bedroom?" he asked; and when he was told he bounded up the stairs and, opening the door, confronted Jeanne with her half-packed valise.

Blind terror seized Jeanne. It might have been that she had a superstitious fear that one day she would be called upon to pay for all the lies she had told. She saw the prison gates opening for her and this time there might be no escape.

She looked about her in terror. She could not escape by the door, but there was the window.

She ran to it, flung it open and scrambled out.

Her nails broke as she tried to clutch the sill; she slipped and fell, and lay groaning on the ground.

Before that day was over, Jeanne, who had stolen more than a million livres, died for the want of thirty.

*   *   *

Cagliostro, in his Italian prison, had but four more years to live. The Cardinal de Rohan had longer. He saw the fall of the monarchy and the rise of Napoleon. De la Motte had a long life before him during which he enjoyed a pension from Louis XVIII, presumably for his assistance in helping to remove his, Louis', brother from the throne. Marie Leguay married a nobleman who at one time had been attached to the house of the Comte d'Artois and later became Captain of the National Guard Company of the Temple; she wrote her memoirs (or someone wrote them for her) which, on account of her participation in the affair of the diamond necklace, were read with eagerness.

Thus all the chief actors in the drama.

In those fateful days, when Louis XVI and Marie Antoinette made their last journeys to the Place de la Révolution, there were still many of the spectators to talk of that thunderclap which had heralded the storm, that first great rumbling of coming disaster; and, in the years which followed, the significance of the mysterious affair of the diamond necklace has not been forgotten.

Jean Plaidy also wrote

The Norman Trilogy
THE BASTARD KING
THE LION OF JUSTICE
THE PASSIONATE ENEMIES

The Plantagenet Saga
PLANTAGENET PRELUDE
THE REVOLT OF THE EAGLETS
THE HEART OF THE LION
THE PRINCE OF DARKNESS
THE BATTLE OF THE QUEENS
THE QUEEN FROM PROVENCE
EDWARD LONGSHANKS
THE FOLLIES OF THE KING
THE VOW OF THE HERON
PASSAGE TO PONTEFRACT
THE STAR OF LANCASTER
EPITAPH FOR THREE WOMEN
RED ROSE OF ANJOU
THE SUN IN SPLENDOUR

The Tudor Novels
UNEASY LIES THE HEAD
KATHARINE, THE VIRGIN WIDOW } Also available in one volume:
THE SHADOW OF THE POMEGRANATE }   KATHARINE OF ARAGON
THE KING'S SECRET MATTER
MURDER MOST ROYAL (Anne Boleyn and Catherine Howard)
ST THOMAS'S EVE (Sir Thomas More)
THE SIXTH WIFE (Katharine Parr)
THE THISTLE AND THE ROSE (Margaret Tudor and James IV)
MARY, QUEEN OF FRANCE (Queen of Louis XII)
THE SPANISH BRIDEGROOM (Philip II and his first three wives)
GAY LORD ROBERT (Elizabeth and Leicester)

The Mary Queen of Scots Series
ROYAL ROAD TO FOTHERINGAY
THE CAPTIVE QUEEN OF SCOTS

The Stuart Saga
THE MURDER IN THE TOWER (Robert Carr and the Countess of Essex)
THE WANDERING PRINCE }
A HEALTH UNTO HIS MAJESTY } Also available in one volume:
HERE LIES OUR SOVEREIGN LORD }   CHARLES II
THE THREE CROWNS
(William of Orange) }
THE HAUNTED SISTERS }
(Mary and Anne) } Also available in one volume:
THE QUEEN'S FAVOURITES }   THE LAST OF THE STUARTS
(Sarah Churchill and Abigail Hill)

The Georgian Saga
THE PRINCESS OF CELLE (Sophia Dorothea and George I)
QUEEN IN WAITING }
CAROLINE THE QUEEN } Caroline of Ansbach
THE PRINCE AND THE QUAKERESS (George III and Hannah Lightfoot)
THE THIRD GEORGE
PERDITA'S PRINCE (Perdita Robinson)
SWEET LASS OF RICHMOND HILL (Mrs Fitzherbert)
INDISCRETIONS OF THE QUEEN (Caroline of Brunswick)

THE REGENT'S DAUGHTER (Princess Charlotte)
GODDESS OF THE GREEN ROOM (Dorothy Jordan and William IV)
VICTORIA IN THE WINGS (End of the Georgian Era)

The Queen Victoria Series
THE CAPTIVE OF KENSINGTON PALACE (Early days of Victoria)
THE QUEEN AND LORD M (Victoria and Lord Melbourne)
THE QUEEN'S HUSBAND (Victoria and Albert)
THE WIDOW OF WINDSOR (Last years of Victoria's Reign)

The Ferdinand and Isabella Trilogy
CASTILE FOR ISABELLA
SPAIN FOR THE SOVEREIGNS }   Also available in one volume:
DAUGHTER OF SPAIN   ISABELLA AND FERDINAND

The Lucrezia Borgia Series
MADONNA OF THE SEVEN HILLS }   Also available in one volume:
LIGHT ON LUCREZIA   LUCREZIA BORGIA

The Medici Trilogy
MADAME SERPENT
THE ITALIAN WOMAN }   Also available in one volume:
QUEEN JEZEBEL   CATHERINE DE'MEDICI

Henri of Navarre
EVERGREEN GALLANT

The French Revolution Series
LOUIS THE WELL-BELOVED
THE ROAD TO COMPIEGNE
FLAUNTING, EXTRAVAGANT QUEEN

The Queens of England Series
MYSELF MY ENEMY (Henrietta Maria)
QUEEN OF THIS REALM (Elizabeth I)
VICTORIA VICTORIOUS (Victoria)
THE LADY IN THE TOWER (Anne Boleyn)
THE COURTS OF LOVE (Eleanor of Aquitaine)
IN THE SHADOW OF THE CROWN (Mary Tudor)
THE QUEEN'S SECRET (Katherine of Valois)
THE RELUCTANT QUEEN (Anne Neville)
THE PLEASURES OF LOVE (Catherine Braganza)
WILLIAM'S WIFE (William & Mary)
ROSE WITHOUT A THORN (Katherine Howard)

General historical novels
BEYOND THE BLUE MOUNTAINS
THE GOLDSMITH'S WIFE
THE SCARLET CLOAK
DEFENDERS OF THE FAITH
DAUGHTER OF SATAN
MADAME DU BARRY

Stories of Victorian England
IT BEGAN IN VAUXHALL GARDENS
LILITH

Non-Fiction
MAY QUEEN OF SCOTS: *The Fair Devil of Scotland*
A TRIPTYCH OF POISONERS
(Cesare Borgia, Madame de Brinvilliers and Dr Pritchard)
THE RISE OF THE SPANISH INQUISITION
THE GROWTH OF THE SPANISH INQUISITION
THE END OF THE SPANISH INQUISITION